CITY BY THE BAY

Stories of Novaya Rossiya

By Walter H. Hunt

11/2022

Justin —

with best regards

Walter Hunt

note on
BGG

Cover designed by Laura Givens

Walter H. Hunt
Visit my website at https://www.fantasticfiction.com/h/walter-h-hunt/

Printed in the United States of America

First Printing: Aug 2019
Eric Flint's Ring of Fire Press

ebook ISBN-13 978-1-948818-44-5
Trade Paperback ISBN-13 978-1-948818-45-2

Dedication

To Lisa, my fellow traveler.
Thank you for everything.

Acknowledgement

Thanks to Alex Shvartsman for his valuable assistance with Russian vernacular.

CONTENTS

UNSHAKABLE FAITH
1816

CHAPTER 1

With a sigh, Father Mikhail dropped onto the rudimentary bench set along the partially-built wall. He reached within his cassock and drew out a set of polished wooden rosary beads, examined them, and then let them fall into his lap. He wiped his brow with his sleeve and looked around, his gaze finally landing on Brother Gennady, who was engaged in a conversation with a workman in halting Spanish.

"You are working too hard, Brother," he said, after a moment.

The young monk gave the workman a slight bow, and came toward Mikhail, his sandals kicking up dust.

"And you should take better care of yourself, *Otyets* Mikhail." Gennady smiled, wiping his hands on the front of his cassock. "Are you feeling unwell?"

"No, not really." Mikhail sighed again. "I am just tired."

"Perhaps you should go back inside and rest."

"And pass up the opportunity to see you work so hard? I would not miss it. What has the *brodyaga* Spaniard to say? More delays?"

Gennady sat next to the older man. "As you know, my Spanish is a work in progress, so I'm not sure I got the full meaning. But apparently they are having trouble with the mortar—it is too watery, I think."

"I would not be surprised if they were watering it themselves."

"That is most uncharitable of you, Otyets. These are good men. They take great pride in their work."

"They do not work here for the glory of God, Brother Gennady. They work for roubles, just as they once worked for pesos. Even when this church is built, and God willing it will someday be finished, I hardly think we will ever see any of them come in to worship."

"That is what <u>Kapitan</u> Donatiev said. 'They are scarcely Catholic; they are unlikely to become Orthodox . . . but build your church anyway, Brother.'" His intonation was a perfect mimicry of the commander of the garrison here at the tsar's newest outpost; it was enough to bring a smile to Father Mikhail's face.

"Mocking is unbecoming a servant of God," Mikhail said, but he couldn't help but smile. "The archbishop sent us to build a church," he continued, "and we will do as directed . . . whether anyone comes to visit or not."

* * *

The terms of the treaty between the crowns of Great Britain and Russia had been agreed upon as early as 1809, but it had taken seven years for the details to be fully worked out. The Great Autocrat, the Tsar of all the Russias, had been granted—with British approval—a large swath of land that had formerly been the northern part of the province the Spanish called Alta California. This was not out of any great love that King George had for his cousin, Tsar Alexander: indeed, it was not even his decision, given his advanced state of madness—but the regent was also none too fond of the tsar. It was merely political expediency, a way to keep the rich boundary of the Pacific out of the hands of the French. Poaching territory from the crumbling Spanish Empire had been done in the face of an earnest embassy from First Minister Lafayette to the Court of Saint Petersburg, which was turned away when the treaty was announced.

The Court of Saint James might have wanted Alta California for itself—but they, like the Russians, might have found it difficult to defend. In any case, it was better to have an ally in Russia than to have the tsar find common cause with the Bourbon kings. Alta California—at least the northern portion—would be converted into *Novaya Rossiya*. The *californios* mostly met the change of authority with indifference, and even though the viceroy in San Diego recommended that they withdraw, the most devoted of the friars in the various missions up and down the coast remained, pursuing their evangelical mission despite the absence of Spanish troops from the abandoned *presidios*.

In the spring of 1816, after the establishment of Fort Ross in the north to manage the fur trade, Gyorgy Nikolaievich Donatiev, the eldest son of Baron Donatiev, was given command of an expedition to the south to plant the double-eagle flag of the Russian Empire on the site of the small village that the Spanish called Yerba Buena. In addition to soldiers, the expedition included carpenters and blacksmiths and other craftsmen—and an aged Russian Orthodox priest, Father Mikhail, and his young acolyte, Brother Gennady.

To himself, Donatiev wondered who Mikhail might have angered to be sent ten thousand miles to be buried so far from home.

* * *

The little settlement—still called Yerba Buena, since Donatiev had no particular desire to invent a name for it—slowly grew with the arrival of craftsmen, settlers, and farmers from the Pacific rim of the Empire. As spring turned to summer, it began to be a regular stop for trading vessels coming from the treaty port of Lahaina in the Sandwich Islands. Brother Gennady heard the sailors' tales of the tropical paradise across the ocean, but still found great beauty in the paradise where Yerba Buena was located—but the comparison made Mikhail grumble.

In the meanwhile, the church began to come together, despite the work habits of the californios who had been hired to build it. It seemed that every day there was a shortage of something at the work site: bricks, wooden beams, even nails. Every time something was unavailable, the workmen would leave off to sleep or smoke or just disappear.

He had heard Captain Donatiev tell Father Mikhail in no uncertain terms that there was no spare capacity among the carpenters, brickmakers or blacksmiths to help build the church. He would have to make do with whatever he could find, and in the meanwhile the spiritual needs of the flock—such as they were—could be met in the ground floor of the custom house in the main settlement until the church was ready.

To Brother Gennady's surprise, however, supplies often turned up after a few hours. The carpenters and brickmakers and blacksmiths would never say that they would disobey the direct orders of the commander of the settlement by bringing a few spare beams of wood or a few hundred bricks or a bucket of nails; nor would their casual advice as they stood with Father Mikhail, smoking pipes and looking up at the façade, be construed (at least by them) as *assistance* for what was considered a low-priority project. Yet the church slowly rose, simple and austere, but handsome all the same.

"God provides," was all that Mikhail would say.

Somehow, the gruff old priest had ways of charming the skilled craftsmen of Yerba Buena, many of whom were regular communicants at the church services in the custom house.

Brother Gennady keenly felt Father Mikhail's profound sadness at being so far from the *rodina*—but it warmed his heart to see the joy in his older colleague's eyes and voice when he communicated the sacraments to the flock that attended the services in his makeshift church.

✳ ✳ ✳

A few weeks before the end of June, Gennady took a break from the preparation for the Solemnity of Saints Peter and Paul, the first opportunity to celebrate a major feast day with the congregation of Yerba Buena. Pascha had been quite a makeshift affair, and Mikhail had decided that Peter and Paul would be a good opportunity to emphasize the primacy of the Church and the heavenly blessing bestowed upon the expedition; but there was an afternoon where Gennady was able to get away from the settlement and walk up into the hills along the old Spanish road that led to the Presidio, the little fort that the former colonial power had left behind (and the current one had not seen fit to repair). He took a small skin of local wine, some bread and cheese and a few ripe peaches, and went off on his own.

The day was less hot than he would have expected, and the weather was very changeable. The sun would be high overhead, beating down, and then a cloud would pass in front making the day gloomy. And it was *quiet*: there were the sounds of birds and a few small animals but no axes or hammers or saws, no laughter or cursing or shouting or the drill of military arms.

"This must have been what it was like in the Garden," he said to himself, as he sat on a rock and drew out his lunch.

"Only the first few days," a voice said in badly accented Russian.

Gennady was on his guard at once, standing and grabbing his walking staff.

"Be at your ease, Brother," the voice continued, and presently a man in a brown robe and stout boots emerged from the trees. He wore a trimmed beard but no tonsure; he carried a loose sack on a strap over his shoulder. "I'm not here to do you harm."

"You surprised me."

"Yes. Well. We don't see too many strangers here. You are from the Russian settlement, sí?"

"Yes. If you would prefer speaking in Spanish—"

"Claro . . . it could not be worse than my Russian." He shifted to the other language at once. "Welcome, Brother. I am Brother Gonzalo, of the Order of Saint Francis. May I sit?" he gestured to the flat, broad rock where Gennady had been sitting.

"Of course," Gennady answered, and Brother Gonzalo settled onto the seat. "I am Brother Gennady, of—"

Before he could continue, the ground began to vibrate very slightly, as if being shaken by a mighty unseen hand.

After the tremor passed, Gonzalo crossed himself in the Catholic fashion and laughed. "You clearly have a better connection to the Almighty than I do."

Gennady crossed himself in turn. "I don't know about that . . . there have been several of those in the last few days, but that seemed very strong."

"A fact of life here." Gonzalo reached into his bag and drew out a small handful of nuts. He handed a few to Gennady, and began to work on the ones he retained. "A few tremors here and there ... but from time to time there's a strong one. A couple of years back there was a temblor strong enough to bring down our barn at the mission."

"Truly?"

"Yes, to be sure." Gonzalo chewed on a nut meat, spitting out a stray shell. "You have to build strong here in Alta California."

"Novaya Rossiya."

"Names." He spat again. "Let the politicos decide them. But you and I—we are men of God, no? What do we care what the land is called."

"So . . . you hold no allegiance to His Catholic Majesty?"

"He is far away," Gonzalo said, "and has abandoned us. The viceroy has his mind on other things—and our order told us to move out.

"And you—do you care what your tsar thinks of your little settlement?"

"Of course!"

"Of course. Well, a bit of advice, Brother—allegiance is earned. Let him show how much he cares for you first."

"That is not how it works, Brother. Perhaps in Spain, but not in Russia."

There was a very mild tremor just as Gennady finished speaking. Gonzalo, without replying, raised his right eyebrow slightly; then he picked up his sack and stood up, sweeping nutshells from his cassock.

"If you'd care to accompany me back to the mission," he said, "perhaps we can discuss it over a glass or two of wine."

CHAPTER 2

"Yes, we've *all* felt the tremors," Donatiev said. He stood up from behind his desk and walked to the large armoire on the side of his office. He opened it and pulled out a bottle and a small glass. He began to turn, then grabbed a second one and brought both to the desk. He uncorked the bottle and poured clear liquid into each glass.

Mikhail frowned, and was about to say something about how early in the day it was, but shrugged and took one of the glasses.

"*Za zdorovje,*" he said, and downed the glass.

Mikhail grunted and drank.

Donatiev sat on the corner of the desk. "What would you like me to do for you?"

"I would not say that I was here to ask you to do anything about them, Captain," Mikhail said. "I just wanted to know whether they were . . . part of your calculations."

"Meaning?"

"We are all building things, Captain. I erect a temple to the Most High: you build an entire colony. I worry that one good shaking will bring it all down."

"You worry too much, Father."

"And I would say to you, Gyorgy Nikolaievich, that you worry too little. My assistant Gennady has learned—"

"Learned? From who?"

"The Spanish monks in the hills. He has learned—"

"He has been talking to the *Spanish monks*? Why was I not told of this earlier?"

"They are our neighbors, Gyorgy. Captain. They mean us no harm."

"That is not for *you* to decide, Father," Donatiev said. He stood up and placed his glass on the desk. "It is your desire to express good will to all men—Spanish, Russian, British—Catholic, Orthodox, and—whatever faith the British profess. But you overlook the danger they present."

"A few monks at a little monastery? How could they possibly pose a danger, Gyorgy Ni—"

"They are *eyes and ears*, Mikhail. They are spies."

"For whom?"

"The viceroy."

"San Diego is hundreds of miles to the south," Mikhail said. He rolled the small glass between his palms, a nervous gesture. "How do you suppose they get messages? A fleet of fast ships? Or horses? Or do they just use their Catholic *magic*? They are abandoned monks, in a mission that their Viceroy has left behind. They pose no threat."

"You are a very poor judge of that."

Mikhail leaned forward and placed his glass next to Donatiev's, then settled himself in his chair and scratched his beard. "I think you underestimate my judgment, as always. The threat is the shaking of the earth, Gyorgy Nikolaievich. Perhaps this place was not such a good choice after all."

Donatiev went back behind his desk and sat down. "So now you question *my* judgment. I think you worry far too much about something over which we have little control. The tremors will stop; the giant under the earth merely shifts in his sleep."

"Making it into a folk tale does not make it easier to deal with."

"No," Donatiev said. "Of course it does not. "But it makes it easier for the men to accept. You tell your folk tales, I tell mine."

Mikhail appeared ready to respond, offended, when Donatiev began to laugh.

"Don't worry, Father. If your little church is ready to celebrate the Feast of Peter and Paul, I can promise you that it will be filled."

The californios worked no harder with the end of their task in sight; if anything, it seemed to Gennady that they moved even more slowly, despite his encouragement and the scowls and complaints from Father Mikhail. Once more, during the last week of June and immediately prior to the feast, there was a slight tremor in the ground; the workmen scattered, but it caused no more than the shaking loose of a few bricks and a single broken pane of glass—enough to make the glazier curse them for their carelessness in an accent from deep in the Steppes . . . until he too was cowed by Mikhail's stern gaze.

Within the little church, Mikhail had arranged a side-chapel with a beautiful little ikon of Saint Helena, the mother of the Byzantine Emperor Constantine, the first imperial to turn to Christianity. Helena's hagiography was an interesting one: it was said that she found the True Cross, and then followed a vision that led her to the burial place of Christ in Jerusalem—the place where the Church of the Holy Sepulchre had been erected.

The night before the great feast—with the church mostly complete, but at least in readiness for the following day's ceremonies—Gennady came upon Mikhail kneeling in the side-chapel. There was a small altar and a rough wooden rail, but no hassock for the old man's bare knees on the rough stone floor.

Gennady stood respectfully waiting for Mikhail to complete his devotions, but when the old man did not rise or acknowledge his presence, Gennady stepped forward and gently touched Mikhail's shoulder.

"We are not destined for great things," Mikhail said without turning. "You know that, do you not, Gennady? We are destined to die here in obscurity, in this distant place for which we have not even chosen a name."

"They call the great bay *Zolotye Vorota*—the name the Spaniards gave to it: Golden Gate. Perhaps that is a good name for the town as well."

"A fine bit of blasphemy, don't you think? As if this were a great shrine to the Mother Church." He laughed, but it was a dry, pitiable thing, hardly a laugh at all. "No, this should be *Bezmanya Zemlya*—the Nameless Land. And this can be the nameless city. Though calling it a city is generous. Help me stand," he added, and Gennady helped the old man to his feet. He made obeisance to Saint Helena, Gennady followed, and the two turned away to face the darkened nave of the church.

"Tomorrow will be a joyous celebration," Gennady said. "Everyone will be here—you told me that Kapitan Donatiev had promised."

"Yes, yes . . . their one and only visit to the church. Then they can go about their business, their duty done."

"Some will attend."

"Most will not," Mikhail replied. "But no matter: I cannot make silk purses from sow's ears. Perhaps they will come and pray when the ground trembles.

"What do you make of that, by the way?"

"I suspect that the land is unstable."

"Brother Gonzalo said—"

"The Spanish monk is now an authority?"

"He has been here far longer than we have, Otyets. He said that such things come and go; a few shakes then nothing for months on end."

"So, we've seen the last of it?"

"I don't know. But he is not worried. So I am not worried."

Mikhail looked over his shoulder at Saint Helena, the gilt of the ikon reflecting dimly from the votive light before it. "I have a feeling that we *should* be worried, Brother. But perhaps Saint Helena will intercede for us here in the Nameless Land."

"I'm sure she is watching, Otyets."

Mikhail looked owlishly at the younger man but did not respond, his face conveying all of his fears and doubts.

* * *

Morning came bright and sunny; the inhabitants of the town began to gather on the shore of the bay, where they found Brother Gennady and Father Mikhail already on hand at a small altar with the ikon of Saint Helena, a small ceramic bowl, and a large beeswax candle placed on it. The two religious men were clothed in their best vestments and were attended by several workers from the church, as well as two brown-robed Spaniards evidently visiting from their mission in the hills.

On the edge of the beach was a large Orthodox cross set in a footing from which it would be removed, so that it could be carried to the church.

When most of the town was assembled, Father Mikhail raised his hands above him and chanted, "Svjatyj Bozhe, Svjatyj Krepkij, Svjatyj

Bezsmertnyj, Pomiluj nas—Holy God, Holy Mighty, Holy Immortal, have mercy on us;" he then proceeded to recite the Trisagion Prayers, with the congregation—at least those that knew the prayers—following along.

Glory to Thee, our God, Glory to Thee.

O Heavenly King, Comforter, the Spirit of Truth, Who art everywhere present and fillest all things, the Treasury of good things and Giver of life: Come, and abide in us, and cleanse us from every stain, and save our souls, O Good One.

Holy God, Holy Mighty, Holy Immortal: have mercy on us.

As was customary, the celebrants repeated the phrase three times; with each repetition, Mikhail dipped his fingers in the bowl and gestured toward the water.

Glory to the Father, and to the Son, and to the Holy Spirit, both now and ever, and unto the ages of ages. Amen. All-Holy Trinity, have mercy on us. Lord, cleanse us from our sins. Master, pardon our iniquities. Holy God, visit and heal our infirmities for Thy name's sake.

Lord, have mercy. Lord, have mercy. Lord, have mercy. Glory to the Father, and to the Son, and to the Holy Spirit, both now and ever, and unto the ages of ages.

When all was again quiet, Mikhail turned away from the inhabitants of the settlement and raised his hands high. "In the name of the Father and the Son and the Holy Spirit, I bless this land and this bay with the name . . ."

Gennady held his breath, wondering if Mikhail would truly call it the Nameless Land in the presence of all of his countrymen, and of the Holy Trinity itself; but he need not have worried.

". . . Zolotye Vorota—the Golden Gate," Mikhail finished. "May it grow and prosper, and may the great Father confer his grace upon it and upon all of us."

From the bay, the people made their way along the wide, flat road into the settlement, led by Gennady carrying the cross. As they walked they recited the Lord's Prayer—the two Spaniards in Latin, the rest in various dialects of Russian. The path was just over half a mile, winding past the workshops and homes of the Russian emigrants who were so far from home. It was more than a day off work that made them joyous: it was the ceremony, the song, the feeling of the presence of the Divine, the completion of the church—whether they planned to visit it or not—that made them smile and brought joy to their voices.

11

The procession reached the little church, and the congregation entered, looking around and exclaiming in little "oohs" and "aahs" how impressed they were with the work. Donatiev remained at the doorway with Gennady, who greeted each person as he or she came through the door.

When everyone was inside, the captain looked at the young monk. "You have done well, Brother," he said, trying to sound gruff, but obviously moved by some emotion he refused to admit.

"It is a dream made whole by the workmen," Gennady answered. "We have—"

But whatever he was about to say was interrupted by the shaking of the ground. Almost as quickly as they entered, people began streaming out of the church—some walking, some beginning to run.

The tremor did not immediately subside. Gennady could see Brother Gonzalo from his spot just inside the door, as Gonzalo kept people moving. In place of his usual sardonic expression, he looked fearful.

Gennady exchanged a glance with Donatiev and went inside, working his way forward against the press of people trying their best to get out. At the far end of the nave he could see Father Mikhail, his arms raised in invocation, his expression stunned—as if the shaking earth was a personal affront, a blow struck against his doubts the previous evening.

"Mikhail!" Gennady shouted. "Otyets! Come, you must leave!"

"Saint Helena!" Mikhail shouted back, and it wasn't clear whether it was an invocation—but he suddenly lowered his hands and scurried toward the side-chapel.

Most of the congregants had made their way out of the church, and Brother Gonzalo tugged at Gennady's sleeve.

"Mikhail—"

Then, without warning, the roof began to collapse. Something struck Gennady and his world went black.

He awoke, choking on dust.

He was lying on a pallet that had been used to carry bricks to the building site; the bright blue sky above him was not marred by a single cloud, but the air was hazy with dust. Brother Gonzalo leaned toward him with a wineskin and helped him drink.

"Father Mikhail," Gennady managed to say, but the Spaniard shook his head.

It took an effort of will to stand, but Gennady managed to do it at last, despite a throbbing head. The church was in ruins and the area was a hive of activity; a number of people were sitting or lying, also affected by some injury. Gennady touched his head and found that it had been roughly bandaged.

Those that could do so reached their hands out, wordlessly or with some whispered prayer; he touched each of them, unable to reply.

Donatiev was at the center of it all, his rich dress uniform covered in dust, his hat lost or discarded somewhere.

"Brother," he said, turning his attention to Gennady. "Thank God. For a time we thought we'd lost both of you."

"Both . . ."

"Mikhail . . .," Donatiev looked down, and then reached within his vest and drew out the tiny ikon of Saint Helena. "He did not want to leave this behind. It was found with his body."

Gennady took the ikon from the captain, and kissed it gently.

For this, Gennady thought. *For you, blessed Helena, my dearest friend died . . .*

No.

"If there is anything I can do—"

"Da," Gennady said. "Oh, yes, Kapitan. There is most certainly something you can do."

He turned away and climbed up the short stairs that were all that remained of the flight leading to the belltower.

"Hear me!" he said, holding the ikon high. The modest height made him very slightly dizzy, but he ignored it. "My friends, my children, hear me."

To his surprise, he commanded the attention of everyone below, working in the rubble, lying on pallets with their injuries—even Donatiev, who had a curious expression on his face.

"We have suffered a terrible loss, far from our homes, far from the rodina. My dearest friend, Father Mikhail, was struck down by a natural event—not a curse from God, not an indication that His face is turned away from us.

"I have in my hands the ikon of the blessed Saint Helena, who found the True Cross, and the place where our Precious Saviour was buried in Jerusalem. My friend—*our* friend—died when recovering it from its place of distinction within our church.

"There is only one way to honor his memory and his sacrifice. We must not abandon our plan to serve Holy Mother Church: we must rebuild our structure, make it grander and greater than this one. We must find a suitable place, closer to heaven—"

He paused and looked out, landward, toward the hills beyond the town. One in particular, a tall, conical hill where he knew Donatiev had talked of building a lookout tower, called to him.

"There," he said, pointing to it. "There we will erect a new, greater church, one that honors the memory of Father Mikhail, and that honors Saint Helena."

Not Bezmanya Zemlya, he thought. *Not the Nameless Land.* "It is the name we should give to our town beside the Golden Gate—Saint Helena. Do you not agree, Kapitan Gyorgy Nikolaievich?"

Before Donatiev could answer, a shout rose from the assembled people—they called out the name of the saint whose ikon Gennady held aloft, its gilt catching the sparkle of the morning sun.

* * *

It took six months for the letter to arrive from the Archbishop of Saint Petersburg, and the rite of consecration was irregular: the abbot of the mission of San Francisco and two of the monks participated—but God, whom they worshipped in different ways, smiled upon their work. But it was Father Gennady who laid his friend to rest in the crypt as soon as a place was prepared for him, even before the official title was proclaimed.

It took another eight months to bring the building materials up to the building site on the lookout hill, to construct the church—again with the help of the Franciscans, who had advice on how to set the foundations and reinforce the walls.

There was never any question whether the church would be built on the lookout hill, or that the town would take its name from the saint to which the church was dedicated; Kapitan Donatiev made no objection, and also said nothing about the effort given to the construction of the edifice, which could be seen from out at sea, the onion dome sometimes ringed with fog and clouds, at others sparkling in sunlight. It was a fitting symbol for Saint Helena, the city by the bay.

A PRIVATE AFFAIR

1831

CHAPTER 1

It was a sailor's lament, Volkov thought: *if only the weather had been different.*

Strelka had been fighting off a wind that was coming from the northeast, making progress along the north coast difficult. It had put them at least three days behind their expected arrival in Saint Helena: and for Captain Leonid Volkov, as for any captain of a merchant ship, time was money. But there was nothing for it: wind was wind, and the sea was the sea.

The first Russian trading settlement had been established at Fort Ross in 1812, nearly twenty years ago; since then, five additional ones had been placed along the coast, one south of the original and four further north. Pelts, particularly of the sea otter, were still the most valuable commodity, and ships bearing the red-white-blue flag of the Russian-American Company delivered them to Saint Helena in exchange for durable goods and food, the pelts traveling onward across the Pacific mostly to China where traders from that ancient, crumbling Empire prized them above gold.

Strelka was a day out of Fort Ross but had been driven out to sea—preferable to being hurled against one of the many rocky promontories, to be sure, but hardly ideal.

Strelka was a sleek little ship, maneuverable and very seaworthy: it could pile on sail and make good speed, but the onset of fog headed toward the coast slowed their progress.

But for that, they might have been able to outrun the privateer.

* * *

Georgy Sharovsky had been at sea for most of his life; he had shipped aboard his uncle's trawler in Alaska when he was nine. When he was a boy, he had been as nimble and agile as the boys who now served aboard *Strelka*. He was a junior officer now, free from some of the lowest of the tasks to which the lads were relegated—including climbing up to the topmast, unnerving in clear weather, and in its way even worse in dense fog. In the moment, Sharovsky decided that he wouldn't send one of the youngsters up in this weather; instead he went up himself, spyglass secured to his belt, holding carefully to the ratlines as he climbed up and up, soon losing sight of the main deck. When he reached the lookout, which swayed in the wind (easily felt, but scarcely seen), he hallooed down to the officer on deck.

"What do you see up there, Georgy?"

"Near nothing. Can't see the waves, can't see heaven either."

"Check every five minutes. Captain's orders."

"Five minutes aye," Georgy said, and took out his spyglass to see if anything became visible.

Just after his second five-minute check, he was scanning to starboard—out into the horizon, out into the invisible Pacific—he sighted something almost ghostlike, cutting through the water. Barely audible, he caught the briefest snatch of conversation and recognized the language—Spanish, spoken harshly and rapidly.

It wasn't clear whether the other ship had sighted *Strelka*: it was a certain thing that if he could hear *them*, they might be able to hear *him* . . . but there was nothing for it: down below would need to know.

As quickly as he had climbed up he descended, and found himself facing Pietrewski, a senior lieutenant, a scowling, intemperate Pole. Before the other could berate him for abandoning the top, Georgy said, "Buzzards starboard. Don't know if they've seen us."

"Heading?"

"East by south."

"They've seen us all right."

"How can you be sure?"

"On this coast, in this weather, no one navigates toward the shore unless there's something he wants to pin up there." He nodded to Georgy. "I'll tell the captain. Get all hands ready; this might not be friendly." Without another word he turned and made for *Strelka*'s pilot-house.

A few moments later, it became clear just how unfriendly it was, when a cannon shot flew past *Strelka*'s bow, and a shout came out of the fog.

* * *

Pietrewski had been right, which was no surprise. Georgy didn't particularly like him, but the Pole was clever and a keen sailor. *Strelka* was no war-ship: it was, in fact, scarcely armed, and was heavily-laden. There was nothing Volkov could do but heave to, and presently a half dozen Spaniards, all mustachios and swagger, had boarded the ship.

Volkov, a dignified man in middle age, kept his anger tightly leashed as the most elaborate mustachio and biggest swagger presented himself, looking around as if *Strelka* already belonged to him.

"Good day, Captain——"" the Spaniard began in heavily accented Russian.

"Volkov."

"Volquez," the man said. "I am—"

"*Volkov*," the captain repeated, letting annoyance creep into his voice.

"Volkev," the Spaniard repeated, and Volkov appeared to just let it go. "I am Don Domingo Alcantár y Rodriguez, captain of *Reina Isabella*, in the service of His Catholic Majesty, and of the Viceroy of New Spain—in whose territorial waters you are presently trespassing."

"These are Russian waters, *gospodin* Don Domingo."

The Spaniard spat on the deck, perhaps a foot from Volkov's left boot. "Nonsense. There *are* no Russian waters, señor. All of this continent—all of Alta California, and its coasts—are a part of New Spain, granted by His Holiness more than three hundred years ago."

"Our respective governments think otherwise."

"Eh, sí, I suppose they do," Don Domingo said. "But they are not here on this deck, are they? At the moment, I am here, and *I* am the government. And as the government, I claim your ship—and all that it carries—as my prize."

"This is outrageous."

"Outrageous." The Spaniard ran a finger down his moustaches, and then let the hand rest on a pistol at his waist. "I suppose you might think so, Captain Volstan. But it really does not affect the matter, does it? Now if you *behave,* I will put you and your fellow trespassers ashore. You may even take a few minutes to gather your effects. If you think to resist, however, I cannot . . . be answerable for the conduct of my hotheaded young *caballeros.*" He looked over his shoulder at the closest "caballeros," who had not seemed to be able to understand most of the verbal exchange, but they grinned, hooking their thumbs in their belts, seemingly understanding the intent.

"You offer me little choice."

"*Exáctamente,*" Don Domingo said, smiling. "I did not come aboard to offer you a *choice,* Captain Volevo. Rather I am offering you *terms.* Now: what is your decision?"

* * *

To Georgy's (and Captain Volkov's) surprise, the Spanish captain was as good as his word. The men were given a few minutes to gather whatever they chose to carry, though the Spanish boarders didn't let them anywhere near the hold: several thousand roubles worth of pelts, along with a few other goods, remained undisturbed in *Strelka's* hold. *Reina Isabella* and *Strelka* put in at a sandy cove, shallow enough that the Russian crew was able to wade ashore. They watched as the Spanish ship, as well as their own, made sail and began to move out to sea.

It was a few miles walk in relative silence to the walls of Fort Ross, the southernmost and oldest Russian settlement along this fairly desolate stretch of coast.

CHAPTER 2

"Say it again, gospodin Captain. But slowly."

"Don Domingo Alcantár y Rodriguez," Volkov said, trying to carefully enunciate every syllable for the young clerk, who wrote it the best he could in block Cyrillic characters.

They had been at Fort Ross for a bit under a day. The thirty men and officers of *Strelka* had made their way along a scarcely-established path that followed the rocky coast, sometimes tracing the very edge of steep cliffs, sometimes descending into deep forests, until they arrived, exhausted and damp, at the settlement.

This was the oldest of the half dozen settlements on the north coast. It had been established a few years before the Russian expedition to what now bore the name Saint Helena. Once rough and primitive, it was now merely rough—the Kashyak village below, on the coast, had grown and expanded, and the walled encampment had a dozen buildings, some with panes of thick, clear glass brought up from the town. More than three hundred Russians made their homes at the Fort, including a dozen married couples; a score of children, ranging from infants to adolescents, seemed to be in constant motion from dawn to dusk, playing and attending to chores. Twenty years on, Fort Ross was thriving.

"That is not a name that I know, Captain. We have had a few Spanish traders this far north—"

"Don Domingo was no *trader*, gospodin. And *Reina Isabella* was no merchant ship. She is a privateer: and she is a threat to anyone traveling in these waters. What I want to know is what the Russian-American Company is going to do about it."

The clerk set his quill down. He took a bit of sand and spread it across the paper to dry it, then shook it off. "There are two answers to that question, Captain."

"Da, of course there are. What are they?"

"I am sure the governor will say to you that the company will extend its efforts to do whatever it can to protect its ships from *privateers*."

"I see. And what is the other answer?"

"The Russian-American Company will do essentially nothing for you, Captain, because there is nothing that can be done."

"I should like to hear that from the governor."

"I am sure that you will. It is what he said the last time."

"*Last time?*"

The clerk sighed, and folded his hands in his lap. "This is the third such incident this year, gospodin Captain. The Russian-American Company has very little power to do anything in these waters. There is no navy here."

"There should be no *Spanish* here. This is our land, this is our coast. There is a governor in Saint Helena—should I protest to him?"

"You might have better luck."

"Is there a ship leaving for Saint Helena?"

"In three days, *Zapodzha* will be arriving from Fort Alexander up north. It's a large fishing trawler, not the most comfortable of accommodations—but also nothing a privateer might care about."

"Who do I need to talk to in order to get passage for my crew?"

* * *

Two and a half days on a fishing trawler was not how Volkov had planned to travel down the coast to Saint Helena; if he was not so angry, he knew, he would be despondent.

A decade before Saint Helena became the capital of Novaya Rossiya, Russian fur traders had been working the coast between Sitka and the Golden Gate Bay, making the Russian-American Company rich. Most of their harvest went west across the ocean to China: it was one of the few things the arrogant, wealthy Chinese Empire wanted. In those early days, when the matter of dominion had not been settled, company ships were better armed and equipped; the company knew that there were clear dangers—from natives, from Spaniards, from weather—that Russian America was a *dangerous place*. Sometime between then and now, Volkov mused, that message had been lost. Saint Helena was prosperous now, with great houses on the hills and four magnificent churches, including the cathedral of Saint Helena on the top of the great hill in the middle of the settlement.

Oh, da, indeed: *very* civilized.

* * *

In Saint Helena, the Russian-American Company headquarters was directly on the Embarcadero, a sprawling complex that had started life as a warehouse but now encompassed six buildings of various shapes, sizes, and styles. The tsar's flag, and the banner of the company, flew over the main one, snapping in the wind.

They had already gotten word of the loss of *Strelka*, days ago; Volkov had no interest in facing that ordeal just yet. He directed Pietrewski and the rest of the officers and crew to go in and report. As Georgy Sharovsky was walking away, Volkov called to him.

"Da, Captain?"

"Come with me, Georgy Stefanovich. I will have greater dignity if I am accompanied by a junior."

"Where are we going?"

"There." He pointed down the wharf to another, newer building. It looked to Georgy as if it had been built according to plan, rather than circumstances, and it flew a banner bearing an armorial device—and the Union Jack.

"The British Embassy?"

"Nyet, Georgy. They would do nothing for us. That—is Astor House."

* * *

When Rezanov first came down the coast from the Aleutians in 1807, he found someone already engaged in the fur trade: a British merchant from the Crown Colony of New York named John Jacob Astor. He had befriended the natives and adopted their methods and means to harvest the valuable pelts, particularly the sea otters.

Through means that Volkov knew were far out of his understanding, when the treaty was signed in 1809 the Astor Company was granted an indefinite license to conduct business in Novaya Rossiya. The patriarch of the clan returned to the east, and Astor House—the west coast affiliate—was established in Saint Helena, capitalized by the wealth the fur trade had brought.

Georgy was not sure what business Volkov would have at Astor House, but he had never been within, and if his captain was planning to visit he was happy to come along.

* * *

The Embarcadero was all noise and bustle, but Astor House was cool and quiet. Volkov and Georgy removed their caps as they entered. The floor of the entry hall was laid out magnificently in glazed brick, and there was a large mural on the far wall showing a view of New York Harbor over which the Astor crest had been hung. Clerks and functionaries moved on their own errands as the two Russians approached a receiving desk, behind which stood a clerk, looking over a large leather-bound ledger. He took no notice of them, even when they came to stand directly before him.

"Excuse me," Volkov said, in English.

The man looked up at last, disdain visible. "Can I help you, sir?"

"Yes, I hope you can," Volkov said. "I should like to speak with gospodin Astor, please."

"Do you have an appointment with Mr. Astor?"

"I have just arrived in Saint Helena. I have no appointment."

"I see." The man ran his finger down the ledger, as if looking for an error. "I do not think he has any openings this week—"

"This is very important," Volkov interrupted. "He will want to see me."

"And why would that be?"

Volkov glanced briefly at Georgy, and though the younger man had not understood most of the exchange—his English was very poor—he saw determination in the captain's eyes.

"Because the matter I must discuss with him threatens his corporation's vital interests. Come, Georgy," he said, and walked away from the desk toward a set of stairs that led to an upper level. The clerk dashed out from behind his desk to try and interpose himself between the Russians and the stairs: but they moved with speed and agility and were on the steps before the Englishman could catch up.

Astor House was not a military facility, and it seemed to catch the employees by surprise for two Russian sailors to come up the stairs at speed. Volkov was not sure exactly where to go, but it quickly seemed obvious where the best, most spacious office must be; and just as he reached it, an impeccably-dressed young man stepped out. The clerk, hurrying behind them, had nearly caught up by the time Volkov found himself standing face to face with the imposing figure.

"You are Mr. Astor," Volkov said.

"I am, at your service, sir. I assume you have good reason for disturbing my place of business."

"If I could have a few minutes of your time, gospodin, I assure you it will be worth your while."

Astor did not answer at once, looking the two Russians up and down. The clerk looked angry and a trifle embarrassed: it was clearly his job to fend off anyone who did not belong, and he might well receive a stern rebuke later.

"You have ten minutes, sir. If that is insufficient, then I bid you good day."

"It will be more than sufficient, gospodin."

"This is most troubling." William Astor had listened carefully as Volkov related the taking of *Strelka* and the response of the governor at Fort Ross. "It is something new."

"Not according to the governor at Fort Ross," Volkov said. "He told us that *Strelka* was not the first ship taken."

"What does the company have to say?"

"I have not yet asked them, gospodin Astor."

"Indeed." Astor raised an eyebrow. "I would expect you would have already asked."

"I came here first. I know what reception I shall receive there."

"Oh?"

"I no longer have a ship, *gospodin*. And the company has lost tens of thousands of roubles in pelts. The burden of command places the blame directly on my shoulders."

"Will they be looking to extract payment from you?"

"They may try." Volkov laughed, with a Russian sort of bitterness and fatalism. "But I do not expect to be given another ship."

"That is a waste of talent, Captain Volkov. How long have you been in the company's employ?"

"Nine years. My father sailed with Rezanov."

"You must know every inch of that coast, sir . . . though you no longer have your charts, I assume."

"Don Domingo was unusually generous, *gospodin* Astor. We were allowed to take things we could carry. I still have my most important charts."

"I assume the company is aware of this."

"I have not yet made my report," Volkov said. He looked at Astor, then removed his watch and examined it—as if to say, *you have given me ten minutes, gospodin. Now you are taking up* my *time.*

Astor picked up a letter opener and toyed with it for a moment, looking down at his desk; he appeared to make a decision and looked up at Volkov, putting the letter opener back in its place.

"If it is not too forward to ask, Captain: what is your compensation with the company?"

Volkov paused a moment and then stated his salary, including the bonuses granted for timeliness.

"I would be prepared to offer you—and your subordinate, should you like—half again as much to work for me."

Volkov did not immediately reply. He was not surprised by the offer: he brought valuable information, experience, and skill—employment with Astor would have been his ultimate goal, given his expectations regarding the Russian-American Company. He just hadn't expected it to happen in fifteen minutes. The Astor Company was known for its sharp business practices.

Still, they operated more or less at the sufferance of the authorities, and he wasn't sure how this would be viewed by the tsar's representative here in Saint Helena.

And there was something else.

"It is an attractive idea, gospodin. But it does not address the central problem: there are still Spanish privateers, and they are as dangerous for your firm as they are for the Russian-American Company."

"They have not attacked our ships."

"Yet."

"Your point is taken. We cannot but expect that sooner or later they will consider us valid targets.

"But this speaks to a wider concern, Captain—it has everything to do with the relationship between the Spanish Empire and the Russian Empire. If the Spaniards are encouraging—or even underwriting—this sort of activity based on a claim of political control, it can lead to war."

"Between the Spaniards and the Russians," Volkov said. "But you are neither, and I am not a diplomat in the tsar's employ. I do not see what I can do, or what you can do, to help this situation. With respect, gospodin," he added.

"You are being honest, Captain. So many people refuse to be direct: they fear how it will be received. But you see to the heart of the matter— and you understand that without an armed force on the high seas, we are at the mercy of the Spanish raiders. The tsar is far away and his governor here cannot assemble one. The Company behaves likewise.

"Therefore, *we* must provide such a force."

"'We', gospodin?"

Astor rose from behind his desk and stepped to his left, where there was a small bookcase that held a set of leather-bound ledgers. He drew one out and placed it on the desk. He opened it to a page toward the front, and turned it to show Volkov. It listed a number of ships and dates going back a few months.

"No Astor ship has been assaulted by the Spanish privateers, Captain, but they have been preying on other ships of other companies— Russian, British, and others of smaller countries as well. Just last week a Prussian ship which had sailed ten thousand miles to join in the Pacific trade was taken just off the Monterey coast. This has been going on for several months—roughly coinciding with the appointment of the new governor in San Diego, Don Pío. Clearly that worthy—" he spoke the word with disdain "—has decided on a new policy." He flipped the page back. Additional pages listed other ships, and even earlier dates.

"You knew of this, before I brought it to your attention. I assume you knew about *Strelka*. I should have realized, gospodin."

"Perhaps so, Captain Volkov. But suffice it to say that your visit to Astor House does not come as a complete surprise to me. It should not surprise you, either—you gained access rather easily, I daresay."

"Whatever reputation for daring I had with my young colleague has been thoroughly dashed, gospodin Astor."

Astor smiled. "Your secret is safe with me, Captain. Particularly because of your willingness to enter here and beard the lion, you have proved to be the man I had been told you were.

"The Russian-American Company will miss you, Captain Volkov. But I think you will feel no need to look back."

CHAPTER 3

Volkov's reception at the Company was less hostile than he had expected; if anything, the *apparatchiki* in Saint Helena seemed indifferent to the matter, as if it was of no moment. As for an assignment, he was given nothing: no replacement ship, no shore-side duties, scarcely any notice at all. They were not completely callous: he and his crew could draw enough owed pay to permit them to find lodging in Saint Helena, at least until they could find other berths.

A day later Volkov presented himself, this time alone, at Astor House. He was told that William Astor could be found at the company's berths, located on the north shore of the peninsula, along a particularly well-constructed stretch of the Embarcadero. There, he came upon a ship being refitted that bore the Union Jack and the Astor banner at the top of its mainmast.

Astor himself stood at the taffrail, and when he saw Volkov he beckoned him to come on board.

"Captain. I did not expect to see you again so soon, but I daresay I am not surprised by your visit."

The Russian nodded. "Da, I suppose I am not surprised either. I do not know why they have so little interest in defending their ships."

"The Russian-American Company is not a military force, Captain Volkov. Perhaps they were twenty years ago, but certainly not now. Still, even if their only motive is profit, they must see that something must be done."

"By someone else, gospodin Astor."

William Astor laughed, as if Volkov had made a great joke. "Yes, yes, that's quite true. And we shall make it true, my friend.

"What do you think of this ship?" He gestured around him.

Volkov glanced around. It was a fine vessel, bigger than *Strelka* and clearly better armed; from where he stood he could see the gun deck below—the main deck was only partially in place—and he counted a number of gun-carriages. Based on his first impression, she would be capable of a fair amount of speed.

"She seems a fine ship, sir."

"She needs a captain."

"To be sure."

"Think you can handle it, Captain Volkov?"

Volkov's eyes widened. He had hoped that Astor might find work for him—and possibly for some of his most trusted crew. But the offer of the command of a brand-new ship, well-armed and well-equipped, came as a surprise he could not conceal.

"Just like that, gospodin Astor—you offer this command to me?"

"I don't see any other skilled captains standing here."

"We have just met, sir. I accept that I come with a good reputation; I am not so humble that I do not believe I would be capable—but still, there must be someone in your present employ whom you could choose—"

"There might be. In fact, I would be a poor manager, and a very poor servant of my company, if there was not. But you are here, and—I expect—available. You are also strongly motivated to take this fight to the people who took your ship away."

"You are using my desire for revenge as a weapon, gospodin."

"I suppose I am. Do you find this troubling, Captain?"

"No," Volkov answered. "I do not."

* * *

Saint Helena had first been settled under military authority, but in the middle of the previous decade the town had passed to civilian control—a *boyar*, usually one out of favor at the tsar's court, was appointed to serve as governor of Novaya Rossiya. There had been three governors since the colony had been turned to civilian rule, all relatively colorless.

The Astor Company had been in Saint Helena for almost a decade, and had more permanence and continuity than the colonial civil government. Though not officially in authority, Volkov was surprised to find out how much influence it actually had; a week after his interview with the Russian-American Company, he received a note from William Astor informing him that if he wanted to be the captain of *Lady Sarah*—named for his mother—then the job was his.

It was an easy decision to resign from the company, take what severance they offered, and walk down the Embarcadero to sign his name to a contract at Astor House. He took a half-dozen of his best men with him, including Gyorgy Sharovsky, per his agreement with Astor. He'd had Sharovsky in mind for first officer—the young man's intelligence (not to mention loyalty) was unquestioned. But Astor had other plans.

Waiting for him on deck was a young Englishman, who bore a letter of introduction from Astor himself.

"Sherwood," he said. "John Sherwood. I am assigned as your first officer, Captain, and the official representative of Mr. Astor aboard *Lady Sarah*."

"You are his spy, da? I don't recall gospodin Astor mentioning anything about this."

"You have his letter," Sherwood said. "Surely that should be good enough."

Volkov grunted, and glanced at Sharovsky, who was trying his best—and failing—to conceal his disappointment.

"You know something of sailing, I assume."

"I was a merchant sailor in China, Captain. I have familiarized myself with the flagship from stem to stern, and am ready to serve as your second."

"'Flagship'?"

"Of the Vigilance Squadron," Sherwood said, with a hint of a smirk that disappeared as quickly as it appeared. "Within the month, Mr. Astor expects to have a half dozen vessels cleared from this port, ready to deal with the Spanish. *Lady Sarah* is just the beginning."

* * *

31

Sherwood could not have been more than twenty-five, but he showed every evidence of having spent considerable time afloat. He climbed the ratlines as well as Sharovsky; he was capable with the charts—and had a fair command of Russian so he could read those that Volkov brought aboard; he even seemed to command grudging respect from the ship's crew, a mix of British and Russian sailors either already in Astor employ or drawn from the idlers in Saint Helena.

Volkov had less than a week to get his crew ready before the word came for them to weigh anchor and clear out for San Diego. *Lady Sarah*'s hold was well stocked with tea chests that had made their way across from China—a prime target for Spanish privateers. Unlike the usual Astor policy, rumors of *Lady Sarah*'s cargo and destination were not kept secret; everyone Volkov met that week knew what they were carrying and where they were headed. He remained tight-lipped and was met with knowing smiles and nods.

Still, when the ship moved out through the Golden Gate into the Pacific under full sail, Volkov felt more at ease than he had been in many months.

* * *

As ordered, Volkov was in no hurry to reach the Spanish capital; he plotted a course that took them out of sight of the coast, to give the crew and the ship "a chance to get acquainted."

On the second day, he made a point to go on deck when Sharovsky was the officer of the watch. He found Sharovsky on the main deck, strolling from place to place, inspecting little things—anchor points, the cleanliness of the deck, the strength and direction of the wind.

A born sailor, Volkov thought. And the born sailor that Sharovsky was, he heard his captain's footsteps, and turned to face him, sketching a salute.

"This is not a military ship, Georgy Stefanovich. Please be at your ease."

"Can I help you, Captain?"

"No, no . . . just checking on things. All is well?"

"So far," Sharovsky answered. "Clear skies and no sign of the Spaniard."

"I feel as if I should be disappointed."

"I think it means that if he's out there, he's keeping his distance. Not a terrible thing, Captain."

"Astor *wants* us to meet up with them."

"Mr. Astor wants us to be bait for pirates, Captain. I don't see how that is a good thing."

"I would not mind a little revenge."

"For *Strelka*?"

"Da. For *Strelka*."

"We will not get her back, unless we attack San Diego. And maybe not even then. But we are not soldiers—*I* at least am not a soldier. We should leave the fighting to others."

"Oh, and who will do that? The tsar's army is not in Novaya Rossiya, Georgy. We should stand up for what is right."

Sharovsky did not answer.

"You don't agree?"

"I did not say that, Captain. I did not say anything."

"You can be honest with me, my friend. You do not think we should be doing this."

"Doing *this*? Sailing to San Diego to make a profit for the Astor Company, and earn a salary for ourselves? Oh, no, I am sure we should be doing that. What I don't know is if we should be acting as the catspaw to draw out the Spanish. Someone should be doing it, but not us."

"You knew that was what he had in mind."

"He sold you on this mission with the offer of revenge, Captain. I know this. It does not mean it was a wise decision."

Volkov snorted. "My friend, I was prepared to give you my sympathy because I had to give young Sherwood the first officer's position—and here you are telling me that I am unwise to do what we are doing. I found you a position, Georgy, and I hope you have not forgotten it."

"I did not mean to give offense, gospodin Captain. But I thought to speak plainly."

"Da, and indeed you did."

Sharovsky remained silent, and Volkov considered what else he might say—and if he was truly angry with his young friend. He had certainly spoken the truth, whether Volkov liked it or not.

* * *

Day turned to night, and *Lady Sarah* continued its southward path along the coast. Volkov retired below; Sharovsky remained on deck, and noticed that the ship was gradually moving to the west, away from the land. It was slow and gradual, but in the space of half an hour they were completely at sea.

Sharovsky went inside the pilot house, where Sherwood was bent over a chart; two lanterns swung slowly back and forth, giving the scene an eerie appearance, like a wavering magic lantern.

"Ah. Lieutenant Sharovsky."

"We seem to be drifting out to sea," Sharovsky said. He glanced down at the chart of the California coast.

"Not *drifting*, precisely," Sherwood answered without looking up. "We are on a course that takes us somewhat further south and west." He took his watch out of his pocket and opened it, tilting its face to catch the light.

"Is Captain Volkov aware of this change of course?"

"I don't know," Sherwood answered laconically. "I suppose not."

"As his first officer, don't you think you should keep him informed?"

Sherwood shrugged, and continued to examine the chart.

"I think someone should tell him," Sharovsky said, turning on his heel.

"Wait."

He turned, and saw that Sherwood had stood upright, his arms crossed.

"Something important is about to happen," Sherwood said. "It will happen whether Captain Volkov is informed or not. It would be better, Lieutenant, if you did not stand in the way."

"Informing my commander that an *underling* is acting without his orders does not constitute 'standing in the way,' Commander."

"Underling." Sherwood chuckled. "I will ascribe that observation to your naïveté. There are things about which you are not aware, intentionally so."

"Is Captain Volkov aware?"

"Of course," Sherwood said. "That is why he is not abovedecks."

Before Sharovsky could reply, there was a shout from above. Sherwood set down his dividers on the chart, donned his cap, and walked past Sharovsky out of the pilot house. Sharovsky turned and followed.

✻ ✻ ✻

Sharovsky's keen young eyes picked it out right away: a close hauled, fast moving ship coming at them from the southwest. It was too dark to see a flag on the topmast, if there was one at all, but he had no doubt that it was a Spaniard—it looked eerily like the ship that had taken *Strelka* several weeks earlier.

Sherwood came up beside him. Sharovsky had not even heard him approach: he started very slightly when Sherwood gave him another chuckle.

"Did you set us up, gospodin Sherwood?"

"If you mean to ask whether I have led us into a trap: the answer, in a way, is <u>yes</u>—but not in the way you think."

"You have insight into how I think."

"Lieutenant, you are an open book."

"I feel I should be insulted," Sharovsky said. "A less tolerant man might want to pitch you overboard."

"Threatening a superior officer is not the sort of thing on which to build a career," Sherwood responded diffidently. He raised a spyglass to his eye, looking toward the foretop of the ship bearing down on them. "Yes," he said to himself, or to no one in particular.

"It's a Spaniard, I assume."

"As expected. In fact, I think it is the *expected* Spaniard."

"Oh?"

"I will prepare for the boarding party, Lieutenant," Sherwood said. "If you would please inform Captain Volkov that we are about to have visitors."

☞

Volkov was unsurprised at being called abovedecks. As they made their way from the captain's cabin, Sharovsky said, "Sherwood is not working for gospodin Astor, is he." It was more of a statement than a question.

"There is no point in denying it."

"Where does his loyalty lie?"

"A good question," Volkov said. "But he may have a closer tie to the tsar than we do."

"You knew this?"

"I suspected it. Think on this, my young friend. Astor House has great power in Novaya Rossiya, clearly even more than any Russian concern. How do you suppose that happens? They made an *arrangement* with the tsar's men."

"The governor?"

"Nyet, nyet—not the governor. He is some old boyar who is enjoying the fine weather and the native food. With the Secret Chancellery, the tsar's police. Gospodin Sherwood is an operative, Georgy. I assume his loyalty lies far from Astor House, and we are now involved in a game we cannot control."

"Are we going to allow the Spaniards to board us?"

"We shall see."

* * *

The Spanish ship was in full view now, its gun-ports open, but it had neither fired a shot nor sent boarders toward *Lady Sarah*. It would have looked like a standoff—except that Sharovsky could see two other ships beyond the Spanish one.

Sherwood approached the captain as Volkov came on deck. He was armed with a pair of pistols at his belt and loosely held a cutlass.

"The boarding party is ready, Captain," Sherwood said. "Permission to depart."

Volkov looked at Sharovsky, who looked surprised: when the young man had gone belowdecks, he'd expected that it would be the Spaniards who would be doing the boarding.

"Georgy, go with the boarders. I will need a reliable man aboard to take command there."

"Captain—" Sherwood began, sounding surprised, but Volkov held up his hand.

"You will return to *Lady Sarah* once the ship is secure, Mr. Sherwood," Volkov said. "You are needed here."

The Englishman looked as if he was ready to object: but he did not. He did not respond at all, except with a nod. He turned and walked away to join the group of crewmen preparing to cross to the Spanish ship.

Volkov put his hand on Sharovsky's arm as he prepared to follow. "Keep your eye on him," he said. "He wants that ship, but I intend to bring it back to gospodin Astor."

CHAPTER 4

*L*ady Sarah came into Saint Helena on the morning tide nine days after it cleared out. William Astor met it at its berth and came aboard while the customs inspectors did their work.

Volkov saw him coming up the gangplank and gestured him to the quarterdeck. At a nod, a crewman interrupted Sherwood, who was headed to join them.

Before Astor could say a word, Volkov said, "Gospodin Astor, while we have a private moment, you will explain to me what you know of gospodin Sherwood's intentions."

"Captain Volkov—"

"Gospodin Astor. You will favor me with the truth, as a condition of my continued employment by your company."

Astor scowled, an expression Volkov knew was intended to wither lesser men. Volkov ignored it: he was not afraid of William Astor—and what was more, the man wanted information that he had.

"Sherwood is a spy."

"Da, of course he is. But who is his employer? I would have thought he was in the pay of the Great Autocrat, but I am not so sure. Do you know?"

"Not entirely. I was directed by the tsar's governor here in Novaya Rossiya to include him in the crew of *Lady Sarah*, but he seems to have an agenda separate from the Russian government. I think he is taking a stipend from another monarch. The British, or perhaps the French."

"You're not certain?"

"Did he hinder your mission?"

"Not truly. We captured Don Domingo's ship; it is at anchor in a secluded bay just south of here. He was generally polite and deferred to me as captain. But there was every indication that he had his own agenda, as you say. I would have thought you might know what it was."

"That is a disparaging tone, Captain Volkov."

"If you find it inappropriate, you may dismiss me from your service. I had thought, gospodin, that we had an understanding that we should be honest with each other—at least when lives were at stake."

Another withering scowl, and another air of indifference. At last Astor said, "I wish I knew more. But I am obliged to cooperate in certain ways with the local authorities, as you can imagine. The governor here in Saint Helena does not want to start a war with the Spanish; but he knows that my Vigilance Squadron could do just that."

"So you will abandon this project?"

"The hell I will," Astor answered. "Let us assume that I am right. If Sherwood is in the pay of His Majesty William III, then a war with Spain—a *Russian* war with Spain—would be just what Whitehall would want. On the other hand if he is in the pay of His Most Christian Majesty, having the Russians fight with the Spanish would give the French a pretext to undertake another war against their greatest rival. It has been scarcely fifteen years since New Orleans—surely they're ready to fight again."

"So on all counts, Sherwood is likely in the employ of a government that wants a war."

"It seems so."

"And you will not hesitate in giving it to them."

"It seems so, on that account as well. Does that trouble you?"

"That depends largely on what you think the objective of such a war might be. If the goal is to end piracy on this coast, to keep the Spanish out of Russian waters, I would be happy to join in such an effort. But if this is about the taking of territory—I am not interested in playing the Great Game, gospodin. Let men in London and Paris do that and leave me out of it."

"What has happened to your taste for revenge, Captain Volkov?"

You seek to goad me, Volkov thought.

"Sea air is remarkably helpful in that regard, gospodin."

"You still work for me, Captain."

Volkov did not look away from Astor's hard glance. "I know that," he said. "And the Embarcadero is right there. If I am dissatisfied with the terms of my employment, I can walk down that gangway and disappear into the crowd. I do not think I would find as comfortable or as lucrative a position, but I am sure I could find work."

The Astor gaze lasted a few more moments, then he looked down. "Very well, Captain. What is your recommendation?"

"If you want the Vigilance Squadron to make a demonstration, then we should sail along the Novaya Rossiya coast and capture every Spanish privateer that we encounter. The governor in San Diego or the Viceroy of New Spain can pay to retrieve them or leave them to rot.

"Within a year, gospodin, ships will be able to travel safely along our coasts, or else Russia and Spain will be at war. But it will be decided by kings and tsars and viceroys, not merchant princes and captains."

* * *

The coast from Saint Helena to Monterey had numerous coves and inlets; the Spanish privateer had been hidden between a small island and the coast. *Lady Sarah* anchored nearby and Volkov had himself rowed to the Spanish privateer.

Sharovsky was waiting for him as he came aboard. They exchanged salutes and handshakes.

"How are things, my friend? All quiet?"

"A Spaniard coaster went past a few days ago, but they didn't see us."

"No other trouble?"

"A few of the Spaniards have received swimming lessons, but other than that, nothing." Sharovsky could not help but smile.

"And our hidalgo. How is he?"

"Fuming. Every day he asks me when I will accord him proper dignity and respect. Now that you are here, Captain, I am sure he will assert his—"

"Ah, Captain." It was spoken in Russian, but the accent was Spanish.

The two Russians turned to face a figure emerging from belowdecks. Don Domingo was dressed in a uniform for which the adjective *resplendent* was wholly insufficient. It was adorned, decorated, and fitted out with every elaboration of medal and award that could be imagined—more a creation of the director of some mad opera than of a military organization. Clearly Don Domingo had had the thing made for himself, and felt the need to make use of it.

"Sir," Volkov said, with the slightest of bows.

"I am moved to inquire," Don Domingo said, "when my vessel and my crew are to be released."

"I am not sure what you mean. I believe this ship was taken in Russian territorial waters."

"So we are prisoners of war then?"

"There is no war."

"Then—"

"Really, gospodin, you are in no position to bargain, and I find your bluster tiresome. I have a simple question for you: what are you worth to Don Pío? What will he pay to have you back?"

"Are you suggesting that Governor Pico *ransom* me? I am an officer in His Catholic Majesty's Navy!"

"Then what were you doing in Russian territorial waters? And I don't mean just here in Monterey Bay—you took my ship near Fort Ross some weeks ago. Surely you must recognize—"

"Spain does not recognize the false Russian claim at all." Don Domingo waved his hand imperiously, as if none of it had any merit whatsoever.

"Your king, the British king, and the Tsar of all the Russias put their hands to a *treaty*, gospodin, that absolutely recognizes the Russian claim. It is not your place to contravene that. And if you claim that you are acting under orders from Governor Pico, then *he* is acting against the explicit desires of His Catholic Majesty—and committing an act of war.

"So are you acting under orders or not?"

"I am trusted to do what I think best."

"Well, then." Volkov turned to Sharovsky. "Lieutenant, prepare a noose for this pirate."

As Don Domingo's face reddened, Sharovsky said, "Aye, Captain. Shall I do so for the rest of his crew?"

"Perhaps the principal officers, Lieutenant. The rest of the crew we can put ashore."

"Captain Volkov—" Don Domingo began.

"Don Domingo," Volkov said, holding up his hand. "If you don't want to be hung like a pirate, then convince me that you are *worth something* to Don Pío Pico. Because if you have value, we will trade you back. If not, a few roubles worth of rope will solve this and we'll send your uniform back instead."

CHAPTER 5

By early spring the Vigilance Squadron included six former Spanish vessels; wherever the orders for Spanish privateers to conduct operations had originated, the orders had clearly been rescinded, allowing lightly armed and unarmed merchantmen to operate along the entire Novaya Rossiya coast.

Lady Sarah was in port following a lucrative expedition to Sitka and the Aleutian Islands; Volkov was supervising an inspection of the cargo when he noticed a colorful display on the docks. A large vessel bearing the Spanish flag, its gunports noticeably closed, rode at anchor in Golden Gate Bay, and a group of fancily-dressed men had just come onto the dock. One of them was Don Domingo, again wearing his highly ornate uniform.

For just a moment the two men exchanged a glance. Don Domingo was in the company of civilians—men of business, perhaps, or diplomats—and was clearly uncomfortable; when he recognized Volkov and *Lady Sarah* his expression turned to one of pure hostility.

God is in his Heaven, Volkov thought. *And the tsar is far away. I would wipe that smile off your face with pleasure . . . but, alas, I have better things to do.*

Za zdorovje, he added. *To your health, Spaniard. May we never meet at sea.*

SUNSET JOURNEY
1843

Make a fortune; a fortune, if you can, honestly;
if not, a fortune by any means.

—HORACE, EPISTLES
(BOOK I: "TO MAECENAS")

SUNSET JOURNEY

In the end, as at the beginning, Martin Van Buren found himself standing on a street-corner in New York. At the end, he wondered if he might have declined the opportunity had he known what lay ahead: but like so many experiences in his life, there was no opportunity to decide, *a priori*, about what might be—there was, and always would be, only a consideration of what *might* have been.

In the end, on balance, after due consideration—when the defense had rested, and the jury had departed to contemplate the verdict—he would not want to have missed it for the world.

CHAPTER 1

The instructions were clear. He was to speak to no one outside of his firm of the interview; the cab was to deliver him to the street corner where Broadway met Prince Street, and not to the doorway of the office; and he was to arrive precisely at eleven o'clock.

As he climbed the short steps of the Doric-fronted building, he could hear the bell of old Saint Edmund's beginning to chime.

He was admitted at once. He handed his hat, coat and walking-stick to a servant, who beckoned him within the great brick building. Like most New Yorkers—indeed, like most people in the world—he had never been within the offices of the richest man in British America, John Jacob Astor: indeed, since a small bit of legal work that Van Allen and Van Buren had done for Astor and Son fifteen years earlier, Van Buren didn't think he'd laid eyes on the man. But when a letter came into the office requesting this unusual appointment, he and his partner, his brother-in-law James Van Allen, had decided that he would be the one to answer.

A middle-aged man, perhaps ten years his junior, stood and extended a hand across the desk to take his own.

"Mr. Van Buren? I'm Fitz-Greene Halleck, Mr. Astor's private secretary. I *do* appreciate your visit this morning under such unusual circumstances. Won't you sit."

"No trouble at all, Mr. Halleck." Van Buren settled himself opposite. Halleck was a poet, he knew—talented and witty, part of one and another literary circle in the city. "One does not receive such—summons—every day."

"No. No indeed. But Mr. Astor has a particular project in mind, and requires the services of a reputable and discreet legal firm. If he can retain you, it will be more than worth your while."

"I am sure we fulfill both the requirements of reputation and discretion, sir."

"Quite. Quite so."

"What is the nature of the work, Mr. Halleck?"

"Mr. Astor wishes to purchase some land. A rather large amount, I daresay; what is more, he requires that the contractual arrangements be such that there is no chance—I cannot emphasize this strongly enough—*no chance* that the sale afterward be challenged."

He already owns half of Manhattan Island, Van Buren thought to himself. Astor had come to the colony in 1784 from one of the German states, taken a loyalty oath to the King to become a British citizen in 1800, and through his business acumen and foresight had built up one of the greatest fortunes in the Empire. What could he possibly want to buy *now*?

"I am sure that we can draft such agreements. Mr. Van Allen and I have considerable expertise with the law, sir."

"British common law."

"Yes, of course."

"Do you have any familiarity with the statutes of foreign nations, Mr. Van Buren? Surely in a city as cosmopolitan as New York, you must have had occasion to acquaint yourself with the law in lands other than our own Empire."

The question took him aback for a moment. He paused to examine the questioner. Fitz-Greene Halleck was of medium height, not particularly stout; he had a receding hairline and affected side-whiskers but no beard. Neatly but modestly dressed, Halleck looked a proper man of business. Like Van Buren himself, he could have been another solicitor appearing before a royal magistrate—he conveyed no information in his eyes or posture.

"On occasion, sir. There are firms that specialize in overseas commerce: Van Allen and Van Buren is not one of them. We do have considerable expertise in land transfer and sale, however— —"

"Which is why I suggested the name of your firm to Mr. Astor," Halleck interrupted. "Let me enlighten you with the reason for my inquiry. Anything I confide to you in this interview, Mr. Van Buren, must remain in the strictest confidence."

"My word is my bond, Mr. Halleck. You have already said that you appreciated my firm's discretion."

"Just so."

"Are there particular nations' laws that you had in mind, sir?"

"Russia."

Again Van Buren was given pause—but upon reflection, it might make sense: Mr. Astor's experience in the fur trade, including a joint venture in the Russian colony along the Pacific Ocean, had helped create his vast fortune. But—a land deal?

"I'm sure that there are resources we could consult, Mr. Halleck."

Halleck's face settled into a smile. He leaned back in his chair. "But. You wanted to say 'but,' Mr. Van Buren—but why would Mr. Astor want to buy land in Russia?"

"Or Russian America."

Halleck slapped the desk with his hand. "Bravo. Bravo, I say, sir. You have struck directly to the heart of the matter. Mr. Astor wishes to buy a considerable area of land in the eastern part of what the Russians call *Novaya Rossiya*—the former Spanish colony of Alta California. Young Mr. Astor—Mr. William—has been there for several years, paying particular attention to this project; but there is not a single lawyer in all of Saint Helena he can trust. Therefore, we will *send* him one."

"What—are you proposing that I *journey* to Saint Helena?"

"I am indeed."

"Mr. Halleck." Van Buren drew himself up straight in his chair. "Mr. Halleck, I am sixty-one years old; I have no more desire for travel than I have had at any time in my life. I summer at my home in Kinderhook; a journey there, a hundred and thirty miles away, is a great adventure. It is out of the question: I am not interested in traveling all the way to Saint Helena."

"Those *are* Mr. Astor's terms."

"I am afraid I cannot imagine why it is necessary."

"It is necessary," a voice said behind him, "because I deem it so."

Van Buren stood up only slightly more quickly than Halleck himself, who came around his desk to assist the man who had just entered the office. It was Halleck's employer and—potentially—Van Buren's client: John Jacob Astor himself.

"Mr. Astor——" Van Buren began, but the old man waved him off along with Halleck, causing his secretary to stand aside.

"Van Buren, isn't it?" Astor said, slowly making his way to the seat behind the desk. "You were solicitor-general for the royal governor a few years ago, weren't you?"

Halleck stood behind him. At a nod, Van Buren took his seat.

"That's right, sir."

"Close the door."

A servant closed the door behind him. Astor looked up at Van Buren; the old man was clean-shaven, stout, and plainly dressed, his expression fierce and expectant.

"Has Halleck named my terms as yet?"

"We had not reached that point in our discussions, Mr. Astor."

Astor named a figure. It was more than three times the prevailing rate for a solicitor at the court of Queen's Bench in New York. "Along with travel and incidental expenses to get you to Saint Helena."

"It is a very generous retainer, Mr. Astor. I do not find fault with it."

"Then we are agreed. You will depart——""

"I beg your pardon," Van Buren said. "I did not say that I had agreed to undertake the commission—merely that I did not find fault with the compensation."

Astor considered this for a moment, never removing his eyes from Van Buren.

"Some of my fellow men of business dislike haggling, Van Buren. I relish it. What is required in order for me to engage you?"

Van Buren wanted to say, *I would not travel to Saint Helena for all of the tea in China*—but he hesitated. Even if the firm had to hire a solicitor to replace him for a year, enough time for him to travel across the continent and back again, the sum Astor proposed would more than cover it.

It wasn't about the money—it was the reason for the journey.

"I need to understand the nature of the commission."

"Didn't Halleck explain it to you?" He cast an annoyed glance at his private secretary, who retained an impassive expression.

"He said that you wished to purchase an amount of land and that you needed a reputable and discreet attorney to draw up defensible land transfer contracts. What I wish to know is *why*."

"Hmm." Astor rubbed his chin. "I must take you into my confidence, Mr. Van Buren. If you were to disclose what I am about to tell you, the consequences would be dire. Dire, indeed. Am I understood?"

Van Buren knew what *dire consequences* must mean, coming from the richest man in British America. A word from John Jacob Astor could completely ruin his firm—and it might already be in jeopardy as he sat here in Mr. Astor's place of business. Two years ago another firm involved with the New Netherland Hotel had made some false step— and within a few months it was shuttered.

"You are understood, sir."

"Bring me the map, Halleck."

Fitz-Greene Halleck inserted a key from his watch-chain into a wooden cupboard. He opened the door and withdrew a large survey map which he unrolled carefully on the desk. It delineated the entire Pacific Coast, from the islands of Russian Alaska to the Spanish fortified mission town of San Diego. The old gentleman took an ornate letter opener with the Astor crest and sketched a line just north and east of the great double bay east of the Russian settlement of Saint Helena.

"There is a vast area here, east of Saint Helena in the foothills of the Sierra Nevada Mountains. This land, Van Buren, which I propose to buy, is at present of no particular interest to the servants of the tsar. They rightly pursue fishing, seal-hunting, and fur trapping. They have taken the collection of hovels that the Spanish called Yerba Buena, and made it into Saint Helena—not a city in the way that my beloved New York is a city, but perhaps someday . . . in any case," he continued after a moment of reflection, "I have learned something about this land that will make it extremely valuable in the coming years—something that the tsar's servants do not know; that Her Majesty's Government does not know, of which even the Spaniards, who claimed the land before the Russians did, remain ignorant.

"Under these hills lies an immense amount of *gold*."

"And if anyone learned this——""

"There would be a scramble for land rights, Van Buren. When it happens—and it *will* happen: some lucky farmer or fisherman will find traces—I want the scramble for mining rights to lead directly to the door of Astor House."

✳ ✳ ✳

Thus Van Buren decided to undertake the sunset journey, as Fitz-Greene Halleck might have termed it in one of his more hyperbolic turns of phrase.

Van Buren had taken up the law nearly forty years before in New York. It was the only career he had ever known: as a solicitor in His Majesty's courts—and now *Her* Majesty's courts—in the Crown Colony of New York. He had established a professional reputation that was the envy of many of his colleagues—they called him *the Little Magician*, as if he was a performer in the court rather than a duly appointed officer—but he took it with good grace. Everyone from old Judge Van Ness to his own sons told him that he would have been a capable politician, either as a part of New York's Assembly or in the great Colonial Assembly in Philadelphia: but the latter remained a place for men with English (and not Dutch) surnames. His world began and ended with the city and colony of New York.

When they were in the city, his sons came to visit him at his Manhattan house. On the Sunday afternoon following his interview with Halleck and Astor, his three eldest sons were at his table—Captain Abraham, Councilman John, and his namesake Martin, who clerked in his office; his youngest, Smith, was up in Albany serving as an aide to Governor Bouck. There had been five, though one—little Lawrence—had died in infancy: he was remembered with a small oval portrait on the mantelpiece in the drawing room, next to a similar one of his dear wife Hannah, the mother of his children, gone a quarter-century earlier to consumption.

Once soup and bread were on the table, he outlined the offer and the plan to travel to Novaya Rossiya.

"It's quite an interesting place, Father," Abraham said. "The Spaniards have been there for more than two hundred years." Abraham

Van Buren was the only one of his sons with any military training—he had served in the Governor-General's guard and was now a militia captain in New York.

"Then why don't they own *all* of it?" Van Buren asked.

"Well, they claim they still do," Abraham said, sampling a piece of the loaf. "Truthfully, they claim that they own all of the New World—except the part that the pope gave to the Portuguese. But His Majesty made an accord— —'"

"The Anglo-Russian Treaty," John said. "Dividing the spoils."

"That's the one," Abraham continued. "It kept the tsar out of the arms of the French King."

"We're not at war with the French," Van Buren said. "No money in it. Mr. Peel doesn't see them as enemies."

"As long as they're near neighbors in Canada, they're enemies, Father," Abraham responded. "We should have knocked them out of America thirty years ago when we had the chance."

John snorted. Young Martin snickered; he had watched his two older brothers argue before—they seldom agreed on anything.

"Jackson's army should have marched right up to Saint Louis in 1816," Abraham added. It was an old argument.

"And Lord Nashville would have spent the next twenty years fighting Indians," John answered. "The French sold off most of their claims in America anyway, without being tossed out by Old Hickory. Better he rested on his laurels as governor general and enjoyed his new earldom than spend the rest of his life kicking over hornets' nests. He had enough on his hands with the Nullifiers in the Carolinas."

"That's utter nonsense— —'" Abraham began, but the elder Van Buren held up his hand.

"I'm far more interested in the *Russian* part of America than what remains of the French part," he said. "So His Majesty's government let the tsar sup at the table when the Spanish Empire was being taken apart, and his share was California."

"*Alta* California," Abraham said. "Only as far as . . ."

"Thirty-four degrees thirty minutes north latitude," younger Martin interjected. The older brothers and his father stopped and looked at him. He took a slow drink from his mug, watching the attention shift to him.

"You had that information at hand?" Van Buren asked, smiling.

53

"I looked it up."

"You looked it up?" Abraham asked.

"As soon as I heard something about California—Novaya Rossiya—I went to the Astor Library and learned what I could. In 1809, His Majesty's government signed a treaty with the tsar that assigned Alta California north of thirty-four and a half degrees north latitude to Russia. Spain protested, because Monterey and a third of their missions were in Russian territory, but the government ignored it—we were at war and the Spanish were allied with the French."

"That was Lord Liverpool, wasn't it?" Abraham asked.

"It was the Duke of Portland," Martin said. "I——'"

"You looked it up," Abraham said, half-scowling, at his younger brother. Martin smirked. "So the Russians have been in California for thirty-five years. You'd think they'd have attorneys out *there*."

"None that Mr. Astor trusts. *Either* Mr. Astor. So——'" Van Buren raised his hands. "So, I am to travel to Saint Helena."

"Alone?" Abraham asked.

"I would not take you away from Angelica and the children," Van Buren said. He was very fond of his son's wife, a southerner Abraham had met during his service in Philadelphia. They had two toddler children—his only grandchildren. "But I thought perhaps young Martin might want to come along."

"He knows the geography," John said, and the four Van Buren men laughed. "Now, if only he spoke some Russian."

✳ ✳ ✳

Travel from the eastern to the western coast was no trivial matter in the spring of 1843. It meant a shipboard voyage either all the way around Cape Horn, a few months at least depending on the weather, or a shorter sea journey to the Isthmus of Darien, several hours on the new (and somewhat perilous) railroad across the narrow stretch of land to Fort Cornwallis on the Pacific, followed by weeks at sea traveling along the Pacific coast to Saint Helena.

Van Buren opted for the shorter travel route. The clipper *Wellesley* was to set sail within two weeks: Astor-owned packets moved between

Fort Cornwallis and the Russian coast at regular intervals bearing cargoes of fur pelts and whale oil bound for British America; Van Buren and his son arranged passage, fitting themselves out with steamer trunks full of clothing and books—law references and so forth, since it was unclear what might await him in Novaya Rossiya—mostly at the expense of John J. Astor and Son. Letters had already been sent overland—by way of rail as far as the western terminus, and then by wagon through the mountains, intending to arrive in Saint Helena a month or so before the party from New York.

Thus equipped, Van Buren father and son took their leave of their home city, unsure when they might see it again.

CHAPTER 2

If the year had been 1743—or even 1793, Van Buren supposed—a sea journey of the sort they undertook might have been a more perilous adventure. In his mind's eye, he had conceived of a trip filled with dangerous passages with French men-o'-war and black-flagged pirates who would fire on and then board *Wellesley* as she made her way from the relatively calm waters of British America's Atlantic coast into the Caribbean—what the stories of a century and more ago had dubbed the *Spanish Main*.

But France was more bucolic these days, intriguing in what remained of the Holy Roman Empire in Germany and Italy, exploring the Pacific and Africa, and intermarrying with the Habsburgs and other royal families. The Royal Navy had sent most of those pirates packing a long time ago, rooting them out from their havens as the Union Jack was planted in more and more places around the Caribbean Sea. It seemed that the greatest dangers were the alien-sounding and often uncivil language of the sailors, and the tendency to smack one's head against low-lying beams across doorways and companionways. For once, Van Buren thanked his Creator that he was small in stature—his son suffered more bumps, but adapted himself much better to the sway and roll of the ship as she plied her way south toward Panama.

Days passed uneventfully for the paying passengers, with largely fair weather drawing them southward. Van Buren father and son dined at Captain Atkins' table; though no scholar he was a well-read man, a Bostonian whose great-grandfather had been introduced to the Prince of Wales when he had arrived in Boston in 1754 for his royal progress.

According to the captain, his distinguished forebear had shaken the hand of Dr. Franklin himself, years before he assumed the title of Earl of

Schuylkill. Captain Atkins was fond of his own genealogy, and seemed able to place an ancestor at every major battle in the long history of British America—Louisbourg, Edenton, Fort Duquesne, Saratoga, Fallen Timbers, Havana, New Orleans . . . it was like a series of lessons at King's College, with a new Atkins (or Paine or Jenness or Conroy) present for every engagement.

Van Buren spent as much time as he was able working with a rather poor translation of Speransky's *Svod Zakanov*, fifteen massive volumes of Russian law that had been distilled from the forty-eight volume complete collection that had been published only a dozen years earlier. The only copy in all of New York could be found at the Russian Embassy; it had taken considerable influence by Mr. Astor to obtain the English-language version of the smaller work, and even more for Van Buren to be able to pack it for the voyage.

If it were not for the ultimate goal, this would have been a wonderful diversion indeed. Yet pack it he did, and on sunny days Van Buren took a volume on deck and found a comfortable spot to sit and study the law, a large and unfashionable hat to cover his balding head.

In the meanwhile, young Martin occupied himself with the rather ambitious task of learning the Russian language from a tutor, a certain Plakhenev who styled himself "Doctor," bound for Jamaica. By the time they reached harbor at Kingston, Van Buren surmised, his son had become sufficiently conversant in the language that he could accidentally insult a Russian of any social class or station.

* * *

The trip across the isthmus was less eventful than might have been anticipated, but in all of his years Martin Van Buren had never experienced the kind of heat that came each day of the train journey from the Atlantic to the Pacific coasts. It was to have taken six hours to travel across the narrow neck of land, but the locomotive suffered a mechanical failure an hour out of New Edinburgh, leaving the train crew and the few passengers stranded for more than nine hours while repairs were effected. Van Buren felt like Vasco de Balboa when he finally sighted the sandstone walls of Fort Cornwallis and the blue waters of the Pacific Ocean beyond.

After four days in the only hotel in Fort Cornwallis worth the title—not coincidentally bearing the Astor name—the schooner *Saratoga* arrived in port, delivering shipments of seal pelts and fruit from Novaya Rossiya. Its accommodations were less spacious than those of *Wellesley*, but she was a faster vessel—Van Buren was no sailor, but he could tell the difference in the way in which *Saratoga* handled the wind; it was confirmed when he made the acquaintance of a fellow passenger, a young Royal Navy officer on his way to Saint Helena.

"Land should belong to those who want to develop it, sir."

Saratoga was two weeks out of Fort Cornwallis, following the outer coast of the long peninsula called Baja California. It was a desolate waste, interrupted occasionally with distant, small clumps of buildings. Sometimes they looked completely abandoned—but a few had marks of civilization: little churches and clusters of houses, perhaps a few plowed fields.

"There seems precious little to develop here, Lieutenant Bartlett."

"Well, not *here*, Mr. Van Buren. But further along the coast the land is wonderfully rich. I imagine we could grow anything there: fruits and vegetables, cotton, tobacco . . . even wine grapes to rival anything the French produce."

"I'm no expert in viticulture."

"Nor am I—but how difficult could it be?" Franklin Bartlett seemed to strike a pose as he stared out across the ocean at the coastline in the middle distance. "I mean, the *French* do it, after all."

While Van Buren was proud of his skill as a rider, he otherwise felt his age—and Bartlett, nearly forty years his junior, could have served as a recruiting advertisement for the Royal Navy. Bartlett was well-read and well-spoken, strong and athletic, tall and full of life.

"There is one small problem—the land doesn't *belong* to us. It belongs to the Spanish Empire."

"For now, Mr. Van Buren. For now."

"Are we planning further war?"

"What, with the Spaniard? No. I don't believe so." He turned away from the rail. "But things change, sir. The Russian was able to obtain his share of this rich land without going to war with the decadent Spaniard;

is there any reason why we might not do the same? We already have parts of Central America—I do not see any reason why His Majesty's benevolent government could not be extended further north and west."

"Without bloodshed."

"I daresay."

"You might enjoy a conversation with my son Abraham. He would certainly find fault with your analysis—things are often far more complex than they seem, particularly when it comes to the affairs of nations. But you must know that, as you are to be attached to the embassy in Saint Helena."

Bartlett smiled and ran a finger along his luxurious moustaches. "The tsar's reach is very long, sir. But Novaya Rossiya is at his very fingertips—where his control is weakest. The American colonies are not far away; the Royal Navy has bases in Central America and in the Sandwich Islands. Sooner or later . . ."

Van Buren smiled.

"Sooner or later it will come to blows. When I was your age, young man, the Crown was at war with the French as it had been for nearly a hundred years. Even if you believe our cause was more just—and I think that I do; and I am sure that *you* do—the effort nearly drove us bankrupt. I am not eager to see us go to war for——" Van Buren gestured toward the barren coast. "For this."

"You have not seen Saint Helena yet."

"Is it New York?"

"No, of course not. Certainly not."

"I would go to war for New York, Lieutenant. But I would stop short of something that did not measure up."

There were further conversations in the same vein. Franklin Allen Bartlett was not really that dissimilar from Van Buren's own son, supremely confident in the mission of the British Crown; but he had instilled a certain amount of pragmatic cynicism in Abraham that Lieutenant Bartlett seemed to lack.

As the ship sailed northward, the land became more genial. Still, it had a certain wild and untamed nature that seemed completely different from the Atlantic shore that they had followed south from New York. At least to some extent what Bartlett said was true: all of this vast land, discovered and claimed by the Spanish more than two centuries ago, remained undeveloped. There were native tribes here, just as there had been when Europeans had arrived in the New World: but here they had not yet been civilized, coerced, or driven off.

As the sun descended to the western horizon each evening and painted the coastline gold and vermillion, Van Buren could not help but notice how beautiful it truly was.

* * *

Lieutenant Bartlett and the Van Burens parted when *Saratoga* docked. The Russian customs officials stomped on board, looking not much different from those in New York (though their English was heavily accented, as might be expected.) Still, the entire inspection process was supervised by a uniformed officer who spoke not a word: he was fitted out in handsome fashion, from the sky-blue tunic and black breeches to the peaked helmet and white gloves. He viewed the proceedings with an intense scowl, as if he were waiting for the moment at which he would express his disapproval—but it never happened.

They had arrived at the morning tide; by noon Van Buren and his son had safely arrived at the Astoria, the best hotel in Saint Helena. It was located at Alexander Square directly adjacent to the main post office, a few streets from the dock area (still called by its Spanish name: *Embarcadero*). There was no one there to welcome them, but a letter was waiting on hotel stationery.

My dear Mr. Van Buren,

Welcome to Saint Helena. Please accept my regrets for not meeting you personally, but scheduling commitments and your early arrival have conspired to interfere. I expect to be available to dine with you this evening.

By Walter H. Hunt

If there is anything at all that you require, my hotel staff will endeavor to provide it with dispatch.

I remain

Sincerely yours,

William B. Astor

It was signed with a flourish.

The hotel manager—who had received them upon their arrival—had clearly known the sender, if not the content, of the letter; he was courteous to the point of being obsequious—like a barrister before an adversarial judge, Van Buren thought. Their suite was spacious and exceedingly comfortable; he and his son were at last settled and left alone, and within a half-hour were enjoying the best sleep they'd had in weeks.

At the dinner hour they dressed and descended to the hotel lobby. There was a faintly different tang to the air and they could hear the occasional murmur of Russian in the background conversation; otherwise it could have been any elegant hotel in Manhattan: thick rugs, upholstered furniture, the soft sounds of a piano in a drawing-room—the clink of glasses, well-dressed ladies and gentlemen.

As the elder Van Buren stood and surveyed the room, an English voice said, "You've just arrived, haven't you?"

He turned to see a modestly-dressed but carefully groomed man of early middle age, who seemed to just glide into view from the shadows.

"I hope we haven't yet violated any local customs," Van Buren said, wondering what might have set the two of them apart.

"It's always hard to tell." The man bowed slightly, and extended a hand. "John Sherwood, at your service. Or as they call me here, Ivan Shervud." His Russian accent seemed convincing. He bowed again, clicking his heels together. "A pleasure to make your acquaintance."

"Van Buren," he answered. "Martin Van Buren. This is my son, also Martin." He gestured; Sherwood took young Martin's hand as well.

"Welcome to Saint Helena. Other than our gracious *hôtelier* I might well be the first person to actually say that—our Russian friends are not long on British courtesy."

"I could not say, Mr. Sherwood. Are you a . . . native of Novaya Rossiya?"

Sherwood laughed. "A transient only. Here for a time, there for a time. At this time I am here."

"Might I ask your profession?"

Sherwood smiled. "In former times I have worked as an engineer and as a naval officer; at the moment I am . . . shall we say . . . a man of leisure."

"I see."

"And your profession, Mr. Van Buren? What brings you to the Pacific shore? I do not recognize your accent—where in the Empire are you from?"

"I am from New York, sir. And I am a solicitor. An attorney."

"Ah." Sherwood raised his hands slightly. "I shall endeavor to take care. We seem to be drawing lawyers to our town these days. Are you looking to set up practice here?"

"I have a commission, sir."

Sherwood raised his eyebrows. "Is that so. Well, let me give you a piece of advice, worth the paper it's printed on as the wag is fond of saying. There are sharks even here in the shallow waters, sir." He twirled a finger. "Predators all around."

"New York has its share of predators, Mr. Sherwood. I am always on guard against them. They might want to watch out for *me*."

"You are confident about your own abilities, Mr. Van Buren. That's a good feature in an attorney. But please remember that Novaya Rossiya in general—and Saint Helena in particular—is sovereign land of Tsar Nicholas, by the Grace of God, Emperor and Autocrat of all the Russias. I imagine that when you arrived," he added in a soft, almost conspiratorial tone, "that you were under the scrutiny of a blue-uniformed officer?"

"A gendarme," the younger Martin said. Sherwood looked a bit surprised—possibly even a trifle put out, as if some great secret had been exposed at an insufficiently dramatic moment.

"That's right. A member of the Corps of Gendarmes—servants in His Imperial Majesty's Own Chancellery. The great and powerful tsar got the idea into his head when he visited France. Apparently it was quite fashionable, and he was taken with the idea . . ." Sherwood let the sentence trail off. "Of course, it's not about the uniform."

"Then what *is* it about, sir?"

"The gendarmes are His Imperial Majesty's *eyes and ears*, Mr. Van Buren. They are looking for intriguers and spies."

"Espionage is the furthest thing from my mind, Mr. Sherwood," Van Buren responded quietly. "It is hardly the purpose of my visit."

"Ah," Sherwood said, smiling again. "I am sure you are most sincere. But I assure you, that when one holds conversation with a spy, that is the first thing he says. Excuse me," he added, bowing again, and making his way across the lobby before Van Buren could reply.

Van Buren turned to his son, not sure what to say.

"That was interesting," young Martin said in Dutch.

"It was. What do you make of it?" Van Buren answered.

"In order for Mr. Sherwood to know what spies tend to say," his son continued, still in Dutch, "he would have had many conversations with them. As a fellow *professional*, sir, if you understand my meaning."

"You think he's a—"

"Yes. And he thinks the same of you, Father."

"I am not . . ." Van Buren lowered his voice almost to a whisper, even though he was speaking his original tongue, which—he suspected—no one else in earshot other than his son would understand. "I am *not* a spy."

"'The lady doth protest too much, methinks,'" the younger Van Buren said in English, after a moment. "Regardless, he likely *is*. And probably not the only one . . . in this room."

* * *

The dinner hour was later than expected, but well worth the wait. At an hour that Van Buren might have been retiring, he was escorted to the private dining room at the Astoria and there, for the first time, met William Backhouse Astor.

The younger scion of the prestigious family shared his father's piercing gaze and firmness of manner. Unlike the patriarch, however, William Astor seemed to have a stronger inclination toward fine living.

"We're glad to have you here," Astor said, taking Van Buren's hand and welcoming him into the elegant dining room. Chandeliers and glassware reflected and magnified the light from the wall-sconces; the faintest sounds from outside wafted in off the balcony with the cool night air. "Once again, let me apologize for not personally welcoming you both to Saint Helena."

"We've received a fine welcome, sir," Van Buren answered. "Allow me to introduce my son Martin."

Astor took Martin Jr.'s hand. "Your first travel abroad, young man?"

"For both of us, Mr. Astor," young Martin said. "We are homebodies."

"No longer, no longer. I miss New York, but we find many challenges here. Allow me to present my wife Margaret." A handsome woman dressed in a beautiful gown stepped forward. She was younger than Astor—likely in her forties—but careworn, as if her experience belied her true age. "I am sure you will make the acquaintance of our children, but we shall leave that for another time. Shall we dine?"

It was almost beyond Van Buren's vocabulary to describe the meal that was laid out for them. Mussels and crab, a tureen of thick, spicy soup, fresh greens, racks of lamb and the tenderest, most flavorful beefsteak Van Buren had ever tasted. Astor's wine cellar was also well-stocked. All in all it was as fine a meal as Van Buren had ever been served—surpassing a memorable dinner at Delmonico's held by the attorneys of Queen's Bench he had attended a few years earlier. By the time coffee was served, the combination of food and drink had nearly rendered him insensible.

Margaret Astor excused herself shortly and departed, leaving only the three New Yorkers at the dining table.

Astor leaned back in his chair, an unlit cigar in his hand, and said, "I realize that you must be fatigued, Mr. Van Buren, but I wish to speak briefly about our business."

"Of course, sir," Van Buren answered.

"I am informed that you had a conversation with a gentleman in the lobby this evening—a Mr. Sherwood."

"An interesting fellow," Van Buren said. "A trifle evasive on his business."

"Did you discuss *your* business with him?"

"He asked my profession. I told him that I was an attorney with a commission here in Saint Helena."

"Well, sir, there are certainly plenty of those. I had been originally minded to employ a well-known solicitor from the East who has established his practice here in Saint Helena—a Mr. Tevis. I don't suppose you know him."

"I confess that I do not."

"He is . . . predatory. I am not confident that either Mr. Tevis or his partner Mr. Haggin are the sort I would trust with the commission for which you have been retained. Still, that I have not engaged those gentlemen may have aroused Sherwood's suspicions."

"Does he work for them?"

"For Tevis and Haggin? Heavens, no. He works for the tsar."

Van Buren and his son exchanged glances across the table. The elder Van Buren allowed himself a slight smile. "He is some sort of civil servant?"

"The worst sort. He is an intriguer—an undercover agent, working for the Secret Chancellery. It is an indication that the Russian government already knows what we are doing—and why you are here."

"What are the consequences of that knowledge, Mr. Astor? Has my trip been in vain?"

"Oh, no. Not at all, certainly not." He waved the cigar around like a baton. "We shall proceed as planned. But it means that our stated reason for acquiring land in the Sierras must be clarified. I have made no secret of our firm's interest in the land—you see, we have said that we would like to build a railroad."

"Over the mountains?"

"More likely *through* them," Astor answered. "The most powerful locomotives in the world are not equal to the task of climbing the summits, or driving through the snow up there. More likely we would have to build some tunnels."

"Through rock, sir?" young Martin said. "Like a coal mine?"

"Something like it. But it would be a major undertaking—with a large engineering cost. I don't even know whether it can be done."

"It would strike me as a rather dubious proposition," Van Buren said.

"Most people will think so. But our company has invested before where others did not."

"For example," the younger Van Buren said, "land on upper Manhattan Island."

As each of the men was aware, those investments—using money derived from the Pacific fur trade—were the cornerstone of the Astor fortune. When the head of the Astor family began buying land beyond the boundaries of the city of New York, he was derided . . . but the old man had long since had the last laugh.

"Quite," Astor said. "Let people think what they wish. In the meanwhile, you can pursue the goals for which you have been engaged."

CHAPTER 3

There was gold out in the foothills of the Sierras. William Astor had evidence: John Sutter, a trapper and mountaineer in the employ of the Russian-American Fur Company, had found it in a riverbed, and a few nuggets and vials of powder were secured in a safe in Astor's office on Front Street near the Embarcadero.

Where it came from, and how it was found, was none of Van Buren's concern. Over the next few weeks his—and his son's—time were spent in the Saint Helena Land Assessor's office and at the Imperial Chancellery, poring over survey maps and volumes of land grant information. Some of it was in Spanish, and some in Russian—but Astor had native speakers in his employ for both languages.

Land grants were a tricky business. Saint Helena—Yerba Buena, as it had been called when Portolà and the Franciscans had established the Missión de San Francisco here seventy years earlier—was a tiny island of settlement in the middle of a vast area of land that had been assigned to the Russian Empire by convention in 1809, and ceded definitively by the Spanish Empire by treaty in 1831. It had originally been divided into grants called *ranchos*, usually thousands of square miles in size.

These had most often been handed over or sold by the Russian government to *dvarionstvo*—service aristocrats—back home, most of whom had never traveled ten thousand miles to see what they had bought or been given. So there they remained, verdant and wild, often sparsely occupied by squatters or Indians—Ohlones, they were called—or simply retained by the so-called californios, Spanish settlers who had met the change in territorial control with a shrug and a wink. The Russian government took interest in Saint Helena and in the settlements across the bay such as Archangel, as well as whale and seal hunting along the coast—and didn't seem to be in any hurry to develop or even survey the great inland *ranchos.*

To Martin Van Buren, these places were no more than lines on a map—and figures in a ledger. He wondered if John Jacob Astor thought of them thus. If Astor and Son had its way, it would work out much the same as it had on Manhattan island: a capital outlay in the present would yield untold riches in the future.

Somehow, he could not imagine that the Russian Empire would stand by and watch.

* * *

Van Buren usually just wanted to rest his tired eyes after a day spent poring over plats and surveyors' diagrams. A few weeks after their arrival, however, he and his son returned to the Astoria on a drizzly evening, and found John Sherwood waiting for them in the lobby. They had crossed paths with the "man of leisure"—or, if Astor was correct, a *spy*—several times since their first meeting; they had exchanged no more than a polite greeting. This evening, however, he rose and approached them as they came in out of the rain.

He was dressed in the height of fashion: tail coat with a high-rolled collar, single-breasted vest, narrow pantaloons with instep straps over highly-polished shoes, and a simple pure-white cravat above a starched shirt. A polished wood cane, topper, and white gloves lay on the armchair next to the one he had occupied.

"You are marvelously turned out, sir," Van Buren said, as Sherwood rose to greet him. "Are you invited to a soirée this evening?"

"Indeed I am," Sherwood answered brightly. He reached into a pocket inside his tail coat and withdrew an envelope, which he extended to Van Buren. "And so are *you.*"

Van Buren accepted the item and opened it. Within were two pasteboard cards marked CASPIAN SEA ROOMS. Each was inscribed in a small, precise hand: one said LORD VAN BUREN, the other MR. VAN BUREN. There was a printed date: this evening—and a time, 8 PM SHARP.

"'Lord . . .'? I suspect that someone is confused about my station in life."

Sherwood smiled. "It is an error in your favor. You have not been in Saint Helena long enough to know about the Caspian Sea Rooms, Mr. Van Buren—but it is an exclusive place, attended only by those whom the Lady Patronesses permit. Do you know about the famous club Almack's, sir?"

"In London. Yes, of course—are you suggesting that this club, the Caspian Sea——"" he turned the cards over in his hand, then passed them to his son"—is somehow an *homage* to Almack's?"

"Better than that. One of the Lady Patronesses here in Saint Helena is none other than the Princess Dorothea Lieven—who once held that exalted position thirty years ago when her husband was Russian Ambassador to the Court of St. James. Now she resides here, nurturing the same sort of society and promoting the same *ton* that she once fostered in the center of the British Empire.

"And, Mr. Van Buren, the lady wants to meet *you*. If I were in your stead, I should not like to keep her waiting."

✹ ✹ ✹

A long time ago, nearly fifty years before—before he had even met his dear Hannah, before his sons, before he had even come to New York—Van Buren had taken up an apprenticeship with Francis Silvester, a prominent barrister in Kinderhook. The young man was to sweep the floor, build the fires, fill the inkwells—and in return, at age fourteen, Silvester would give him a rudimentary education in the law.

On the first day of his new employment, he had appeared in clothes of coarse linen and woolens, spun and woven by his mother. Over the course of the day, the garments became more and more unkempt and dirty. At the end of the day, Attorney Silvester delivered him a lecture on the importance of proper clothing. Two days later, young Matty turned up in the same expensive suit as the attorney wore, cut to his more modest frame. He had borrowed the money for the suit and worked two months to pay it back. No one would ever accuse him again of a casual attitude toward clothing—he always thereafter paid close attention. Some of his fellow attorneys called him a dandy: well and good—but they would never accuse him of being slovenly.

Though the invitation was unexpected—it had arrived totally without preamble!—Van Buren was not about to pass up the opportunity tossed his way. Within half an hour, father and son were attired in the best suits in their wardrobe: dress coats cut away in the front, handsome vests and pantaloons, shirts and cravats laid carefully in trunks in New York and untouched by the incessant damp of Saint Helena. Van Buren's vest was a bit more of a fashion statement than that of his son—cerulean blue with a faint paisley pattern that rather set off his eyes—but they were otherwise in proper *mode* for a formal reception at Almack's, at a gentleman's club in New York, or even at the club to which they had been invited. Van Buren knew that he could at the very least dress the part. The survey maps and court records of three-quarters of a century were to be put away for the night.

✳ ✳ ✳

A carriage brought them to the Caspian Sea Rooms, an elegantly-done up ballroom on the ground floor of a large house significantly uphill from the harbor area. Van Buren had not ridden carriages or trams around—the hills were so steep and treacherous that it seemed a single misstep would send horses and people hurtling down to their deaths; he had preferred to walk instead. But in evening dress it would hardly be suitable to arrive on foot. Thus it was with some trepidation that he stepped into a carriage with his son and Sherwood to make the journey to the club, which stood at the base of a hill surmounted by an onion-domed Orthodox church – the Cathedral of Saint Helena. There was a tower there with a telescope, and Van Buren had been told that many businesses in the city paid a fee to help keep it staffed day and night to report on the arrival (or demise) of ships in the great Golden Gate Bay beyond.

It seemed almost ironic that a society ball would be held in the lee of a church—but perhaps, Van Buren mused, the Orthodox faith looked more kindly upon such an event.

There was a queue at the door. Despite the light rain, a number of people were standing under the awning of the large two-story building, an ungainly structure that looked like a cross between a goods warehouse and a Grecian temple—huge windows and a flat roof, with the front redone in a sort of Neoclassical style, with pillars and pediments. The gentlemen and ladies held umbrellas to cover their fashionable garb, and the queue slowly moved forward through the double doors. Van Buren could see as soon as he alighted from the cab that there was a lady in a formal gown consulting some sort of bound volume on a lectern just inside the door; most of the guests were being graciously greeted, but a few were politely turned away—though rarely without some sort of argument.

"Don't worry, old man," Sherwood said. He patted his pocket. "We have signed vouchers. I know we are listed in that book. We don't even have to queue." As he spoke, he was leading Van Buren by the elbow along the line, with the younger Van Buren following behind. There was some murmuring, but as soon as they went through the doorway, he was greeted by name by the lovely hostess.

"So nice of you to be with us this evening, Mr. Sherwood. And your companions . . .?" she gestured delicately with one hand, encased to the elbow in a white kid opera-glove; one eyebrow raised itself ever so slightly.

"These are the Van Burens, father and son," he said.

The haughty demeanor of the lady seemed to transform itself at once. "Of course, of course! Please be welcome at the Caspian Sea Rooms, my lord," she said, offering a slight curtsy. "And your son as well."

"I beg your pardon," Van Buren began, producing the vouchers from his pocket and offering them—but they were completely ignored as the two New Yorkers were ushered within. There was a bit more murmuring among the ladies and gentlemen queuing for their turn, but any objections were being ignored. In a few moments, the Van Burens found themselves divested of outer coats, hats, and gloves.

A paneled hallway led into the Caspian Sea Rooms, separating the hubbub and weather without from the genteel accommodations inside. Sherwood nodded politely and disappeared into the crowd, leaving them to pause for several moments while they took stock of their situation.

The ground floor of the club was a series of linked drawing rooms. From somewhere nearby, Van Buren could hear someone softly playing a piano; all around there were people mingling, speaking politely to each other in English, French, Spanish, and Russian—and possibly other languages: he couldn't be sure. The air was faintly tinged with lavender.

In the middle, nearly opposite the door, there was a grand staircase that branched at the top, leading to an upper floor.

"Dancing," Martin Jr. said. "That's where the dance floor is."

"Quite right," a female voice said behind them, in perfect English tinged with a faint, but perceptible, Russian accent. "The upstairs windows can be opened to the night air, and the view of the bay is really quite wonderful."

Van Buren and his son turned to see who had spoken, and for the first time laid eyes upon Doroteja fen Lieven—Her Serene Highness Dorothea Lieven. She was beautiful: tall and lithe, clearly a woman far into middle age but a radiant figure, dressed in an exquisite off-the-shoulder gown in pale blue. A king's ransom in jewels adorned her breast, her ears, her wrists. She seemed to outshine everything in the room.

For all of his skill, with all of his experience and worldliness, Martin Van Buren found himself speechless before her.

"You must be Lord Van Buren," Princess Lieven said. "And this must be your son. We are most esteemed by your presence."

"I . . . am honored to be here," Van Buren finally managed. "But I have a confession, Highness. I am not worthy to be addressed as lord. I am a simple barrister from the Colony of New York."

"You have no title?"

"I must regrettably say that I do not."

Van Buren wondered if he would be escorted from the premises. If so, it would be a disappointment, but such were the vagaries of court life: he would depart with the same dignity he entered.

The princess merely smiled.

"Your honesty does you credit, sir. It is of no matter. Here we do not judge a guest by the title he carries—but rather by the way in which he carries *himself*. I must offer you an apology for taking so long to invite you to be with us."

Van Buren had no reply. The princess beckoned to another woman standing nearby, who came to stand beside her. "Allow me the honor of introducing Vasileva Serastova, who has been my particular friend for several years, and who accompanied me out here to Saint Helena two years ago." Miss Serastova bowed; Princess Lieven conveyed her elbow gently onto the younger Van Buren's hand. "Now," she said. "Shall we dance?"

* * *

She danced marvelously.

Van Buren realized from the first cadences of the waltz that every eye in the ballroom was upon him; he thanked the Lord Most High, and every other intervening power between heaven and earth, that he had taken dancing lessons—for though she was a few inches taller than him even in dancing-slippers, and though she moved with an air of confidence while he was feeling his way through the evening with every step—he was able to carry off his part with dignity.

They spoke only of trivialities while dancing. It was not Van Buren's intention to talk of business, particularly not when it came to his reason for being in Novaya Rossiya; the Princess did not ask—but he could see that William Astor was present, standing among the tailcoated gentlemen at the side of the ballroom, his expression stony as his eyes followed Van Buren's every dance-step.

At last, after two waltzes and a quadrille (during which the lady politely rebuffed attempts by a number of gentlemen to induce Van Buren to yield), she led him off the floor into a side alcove, where a bowl of punch and a light repast—bread, cheese, condiments of some sort, and fresh fruit—was laid out. Beyond, there were French doors open to the balcony, where the early evening rain had yielded to a cloudy moonlit night. She daintily chose a few items, accepted a glass of the pale-colored punch, and invited Van Buren to sit at one of the small tables near the open balcony.

"Your Highness dances very well," Van Buren said, sipping carefully at the punch—which, to his surprise, appeared to be nothing more than lemonade.

"I shall make you a bargain. I will not address you as 'Your Lordship' if you desist from calling me 'Highness.' We are agreed?"

"It is no loss of dignity for me, madame. Your title is yours by right, the other is merely a bookkeeping error."

Her eyes flashed—for a moment he thought he had offended her, but he was at a loss to understand exactly how. But then she smiled and chuckled. "You tread on dangerous ground here, sir," she replied. "The word of the Lady Patronesses, here as it once was at Almack's, is law—and you suggest at your peril that any error was made."

"Regarding the title only."

"We ennoble those whom we choose. We turn away those whose character—or behavior—do not measure up to our standards. Be assured, my dear Mr. Van Buren——" she paused to lay one gloved hand upon his own"—that you exceed our requirements on both counts. We hold our little parties but once a week; your presence would please us all immensely."

"I am flattered, your H——" he looked away. "I beg your pardon. The habit of courtesy is hard to break."

"As it should be. But you must call me Dorothea. And I shall call you Martin, if you will permit."

Van Buren paused and sighed deeply. To his professional colleagues and friends he was *Van* or, sometimes, *Matty*: his sons, and even his daughter-in-law, invariably addressed him as *Father*. No one had called him by his Christian name for many years . . . it had always been the choice of his dear Hannah, now a quarter-century in the grave. The idea that a lady of such standing should want to be on a first-name basis at once was more than a little surprising.

"I have offended you."

"No, no—not at all." Van Buren withdrew his hand from beneath hers, but looked back at her, seeking to steady himself as he spoke. "I am only put in mind of my wife. My late wife."

"We have all lost someone, Martin. If I may call you that. My Kristoph, the Count Lieven—he died a few years ago, along with my two youngest sons. I . . . am no longer comfortable in Saint Petersburg. After my husband died during the tsar's Grand Tour, I left Russia for Paris—but even that was not far enough distant to soothe my poor heart."

"Thus—Saint Helena."

"To be sure," the Princess said. "It remains to be seen if this is far enough. In the meanwhile, it amuses me to recreate what once gave me such great joy elsewhere. These rooms are not Willett's in London, and this club is far from Almack's . . . yet it conveys a bit of the *joie de vivre*, the *ton* of society that speaks of gentility and good manners.

"We have done what we can to bring whatever we can here to the Pacific shore. Why, just last week the renowned ballerina, Miss Elssler, arrived from the east. She will be performing at the Imperial Theater beginning next week."

"Fanny Elssler? The Austrian dancer?"

"Why, yes indeed. Do you know the lady?"

"Not personally—no, of course I have not made her acquaintance." Van Buren smiled. "But my son Martin is an aficionado of the art and was quite taken with Miss Elssler's performance when she was in New York last year. I had no idea that she might travel all the way out here."

"Ah." The Princess smiled in her turn. "She and I are old friends, Martin. I first met her when she came to London, and the acquaintance was renewed when she was on stage in Paris. She has extended her American tour to include Saint Helena . . . at my request." She looked away, the soft candlelight catching her jewelry, then returned her gaze to the New Yorker. Her expression was that of someone who had just shared a precious secret. "I shall endeavor to obtain an introduction for your young man."

"He will be gratified beyond words."

"It shall be my pleasure."

"All of this is a wonder," Van Buren said at last. "I could not have imagined such a thing here."

"Did you expect different?"

"In Saint Helena? I . . . well, I confess that I did not know *what* to expect. A place of fur traders and seal hunters and whalers; a distant outpost of the Russian Empire——"

"Filled with Russians."

"I have never seen London, madame. Indeed, I have never been abroad until now. But we tend to measure every city by the standards of our own New York. And Saint Helena is *not* New York."

"No." She patted his hand again. "I do not think anyone believes otherwise. But what—did you think this would be a group of squatters' huts filled with _esquimaux_ and ribald sailors? Society is what we make it, Martin. If this establishment can help improve gentility here, then it is more than worth its while." She glanced across the room at the staircase;

William Astor was still there, keeping a watchful eye on Van Buren and the princess. "Your employer has been very generous in assisting us thus far."

"Mr. Astor is a fine gentleman."

"And a good businessman. And clearly your work here is part of that business. I have heard that he wishes to buy some of the land across the bay, near the mountains. Why would he wish to do that?"

She asked it in a light, offhand way—but it put Van Buren immediately on his guard. His first reaction was suspicion—*why should she want to know?*

Then, upon consideration—or perhaps after a few moments of contemplating the lovely woman who was sharing his evening—he dismissed the thought. Society gatherings were all about the exchange of gossip—and surely any undertaking the size and scope contemplated by William Astor could not remain secret for long. What was more, she would not demean such a setting with such a discussion. Almack's—and the Caspian Sea Rooms—were no place for business.

But he still did not wish to answer the question directly.

"Mr. Astor is a clever man, Dorothea. He felt that my firm's services were more dependable and respectable than those of others who practiced law here in Saint Helena."

"Like Mr. Haggin and Mr. Tevis."

"Those names were mentioned, yes."

"Rest assured, my friend Martin," she said haughtily, "that is the only time you will hear *those* names spoken in this club. They are not welcome here—they are *not* the sort of person we wish in our company. They are said to be skillful at what they do. But I am sure that your knowledge and skill is superior, and that Mr. Astor made a wise choice."

"You are most complimentary."

"Thank you. Well. I hope that we will have many other opportunities to speak—and to dance." She rose gracefully from her seat; he was on his feet at once as well.

She offered her hand; he bowed over it and offered the merest touch of his lips, *à la française*—and she presented him another radiant smile.

"Thank you very much . . . Dorothea."

She graced him with a regal nod, and then turned away.

CHAPTER 4

The days flew by, interrupted each week by a visit to the Caspian Sea Rooms. Van Buren and his son prepared an ever-increasing number of land transfer agreements between the managers for the absentee *dvarionstvo* and several holding companies, entities that Astor had created to cloak their activities.

At the beginning of the following week, and nearly every night thereafter, young Martin attended the Imperial Theater, enthralled by the dancing of the great ballerina Fanny Elssler. True to her word, Dorothea Lieven arranged for the young man to meet her at a British Embassy reception, and invitations duly arrived at their hotel.

Tens of thousands of square miles of vacant land lay between the Golden Gate Bay and the Sierra Nevada Mountains, the great range that separated the Pacific coast lands from the sources of rivers that flowed into the Atlantic and the Gulf of Mexico. As their work progressed, the rights to the lands moved more and more into the hands of William Backhouse Astor.

* * *

On a foggy Saturday morning three and a half weeks after their first visit to the Caspian Sea Rooms, Van Buren's mail included a personal letter bearing a local stamp.

A carriage will call for you at ten o'clock. I have a marvelous spot for lunch.

D

"I think this is a *personal* invitation, Father," young Martin said, lowering his teacup and the daily newspaper. He looked out through the bay window of the breakfast room. "It doesn't look much like a picnic day."

"I'm sure the princess knows what she's about."

"And I'm sure that she doesn't need *me* around to—I don't know, hold a parasol for Her Serene Highness. Besides, there is a matinee this afternoon at the Imperial." His eyes shone with the light of the recently smitten.

"I'm sure she has servants for that."

"If she brings them along." Martin smirked.

"You should be ashamed, young man. She would not be unescorted. There will be someone to hold her parasol, and someone to lay out the blanket, and someone to . . ."

"I have the general idea." He pushed out the chair next to him and beckoned for his father to sit. Van Buren drew out his pocket-watch and consulted it: a quarter to ten. He smiled and sat.

"Would you like breakfast?"

"I dined and had a constitutional earlier. Thank you."

"Father, I've been thinking. Your friend the princess——'"'"

"Dorothea."

"The princess. She seems a gentle, kind lady."

"And beautiful," Van Buren said. "Don't forget that she is beautiful."

"I hadn't. But had it occurred to you that she is, well . . . a bit above your rank, Father. Why has she taken an interest in *you*?"

"I think I still cut a reasonable figure at my age." Van Buren reached for the teapot and poured himself a cup. He considered a sweetroll, but decided against it. "I don't see—"

"No, Father, *I* don't see. Of course you're a handsome man, an accomplished and intelligent man . . . but for the princess—a Russian aristocrat—to suddenly be taken with you, doesn't that strike you as a bit suspicious?"

"Should it?"

"It does for me. I am concerned about her motives, Father."

"It may not have occurred to you, my son, but her motives might not be what you think. She has suffered great loss, Martin. Her husband—her two youngest sons . . . and her country. She is on the other side of the world from everything she knows.

"She looks confident and strong, Martin, but she is wounded. There is an inner sadness."

Young Martin Van Buren clearly saw the sadness in his own father's eyes. It had always been there, of course: it had never been absent, not as long as Martin had been old enough to notice.

"You think that she sees you as a . . . kindred spirit."

Van Buren sipped his tea. "Something like that."

Martin considered a reply, but saw the light in his father's eyes.

"I just want you to be careful, Father," he said at last.

✳ ✳ ✳

A road led over a series of hills west from the town gate. The great bay was intermittently in view below, partly shrouded in fog; it was, as Martin had said, hardly the sort of day that made one want to picnic. But after they passed by the Presidio, a fort converted for use by the Spanish ambassador, a marvelous thing happened. The road led up over a final hill and suddenly they emerged from the fog into bright sunlight, as radiant as a summer's day, that had appeared before its time in late spring. There was not much of a road here; the peninsula came to an abrupt end not far beyond, dropping sixty or seventy feet to rocks below. While a shore could be discerned in the distance to the north, to the west there was nothing—pale-blue ocean rolling down onto the rocks, visible all the way to the horizon.

The driver had pulled the carriage onto a wide verge that gave a beautiful view in both directions, right about where the road—if there ever was one—would change its direction from west to south.

After a moment, the driver and footman opened the carriage-doors and assisted the princess and Miss Seratova down, and then offered their assistance to Van Buren; he accepted a single hand but otherwise descended without help.

"We have arrived," Princess Lieven announced.

While the servants set out a blanket and folding stools, the princess offered Van Buren her arm, and they walked near to the brow of the hill to look out over the ocean. Her friend followed, but at a distance.

"Isn't it beautiful?" she said. "There are two great hills and a range of smaller ones off to the south. On this side, the weather is almost always different from what they have in the town. So even though it's dismal there—"

"It's bright and sunny here. Yes," he agreed. "It's breathtaking."

"I understand that some enterprising soul in Saint Helena is thinking that he might build a tea room here. Imagine—miles from anywhere, at the side of a cliff. I think that's what he wants to call it—'Cliff House'."

"It *would* be quite a view."

"Yes, I suppose it would be. In fact, we've packed a telescope to get a better look. I wanted you to see this, Martin—you don't have views like this in your New York."

"We have our own landscapes."

"Yes, yes. Everywhere does." She gazed out over the ocean, not speaking for a time. "This is the edge of the world, Martin," she finally said. "Beyond here—" she gestured out across the ocean—"there is nothing but ocean for thousands of miles. Nothing from here all the way to the islands of Japan and the mainland of Russia. The Sandwich Islands are out there somewhere as well."

"The edge of the world. That's very prosaic."

"But very accurate. The Russian Empire clings to its small part of North America—nothing like the expanse over which your Queen rules. But it is a golden land." She looked at him. "Wouldn't you say?"

It was another comment presented in an offhand way, but the choice of words made him alert at once. His courtroom experience, however, allowed him to retain a mask of serenity.

"I am told that wine-grapes as fine as those of France grow here," he said. "And fruits and vegetables of every description. No harsh winters. I would venture to say that makes it a golden land, Dorothea."

She seemed to be recounting his response, studying him, trying to determine what she thought of it.

"I don't miss the winters, Martin. Not at my age."

"Each season has its own beauty. Any farmer can tell you that."

"Not when the winds howl across Lake Ladoga," she answered. "Come, I think our luncheon may be ready."

They sat on folding stools at a little table under the shade of an umbrella. There were small sandwiches, crackers spread with some darkish substance Van Buren could not identify, cheese and fresh fruit, all accompanied by an excellent wine. A gentle breeze stirred the air, but not enough to cause discomfort. Miss Seratova ate daintily but did not speak; Van Buren could find nothing in particular to say.

After eating, they walked to where the telescope had been set up. The footman had been looking through the eyepiece, but stood straight as Princess Lieven approached; they exchanged a few sentences in Russian, of which Van Buren understood not a word.

Before she bent to look through the glass, the princess glanced up curiously at Van Buren. She looked, then adjusted the eyepiece and the angle of the tube and stood erect.

"Martin, I think you might find this of interest."

"What is it?"

"I should be gratified if you could tell me."

Van Buren stepped around to stand close beside the princess. He removed his handkerchief and wiped his eyes and brow, then bent to place one eye on the eyepiece.

Through the telescope a scene swam into view: two, and then three broad two-deck warships, their gunports closed. Each flew the Union Jack at the topmast.

He gazed out across the ocean, shielding his face with one hand. He could just barely pick them out—they must have been a few miles out to sea.

As he did so, he realized that those ships would have been nearly invisible unless one knew where to look for them—and the princess, or perhaps one of the servants, had known. Though it was clearly a beautiful spot, and though her affection for the place was genuine, she had brought Van Buren out here so that he could see what she had just shown him.

"Those are Royal Navy ships, madame," he said.

"Yes, that much is clear. I am minded to ask—why are they here?"

"I do not know why you are asking *me*," he responded at once. "I am an attorney, not a naval officer." *And I do not know why you are asking me,* he thought to himself. *What does this mean?*

"I ask," she said quietly, "because you are a citizen of the British Empire. You, Mr. Astor, and a dozen others in Saint Helena who might have an interest in seeing our land added to the vast territories that already belong to that Empire—at the expense of my own."

"I have no such interest," Van Buren said. This conversation had suddenly changed: it had been bucolic and pastoral, and of a sudden it seemed threatening. "I am part of no such plot, and will not be party to one."

"I am gratified to hear you say that."

Van Buren turned at the sound of the voice to see John Sherwood approaching. He was casually dressed, but was accompanied by four men in the uniform of the gendarmes, one obviously an officer. He stopped and offered a deep bow to the princess, then took Van Buren by the elbow and led him a dozen feet away.

"Unhand me at once," Van Buren said, shaking loose from Sherwood's grasp. "I demand to know the meaning of this."

"Listen very carefully to me, Mr. Van Buren," he whispered. "I want to reassure you of two things. First, I am convinced that you are *not* intentionally involved in any plot against the Russian government of Saint Helena. There are others who do not share that view, but I am doing my best to disabuse them.

"Second, the project that your Mr. Astor has undertaken out here in Novaya Rossiya is no secret. His Serene Majesty Tsar Nicholas, Emperor and Autocrat of all the Russias, is aware that there is *gold* in the hills of the Sierras, and there is no possible scenario in which the Astor family can acquire all of the land without involving the Russian Government."

"I see," Van Buren said. He was not interested in confirming or denying anything. "Was there anything else?"

"Oh, yes, one more thing." Sherwood smiled, his lips pulling back from his teeth in a rather unpleasant rictus. "It is possible that there may be some sort of conflict between the tsar and Her Majesty Queen Victoria. It is a matter of no great importance to me which side ultimately wins."

Without another word, Sherwood turned and walked back to the group of people standing near Princess Lieven. Van Buren followed warily, not sure what had just happened.

"Thank you very much, your Serene Highness," Sherwood said, bowing again. Princess Lieven's face was a mask of tightly-controlled fury. This was not the scene she had expected—and this was clearly not the role she had planned to play.

"Perhaps we should return to Saint Helena," Van Buren ventured.

Sherwood nodded. "Yes, by all means. Please do not trouble yourself, madame," he said to the Princess. "We will be more than happy to convey Mr. Van Buren back to his hotel."

✳ ✳ ✳

They only got as far as the Presidio.

A messenger was waiting when they reached the fort. The gendarme officer was handed a dispatch; there was another brief conversation in Russian, to which Sherwood listened intently (and of which Van Buren understood not a word, except the name *Astor*, which was mentioned twice). The officer was not at all happy with the result. He dictated a curt reply, which the messenger repeated once, then mounted his horse and spurred off toward the town.

"We will wait here for a bit," Sherwood said. The Presidio was a small, stout fort, not built to withstand much but rain and the occasional Indian; it was situated on a high enough hill that a spyglass could give a view of the nearby bay, but not much else. The Spanish ambassador, an officious little man, seemed put out by the presence of the Russians, but made no protest, retreating to his residence and leaving Van Buren and his escort in the reception area.

"I wouldn't suppose," Van Buren said, "that you could let me know what's going on."

"You'll learn in due time."

"Mr. Sherwood," he said, "if that is indeed your name, my *son* is in Saint Helena. If he is in any danger—"

"There is always that possibility," the other replied. "But unless he causes some sort of provocation, I suspect that he is quite safe."

"I am hardly reassured."

Sherwood seemed to consider this for a moment. Then he said, "Your Mr. Astor—or the patriarch, or perhaps both—have turned out to be more clever than anyone expected. Apparently they had friends in the Royal Navy."

"I am not surprised. Pray continue."

"I have to admit, the plan was a clever one: permit Astor and Son to invest heavily in the gold fields to the north and east, then seize the lands for the tsar. Astor would be compensated, of course—but it would be the Great Autocrat's government that would reap the benefits of land leases, after all of the work had been done to locate the sites.

"But evidently *that* was anticipated. Rather than having no recourse, Mr. Astor's connections in the Royal Navy offered a source of leverage. Either Astor would be paid handsomely—perhaps by becoming a partner in the gold land business, or by being bought out at a much increased price by the tsar—or else the Royal Navy would step in to defend the rights of a British citizen. It is my belief that all of this was foreseen."

"By everyone but me."

"Forgive me, Mr. Van Buren, but you are not acquainted with the rules of the game. New York's Court of Queen's Bench is one sort of arena; while the field of international diplomacy—"

"Espionage, rather."

"A turn of phrase. The field of international diplomacy is quite another. You played your part very well. All of it—even the part with the lovely Princess Lieven."

Van Buren stared at him angrily. "I should like you to clarify exactly what you mean by that statement, sir."

Sherwood did not answer for a moment, then rubbed his chin thoughtfully. "You don't know, do you?"

"Know what?"

"Dorothea Lieven is a socialite, of course. For more than twenty years she was the wife of the Russian Ambassador at the Court of Saint

James. But her maiden name is von Benckendorff. Her older brother, the Count von Benckendorff, is the commander of the Corps of Gendarmes—and the head of the Secret Chancellery.

"What it means, Mr. Van Buren, is that the woman who has so captured your affections . . . is a *spy*."

* * *

Van Buren returned to Saint Helena after sunset, where he was met in the lobby of the Astoria by his son and by William Astor. The younger Martin looked visibly relieved; Astor seemed to be scarcely perturbed by the entire turn of events. He escorted them both to the lift and to the private dining room, which was empty except for a servant, who made them stiff drinks.

"I believe that I owe you something of an apology, Van Buren," Astor said. "You will receive none from my father, I'm afraid: he's not in the habit of dispensing such things."

"I do feel as if I have been a pawn in some game."

"And you have been. But this outcome was by far the most likely—and you have done your part admirably. There will be some details, but the Governor-General of Novaya Rossiya has agreed to compensate my firm for quite a sum of money to acquire most of the land that you have under agreement. It was either that or . . .'"

"Cannonades, I suppose."

"Or perhaps more than that. I don't think that the Russians truly have a long-term interest in North America, but it might take decades for them to decide that. Another tsar, perhaps."

"And another Astor," Martin said.

"Young man, everyone walks happily away from this—the Russians, my firm, Her Majesty's government for having protected the interests of her subjects—"

"Everyone?" Young Martin looked disgusted, unhappy at being presented with ugly truth.

"I intend to send you two home with a substantial bonus, young man. As I told your father, he has played his part admirably. This is not the end of the Astor business here in Saint Helena—no matter who ultimately governs it. Your legal work has assured us of a position here on the Pacific coast—and there are innumerable business opportunities awaiting us. I think . . . I may consider the Sandwich Islands."

"Palm trees and tropical breezes?"

"Well, sugar, certainly . . . but more importantly, the Sandwich Islands are roughly halfway between Saint Helena and the Russian coast in Asia. Between British and Russian interests, I'm sure it will be an interesting port of call for years to come. Would you have any interest in working with me in Honolulu, Van Buren? I'm told it's a paradise."

"I would like to be back in New York, Mr. Astor. I will be content to go home."

"I'm sure we can wrap up our business here in a matter of weeks. You shall have the best accommodations on your return journey."

CHAPTER 5

It turned out to be as simple as Astor had described it. There was a British presence in the harbor, anchored well offshore; the gunports on the six—*six!*—warships remained closed, and it was reported that the tsar's governor had received Commodore Sir Stephen Decatur with all due honor and ceremony. Within days of the abortive picnic, reports of the discovery of gold were streaming into Saint Helena, and the government was issuing prospecting licenses as fast as it could print them.

* * *

On the day he was to depart, Van Buren stood at the dock on the Embarcadero watching his luggage being brought aboard, when he spied a familiar figure—Lieutenant Franklin Bartlett, who had shared his journey northward. The young man was in even better spirits than when he had last seen him.

"Headed home, sir?"

"Yes, Lieutenant. I have drunk my fill of Saint Helena, I believe."

As if testing the air, Bartlett drew in a deep breath. "I think it will take me considerably more time to tire of it, Mr. Van Buren. I think the place is quite charming."

"In its own way."

"I had hoped to meet you at the Caspian Sea Rooms. I was told that you were a member there."

"I was. We attended . . . for a time." Van Buren adjusted his hat on his head, as a sudden breeze threatened to carry it off. "Its charms dissipated as well."

"I'm sorry to hear that. It's really quite a wonderful place—particularly if a man wishes to establish . . . long-term relationships. If you understand my meaning."

"My long-term relationships are all in New York, sir. But I wish you the best of luck in all your endeavors." The two men shook hands; Bartlett seemed to want to say more, but also seemed to sense that the conversation was at an end. He turned and walked away along the Embarcadero. Van Buren watched him until he was out of sight.

Martin had already gone aboard to see to their things, but the elder Van Buren—for all of his stated desire to return home—felt no great desire to go onto the ship and surrender his last minutes of fresh open air. He walked to a wooden railing and looked out across the inner bay. Somewhere beyond the far shore, out of sight, were the golden hills that had provided William Backhouse Astor with his desired coup. While he had worked here in Saint Helena they had existed only as items in his mind's eye: plats and surveys and deeds of sale, chimeras of his imagination. For all he knew they might as well not even exist.

"I am so glad that you haven't gone aboard yet, Martin."

He turned at the sound of the woman's voice interrupting his reverie. Princess Dorothea Lieven stood there, the late-afternoon sun perfectly setting off her complexion; a carriage stood some distance away—obviously it had brought her hence.

"Your Serene Highness," he said, bowing. "It is a pleasure to see you again."

"I thought we had agreed to dispense with titles."

"It would be inappropriate at this point, I think. I apologize for any misunderstanding we may have had."

"It is I who owe you an apology. I . . . did not intend things to happen the way they did."

"I cannot conjecture how Your Highness intended *things* to happen. In fact, I am sure that my powers of deduction have atrophied as a result of the Pacific air, or my advancing age, or—or something."

"Mr. Sherwood was precipitate and unpleasant. Be assured that he is not welcome in the Caspian Sea Rooms. His name has been stricken from our books."

"I cannot convey how gratified I am to hear that."

"Sarcasm ill becomes you."

"This exchange ill becomes either of us, madame. It is clearly beneath you to prevaricate about any intimacy between us, and it merely reminds me how much a fool I have been."

Princess Lieven looked genuinely hurt; but her face also conveyed sympathy.

"You were never a fool, Martin. My affection for you was genuine. Is genuine."

Van Buren did not answer. It was another indeterminable statement following a few months of intrigues and lies: more games in which he had been not a player, but merely a pawn.

"You don't believe me."

"My son told me that he saw no reason why a lady of your station would take any interest in a man in mine. I should have listened to him: I know why you did so—it was because of the gold. It was always because of the gold, all of it: my commission here in Saint Helena, my invitation to the Caspian Sea Rooms. And . . . all the rest."

"You are mistaken, Martin. Not completely: I admit that. But not completely."

"Princess, this is unendurable. I shall board my ship soon and leave all of this behind. I beg you to let me go in peace."

"You can choose to believe me or not, but though I pursued you because of your involvement with Astor, I truly did enjoy your company and your attentions. You are a gentleman, Martin: witty, intelligent, courteous, and kind. I cannot tell you how many men I have met who have none of those qualities.

"I never wanted to hurt you, not in any way. You must believe that I am telling you the truth."

"It was just business."

"Yes. I suppose that it was."

Van Buren considered how to answer that. There were so many possible choices: he could be conciliatory, he could be cutting, or he could simply be indifferent.

No, he thought. *Not indifferent. If she truly felt him to be a fool—why come here to say goodbye? They would likely never see each other again.*

"I will treasure the memory of our time together, madame."

"Will you not address me by my name?"

"I will remember you always . . . Dorothea."

✳ ✳ ✳

New York was much as he had left it. Spring and a good part of summer had been left behind, but it was a seasonable day when *Charleston* docked at lower Manhattan. All of Van Buren's sons were present for his homecoming.

A few days after they were settled, Van Buren found his way down to Prince Street following a message from Fitz-Greene Halleck. John Jacob Astor's secretary met him in his office; the poet had not changed very much either.

"I trust you have found that your practice has thrived in your absence, Mr. Van Buren."

"I understand that Mr. Astor has steered some clients our way."

"One hand washes the other, sir."

"I suppose it does."

"Our latest word from young Mr. Astor is that your work was exemplary—none of the land purchase contracts were struck down. Capital, Mr. Van Buren; capital."

"I am gratified that we are appreciated."

"More than appreciated. Mr. William said that he offered you a chance to participate in a new venture in the Sandwich Islands."

"Which I refused." Van Buren held up his hands. "I'd prefer to remain here in New York, Mr. Halleck. No more journeys for me."

"I understand." Halleck reached for a rolled paper on his desk and began to spread it out on the desk. "But I should like to show you something—again, in strict confidence."

"It doesn't commit me to—"

"No, not in the least. It is for the venture just completed."

Van Buren leaned forward to see what Halleck had to show him: it was a diagram, a sort of engineering plan annotated with specifications. It was a locomotive—a powerful-looking one, bigger than anything he had ever seen.

Halleck smiled. "This is being built in our works in Wilmington. Over the next few years, Mr. William will be building a locomotive works on the east side of the bay near Saint Helena—and they will produce one there every three to four months."

"I didn't realize that Mr. Astor was interested in being a railroad man."

"Not here in the east, Mr. Van Buren. But in the west, there will be a great need—once tunnels are built through the mountains."

It took several seconds for the idea to sink in, then Van Buren sat forward. "Wait. You mean . . ." He tapped the locomotive diagram. "You mean that Astor intends to actually *build* a railroad in Novaya Rossiya? That wasn't just a cover?"

"That's right. We retained a small number of land parcels in the gold fields with the specific intention of building a rail line that will ultimately connect Saint Helena with the mines. And eventually—that line will stretch all the way across the mountains. Someday, sir, you will be able to board a train here in New York and debark in Saint Helena a week later. Or, even sooner than that. It will require powerful engines; but this is an excellent start."

The idea of it left him speechless. Buying up land claims to steal a march on a search for gold was devious enough. Arranging for the Royal Navy to be on hand to make sure claims were enforced was even more forward-thinking than he had anticipated. This third level of indirection—actually carrying *out* the plan that had been no more than a cover story—was more cleverness than he could have expected, even from the very clever Mr. Astor.

He did not betray it, though—for an attorney, there was never a reason to cast doubt in the jury's mind. But he was deeply impressed with the way in which John Jacob Astor had thought this through—and past—the end. It was as fine a piece of chicanery as he had seen in forty years before the bar.

He thanked Halleck for the glance at the locomotive, promised that he would be willing to entertain further commissions in the future (so long as no more sunset journeys were contemplated!) and took his leave.

And, at last, he found himself on the street corner, breathing the warm air of a summer day in Manhattan, regretting nothing and glad to be home.

There was, after all, nothing to regret.

CAT'S PAW

1853

CHAPTER 1

Near midnight, at the end of summer. A full moon overhead.

The three-master *Nevsky* rode serenely in the gently-rolling waves in the middle Pacific, Saint Helena behind and the Sandwich Islands ahead, her bow parting the water quietly, invisibly, from the deck. A man stood there alone, leaning on a stanchion, a briar pipe clenched in his teeth—though it had gone out and had remained unlit for quite some time.

The men of the watch left him alone. He might or might not have actually been master on board, but the captain treated him as such, and had assigned him the second-best cabin (after the captain's own) for this journey across the water.

Truly, all of *Nevsky*'s crew was content to steer well clear of the man: he was no sailor, though he clearly showed signs of having been to sea before—no landsman's sickness, no fear of storms, good sea-legs from the time they'd left the Embarcadero for the journey across from Novaya Rossiya to the island kingdom of Hawai'i. Yet he seemed to take no pleasure in it, as if the prospect of coming to the tropical paradise held no attractions. *Nevsky*'s sailors held a quite different position: liberty, even in the Russian treaty port of Lahaina, was one of the highlights of their route . . . for most of the men, a combination of Russians, Poles, Ukranians, and even a few men from the steppes who had somehow found themselves in merchant service, the balmy, bucolic Sandwich Islands were stark contrast to their native lands, and a welcome departure from the rainy, changeable weather of hilly Saint Helena by the bay.

But not for the civilian aboard *Nevsky*. By day he kept mostly to himself, his endlessly scratching pen audible to any who passed the cabin door; by night he sat or stood in solitude, looking into the night as if his doom were out there, waiting to swallow him up.

It was enough to make a man shiver, even under the summer sun. Or to turn aside the evil eye. Or to take another drink.

The one exception to this rule was the captain of <u>Nevsky</u>—the crew of the watch, if they looked up to see, would have noticed him stumping along toward the solitary man on his foredeck.

At the sound, the man turned; he removed the pipe from his mouth, noticing—perhaps for the first time—that it had gone out. He rapped it on the heel of his left boot and tucked it into an inner pocket of his coat.

"Good evening to you, gospodin Norton," the captain said.

"Captain Sharovsky," Joshua Norton answered, nodding. "You are up late."

"The youngest of our crew thinks I never sleep."

"Do you?"

"Deeply," Sharovsky said. He smiled tightly, seemingly pleased at his minor attempt at wit. Like Norton, the captain of *Nevsky* was not a particularly jocular man.

How very Russian, Norton thought, then dismissed it: he had traveled the world before coming to Novaya Rossiya's Pacific coast, and he'd met all kinds of Russians—from the dour ones who had served their tsar in the wilderness of Siberia to the ones fortunate enough to make their home in the pastoral lands in America. There was no typical Russian, not these days.

"Yet not tonight."

"Nyet," Sharovsky answered. "Not tonight. We have . . . a matter to discuss."

"Have I offended?"

"No, no, not in the least, gospodin Norton. You are a model passenger. I have had the honor to carry a great noble, a nephew of the mighty tsar himself, who chose to grace our fair colony with his presence. Now *there* was a passenger." Sharovsky turned aside and spat to punctuate his comment.

"I see," Norton said. "I understand."

"Da. It is another reason."

"Ah." *Get to it,* Norton thought.

The captain might have sensed the other's impatience. "Well. I was surprised to find that we have a stowaway aboard, gospodin. It would not be necessary to trouble you with this news, but . . ."

Norton frowned. "A stowaway?"

"If we were merely traveling along the coast, I would pause our journey and place him in the hands of the constabulary. This far at sea, he cannot be thrown overboard . . . not that it was not threatened, of course." Sharovsky smiled again.

"Did he explain himself?"

"Yes he did, yes he did. And he asked for *you*."

"Did he say why?"

"I think that it might be better, gospodin, if he explains himself to you directly. If you could spare the time now, I will take you below."

Norton looked up at the sky, then out to sea. "Aye, I can. The moon and the sea will still be here when I return."

✳ ✳ ✳

Nevsky was a good-sized vessel, but it was still cramped below. The prisoner—the stowaway—was confined to a section of the crew quarters near the orlop, so it was dimly lit and a bit foul-smelling. Norton was fairly sure that no nephews of the Great Autocrat would have visited this part of the ship.

Most of the nearby crew was awake, watching from their hammocks; others, further forward, were snoring steadily as Sharovsky and Norton made their way back.

The scene was lit by a lantern swinging slowly to and fro from a hook in the ceiling. A burly able seaman sat opposite on a sea-chest, idly whittling, keeping his eyes on the man sitting on the deck. The stowaway clearly had no thoughts of escape; he sat leaning back against a bulkhead, one knee raised, hands in his lap; the headroom forced all of them to bend down as they approached.

"Our unwanted guest," Sharovsky said. "I still haven't heard anything that is keeping me from tossing him overboard, gospodin," he added to Norton.

Norton stopped a few feet from the stowaway. "The captain said that you know my name."

"Indeed I do, Monsieur Norton. And I have some information for you."

"'Monsieur?' You are a Frenchman?"

"I am. Jacques Damon at your service."

"Not your real name, I am certain. Knowing your nationality does not make you more trustworthy," Norton said. "Rather less."

"Even given the 'auld Alliance'? You are a Scotsman by birth, I know."

"The auld Alliance died at Rotherham and Edenton a century ago, Frenchman. The Pretender wasn't killed in the Carolinas like his father was, but no one flocked afterward to his cause. It's dead and buried now no matter how many trumped-up Stuarts may turn up to wave the rebel flag. Now explain your interest in me or I'll toss you in the sea myself."

Damon seemed to think about this for a few moments, trying to decide if Norton—or the captain—would actually contemplate doing so.

"I know why you are on board *Nevsky*, Monsieur Norton. I know what you were promised for your efforts: that your losses—your *extensive* losses—would be made whole as long as you did what you were told on both legs of the journey, kept your own counsel, and asked no questions."

Norton said nothing, but did glance at Sharovsky; the captain was listening attentively, but gave no indication of his opinion of the matter.

"You seem well informed."

"Oh, I am, I am. But it should seem blindingly clear to you, sir, that you are vulnerable. You are being used—and it will not end well."

"Because . . ."

"Because this matter is *bigger* than you." The Frenchman spread his hands apart. "Once you have done the bidding of your employer, he has no reason to honor his part of the deal; and if anything goes wrong, you provide a convenient target for blame.

"After all," he added, "you are alone. No alternatives, no funds, no partner. Too bad about Thorne."

Norton stepped forward and grabbed the Frenchman by the bunched front of his shirt. "What do you know about Thorne?"

Damon smiled, which made Norton want to strangle him, and he waited almost too long to reply.

"He does not share in the joy of your distress, Monsieur Norton. The reason that you could not find him when matters became serious is that he sold his interest in your clever scheme and left Saint Helena.

"He is comfortably situated. Veracruz, I think, the guest of the viceroy."

Norton once again considered how much he might enjoy strangling the Frenchman. It would be easy, but the pleasure would be short-lived.

He shoved him back roughly against the bulkhead, where his head struck with a satisfying thump.

"Veracruz," Norton said.

"At last word. But, in any case, a long way from Saint Helena."

Norton stepped back, wiping his hands on his trousers as if he'd gotten something on them during his rough treatment of Damon. Finally he said, "I expect you have an offer to make."

"I do," he answered, settling himself more comfortably, reaching one hand to the back of his head to determine whether any damage had been done in the exchange. "On behalf of His Majesty, my king."

"What do you want?"

"Something simple. A quid pro quo. You do something for us, Monsieur Norton, and we will provide you some surety."

"I have no more reason to trust you than to trust those who hired me in Saint Helena."

"Oh, but you do," Damon said. "And I can prove it."

"Then prove it."

"*Certainement*," he answered. "In the Islands. I will provide you with a . . . retainer, sufficient to assist you in your predicament. Not enough to solve the problem, but enough to put off the day of reckoning."

"I could simply take your money and refuse to honor my end of the bargain."

"We rely on your well-known probity, Monsieur Norton. You would do nothing to sully your good name. And the task we ask is very minor, a mere bagatelle. For you, at least."

"You seem very sure."

"What is it you British say? I have . . . bet my life on it. His Majesty was confident that you would be receptive to the offer and that, upon reflection, you would agree."

"I would want to know terms."

"Of course you would," Damon said, smiling. "Those need not wait until will reach the islands.

"Shall we begin?"

CHAPTER 2

Across the great bay, in the hills beyond the oceanside villa of Prince Gregori Andreivich Gyazin, fortieth (or forty-first or forty-second) in line for the throne of the Tsar of All the Russias.

A brisk late-spring day, clear and—by the standards of Russians from the old country—balmy. The local residents, peasants who still mostly spoke Spanish or some hideous Indian tongue, might have thought otherwise, but the aristocrats in Novaya Rossiya never considered their opinion.

A mounted party was slowly making its way down the hill to where Joshua Norton and his business partner, Zachariah Thorne, waited for their arrival.

The Russian patricians who had gone up in the hills in search of a fine black bear had met with good success, it seemed: Norton and Thorne could see several large pelts stretched across the backs of servants' horses, and the finely-dressed Russians had a look of being very pleased with themselves.

Thorne could scarcely conceal a sneer, even after a sharp look from Norton, who stood up from his comfortable spot near the small fire they'd built and began to walk slowly up the trail.

"They've done well," Norton said as Thorne caught up with him.

"You expected otherwise?" The sneer was very near the surface now. "With the number of servants and beaters and men to hold their weapons and respond to their every whim—of course they did well."

"Bear-hunting isn't a ride in the park, Zachariah."

"Big brave hunters. You give them too much credit."

"I do no such thing."

"You are a sycophant, Norton, for all your attempts to ingratiate yourself. You know what they think of you."

Norton stopped walking. "I do. What do *you* believe that they think of me?"

"That you are no better than a peasant. You may be a fine and upstanding man of business, but you are no more than that. Back in Hartford we have a saying." *They have a saying back in Hartford for every occasion,* Norton thought to himself. "'Dress him up in tails and a top hat and he is still Mister Pig.'"

"You North Americans and your sayings. If I could make sense of that, I suppose I would find it insulting."

Thorne scowled but didn't reply, as if he was trying to decide whether Norton didn't actually understand and was fooling himself, or was simply sparing his business partner's feelings.

Finally, Norton said, "I consider Gregori Andreivich to be a friend. I have done him several favors, and he has materially affected our ability to do business in Saint Helena. I will ask you to remember that, and be polite."

"We do not bow and scrape where I come from."

"Of course you do, Zachariah. You just don't recognize it when you do. Now, let us go meet the mighty hunters, and I will ask you to be polite—especially when we will be eating and drinking at their expense."

"It won't be bear meat, that's for sure," Thorne said. "They most likely left the carcasses rotting in the woods somewhere after they bravely killed their prey."

Norton nodded. "You're probably right. But it isn't as if the woods here are running out of bears."

* * *

Gregori Andreivich Gyazin, at age twenty-five, had arrived in Novaya Rossiya a bit over a year ago. Unprepared for the long sea voyage—he'd come by way of Aden with his even younger wife and their three little children—he had been deathly ill and, despite being the son of one of Novaya Rossiya's wealthiest absentee landholders, had a difficult time accustoming himself to life on the frontier.

Saint Helena, of course, was hardly the frontier in the early spring of 1853. It was not Saint Petersburg, but it had come a long way since the Anglo-Russian Treaty of 1809, which had officially transferred the central and northern coasts from the crumbling Spanish Empire to the surging Russian one. In half a century the shabby town of Yerba Buena, its unkempt Presidio and its Catholic monastery and mission had been transformed into something resembling a city, one named for the blessed Saint Helena, the mother of Constantine the Great.

Norton and Thorne met the young nobleman and his party on level ground, in a clearing a few hundred yards from the small hunting lodge Gyazin had had built not long after his arrival. From where they stood, the wide sweep of the bay presented a gorgeous sight; most of Saint Helena was swathed in fog, though the top of the onion-domed Cathedral of Saint Helena on Telegraph Hill poked through.

"I should be grateful I am not kneeling, I suppose," Thorne said, under his breath.

"We are Britons," Norton answered, "not serfs in Gyazin's thrall. We could even be on horseback, but I think a little deference is in order."

"All this for an opportunity to sup at his table." Thorne snorted. "I doubt he'll even notice I'm here."

"He wanted to meet you, Zachariah," Norton said, and wanted to say more, but did not have a chance. Gyazin had come into the clearing, and he jumped from his horse and strode forward smiling to grasp Norton's hand.

"Norton, my friend," he said. "I am pleased you could take time to meet me. We have had a fine day, a fine day."

"I can see, Excellency. Those are excellent specimens," Norton added, gesturing toward the pelts draped over the horses.

"One of them was from a great beast. I don't think I've seen its like here in Novaya Rossiya. I think it will make a fine rug, don't you think?"

"I am sure."

"And the other ones—one for my little Mishka's bedroom, and the others . . . Andrea will decide what to do with them, I suppose." The nobleman rubbed his hands together.

Thorne cleared his throat, a bit too obviously, and Norton resisted giving his business partner a sharp look.

"Excellency, I have the honor to present my partner Zachariah Thorne. Zachariah, His Excellency Gregori Andreivich Gyazin."

The two men shook hands. Thorne's expression was guarded but polite: whatever his annoyance, he knew how to comport himself before nobility. Gyazin looked him up and down, as if trying to make some judgment of his own.

"Gospodin Thorne. I have heard much about your . . . business acumen. I understand you are an American by birth, from the eastern colonies."

"I am from Connecticut, Excellency," Thorne said. "I came out to Saint Helena some years ago as a factor for the House of Astor, but found other opportunities."

"Novaya Rossiya is full of opportunities," Gyazin answered. "And you are here *voluntarily*." He laughed. "My father and uncle sent me here to look after the family estate. And to keep me out of trouble, I suppose. It is not the rodina, but I have come to like it."

"Most gratifying," Thorne said.

"Yes, yes. Well. I am glad to make your acquaintance. Norton and I have known each other almost since I arrived—he offered his services and helped me obtain our house on Odessa Street. My Andrea is eternally grateful." He slapped Norton on the back; out of sight of the young man, Thorne scowled at Norton, as if disdaining the false camaraderie.

"It was my pleasure," Norton said. "I am glad that the Lady Gyazin continues to enjoy it."

The three men began to walk toward the lodge. "It suits us well. Though if the family grows any larger, we may need to find a more suitable place."

"Larger?"

Gyazin shrugged. "Andrea loves her daughters . . . but thinks perhaps that Mishka could use a younger brother."

"Do you mean . . ."

"If the Lord grants her health—in the spring. Da," Gyazin said, beaming. "She lights a candle every day that all goes well."

"My congratulations, Excellency!"

"Not yet," Gyazin said, placing a finger over his lips. "We shall see. We have both had the inoculations against the smallpox and measles, but

CITY BY THE BAY

there are so many things that can happen. Still, Andrea is young and strong, and God is merciful. Don't you think so, gospodin Thorne?"

"No man can know God's will, Excellency," Thorne answered. "His power is great and just—no matter how many candles are lit."

Gyazin's face darkened for just a moment. Norton quickly said, "My partner is a severe Protestant, Excellency. They came to this continent so that they could take pride in that severity."

"I recognize the sentiment. There is a priest in our church who has the same outlook. I do not think he sees any sunny day without thinking about the storm to come."

"Just so, Excellency." *You arrogant fool, Thorne,* he thought. *Are you trying to antagonize him?*

"Well," Gyazin said as they reached the door of the lodge, where a liveried footman opened the door with a bow and flourish. "Enough of this talk. I am famished—aren't you?"

* * *

It was no surprise that Gyazin set a good table. It was a matter of keeping up appearances, even across the bay and in the hills: people talked, and society in Saint Helena was small and talkative.

And wealthy, Norton reminded himself.

A sleepy little town at the far end of the Russian Empire, Saint Helena had been completely transformed by the discovery of gold not far from where they dined this afternoon. From what he had heard, it had been found at a mill belonging to the Astor company, and the patriarch had tried to secure title to all of the land before news got out—but there were some complications and very nearly an international incident.

By the time he arrived a few years later, drawn—along with people from all over the world—by the lure of the gold fields, Saint Helena had blossomed into a boom town, though the presence of the constabulary curbed the very worst of it. Still, more money came into the hands of more unlikely sources . . . sometimes unscrupulous and devious ones.

And wealth had also attracted society—not only because it provided the sorts of amenities they wanted and required, but also because the imperial bureaucracy wanted very much to put its hands in the stream to obtain its fair share.

"Norton."

He felt his elbow being jostled, and he realized that his name had been called, probably more than once.

He looked up the table and saw Gyazin, his chin tilted up. The nobleman was used to being the center of attention at all times.

"I beg your Excellency's pardon. I was lost in thought."

"Thinking about making money." There were chuckles and titters around the table. "Is that all your people think about?"

My people, Norton thought. *Scotsmen? Jews?*

Sometimes it was easier to simply pretend that nothing had been said. "How may I be of service?"

"I wanted to have you try a delicacy." He gestured toward a servant, who placed a small, delicate bone-china plate before him and then added several square chunks of a yellow fruit, arranging them carefully with a pair of silver tongs. "Pineapple. From the Sandwich Islands: they arrived on a steamer just this morning. As fresh as they can be."

Norton realized that conversation had stopped at the table. Six Russian aristocrats, Gyazin's chaplain, two highly-regarded retainers, and Thorne were all waiting for his reaction to this mark of Gyazin's favor.

It would have been more dramatic had Norton been more the man he portrayed himself to be, and less the man who had traveled the world before coming to Saint Helena. He'd never had pineapple, but was no stranger to tropical fruits.

He tasted one of the chunks: it was sweet and juicy, like a bite of sunshine. This would be very popular in Saint Helena; people here, both Russians and gold miners had quite a sweet tooth, enough to keep Ghirardelli, the chocolatier and proprietor of the Cairo Coffee House and the huge general store on the corner of Battery and Kalinin, in business.

"Exquisite," Norton said at last. "I thank you, Excellency, for the favor."

Gyazin beamed. "I think there's a market for this," he said, gesturing with a fork. "But I am not a man of business, of course. What do you think?"

"There are many variables," Thorne cut in. "Fruit export is a notoriously fraught trade, Excellency. I would—"

"I think it is worth investigating," Norton said. He leaned in slightly and pressed his right boot heel on Thorne's left shoe. "If you would give me a few days I will be happy to let you know."

"Capital," Gyazin answered. Around the table, Norton could read the reactions of the others. *Man of business*, they were thinking with disdain. *Britisher.*

And probably, also, *Jew.*

But while Lord Gyazin was content to have Norton and his business partner sitting at his table, nothing would be said.

CHAPTER 3

Late morning. A squall darkening the sky, *Nevsky* sailing close-hauled and making very little headway west, the storm driving it south.

The weather prevented Norton from contemplations in solitude; he had been largely confined to the (second-best) cabin at most hours, bounded by the narrow walls and constrained by his thoughts.

Veracruz, he kept thinking. Thorne was in Veracruz. A guest of the viceroy.

This matter is bigger than you.

What he wanted to do—what he *really* wanted to do—was to go belowdecks and have words, possibly more than words, with the Frenchman. Not only had he illuminated Norton's distress in a way far more public than he might desire, he had suggested that there were dimensions to the situation that he had not known or considered. He didn't like it, and he didn't like that Captain Sharovsky viewed him suspiciously.

That, at least, he could address.

Sharovsky came down the stair, rain streaming from his oilcloth and clinging to his beard. He did not meet Norton's eyes, and might have wanted to ignore him entirely; but the gangway was too narrow, and Norton did not get out of his path.

"A word, Captain."

"I am busy, gospodin Norton," he said.

"I will not keep you long."

Sharovsky stood, slightly bent over, and looked at Norton. "Da, very well. In my cabin." He gestured. Norton stepped aside, and followed the captain toward the fore end of belowdecks.

The captain's cabin was slightly larger than Norton's own, and extremely tidy. Sharovsky shrugged off his rain gear in a cloud of droplets and hung it on a peg; he stepped over to his sea-chest, which had an embroidered cushion laced onto it, and sat down to face Norton.

He reached above his head without looking, unhooked the door to a cubby-hole, and drew out a flask. He unscrewed the top, made a gesture toward Norton and took a healthy drink, then wiped his mouth with the back of his sleeve.

"Drink?"

"No, thank you."

"Then tell me what you want, gospodin."

"I fear that I have offended you, Captain. We are still three days from landfall, and I find this a difficult situation."

Sharovsky frowned, and took another short drink from the flask, then capped it and secured it in its place.

"You seem willing to accept the French stowaway's offer, and his king's money, gospodin Norton. I do not know what to make of it, nor do I know what my employer will think."

"Listening is not accepting, Captain. I have made no commitment. I told him that I did not trust him."

"Da, so you did. But you did not tell him no, either."

"I keep my own counsel. He does not need to know whether I will cooperate or not."

"But you need the money, and the Frenchman's gold is as good as . . ."

"As your employer's. Yes."

There was a long silence, as Sharovsky considered that answer and where Norton's loyalties might lie.

If I am in the tsar's employ, Norton thought, *it is a temporary thing. And if I take the French king's shilling . . .*

"I would not toss you overboard," Sharovsky said at last, "and I would not put you adrift in one of my boats. Waste of a good boat."

"You are the soul of thrift."

"What shall I do with you?"

"Nothing more than you have done," Norton answered. "Our employer has hired you to transport the cargo, and has hired me to escort it. We go to Lahaina and then Honolulu, and then we go back to Saint Helena. Nothing is changed."

"Are you sure?"

No, Norton thought. "Yes," he said.

"For your sake, gospodin, I pray this is true. I pray by . . . Saint Helena," he added, gesturing to a tiny framed icon of the mother of Emperor Constantine on the opposite wall. The gray light that filtered through the tiny window caught the gilt paint on the picture, punctuating the comment.

* * *

The storm cleared while they were still in open sea. There was no apparent damage to *Nevsky*, neither hull nor masts nor rigging; still, Sharovsky had the ship heave to; in the bright tropical sunlight the crew went all over the ship, patching, tightening, ordering.

It was a welcome relief for Norton to be on deck; he found a place out of the way on the foredeck, smoking his pipe and watching the bustle.

To his surprise, the French stowaway Damon was brought up, escorted by a seaman—the same one who was present at the first interview. It was either as a convenience for the work or as an indication of their separate status. Norton did not choose to interpret it as any more sinister than that.

He and Damon were quiet for a time, and then the man said, "I am surprised to be given fresh air and liberty. Do you suppose they want to catch us conspiring?"

"You must be looking for me to shut your mouth for you, Frenchman," Norton said.

"We could converse in French, I suppose . . ."

"I do not speak French."

"Ah, well. Learning a new language is difficult."

"I have managed to become conversant in Russian."

"Unlike Thorne," Damon said. "Perhaps he is finding Spanish easier."

"I doubt it. You delight in trying to provoke me—don't waste any more breath. Thorne moved out to Saint Helena in the 1840s and never made any progress with Russian. He should go back to Connecticut. But maybe he betrayed someone there as well."

There was another pause, as the two landsmen watched the crew of *Nevsky* scurry around to bawled orders in Russian from Captain Sharovsky and his first officer.

"Have you been to the Sandwich Islands before, Monsieur Damon?"

"Oh, yes. Several times."

"Ah. So you have experience as a stowaway. Is this the first time you have been caught?"

"This was a special assignment," Damon said, settling himself more comfortably on the deck where he sat. "I do not always travel this way— I think I am not very good at it."

"They caught you."

"This time," he answered, smiling as if he had something to conceal. "When I was last in the Islands, it was in different circumstances. Now that I am not to be thrown overboard or set adrift in a boat—"

"Waste of a boat," Norton said.

"*Bien sûr,*" Damon said, smiling again. "Now that I am past the point of violent death or abandonment to the sea, I think I can say with some assurance that I serve an important role . . . as do you."

"I have not consented to any arrangement."

"If you say so. But once you ask terms, it means that the matter will be concluded—it is only a matter of determining the price."

"You seem very sure of yourself."

"It is only because I am. We—I—know a great deal. More than your Secret Chancellery suspects.

"Yes, Monsieur Norton. We will come to terms. And if properly done, you can still receive whatever the gendarmerie has promised you, assuming they keep their end of the bargain."

"On which point you are doubtful."

"The Russians may yet surprise," Damon said. "If it was your government I might be more sanguine. But the servants of the Great

Autocrat, particularly those in the Secret Chancellery, will feel no compunction to be men of their word. Not to you."

"And you seem very sure of that as well," Norton said, looking away from the Frenchman and out to sea.

"*Bien sûr*," Damon repeated. "We have been playing this game with them for quite a long time. If they want to win at it, they should stop letting their ally call the tune."

✳ ✳ ✳

Nevsky's first port of call was Lahaina on the west coast of Maui. Their first sight of the Islands overall was the smoldering peak of Mauna Kea on Hawai'i Island, which served as a navigational beacon day and night; the prevailing wind pushed them around the southern tip of the roughly triangular island, after which the wind pushed *Nevsky* north by northwest and then through the Maui Channel, along the island's north coast, arriving at Lahaina from the north on the evening tide.

On a map, it was the sort of course that was incomprehensible to landsmen—but to sailors it made perfect sense, given the wind. Thus they came to Lahaina from the north, getting their first look at the Russian treaty-port, a quite modern facility filled with whaling ships.

"Quite a pretty town," Damon said to Norton, who was standing at the rail. *Nevsky*'s crew was all a-bustle, but there were still two hands near the Frenchman, who had his back to the mainmast: they had no interest in seeing him go overboard into the clear blue water of the harbor and swim to freedom.

Norton didn't turn around; after his conversation with the captain, he'd been left to converse with the stowaway whenever he liked. As the only two non-Russians aboard they had seemed natural companions, he assumed—but Norton had no interest in considering the amiable, supercilious Frenchman as anything approaching a friend. He was not sure he could apply that term to anyone at the moment.

"It's rather more built up than I would have expected," he said at last. "Didn't the king move his capital away from here?"

"Oui, to be sure. Years ago. The young King decided that he liked the view of Pearl Harbor better than the Ka'anapalli coast, especially after

Her Majesty's father's engineers so graciously dredged the anchorage for him."

"Then why so much traffic here at Lahaina?"

"He was more than happy to accept favors from the Great Autocrat as well. His Majesty Kamehameha is a wily one," the Frenchman added, "and he knows that granting what Russia wants in exchange for their help benefits him as well, showing that he is no mere puppet of the British Crown. It makes both great powers more eager to please."

"They are allies," Norton said. He turned around at last, somewhat annoyed at being drawn into a conversation he did not want, with a man he did not like. "Are they not?"

Damon smiled, as if he were considering this point—though Norton suspected that the Frenchman had an answer already prepared. He rummaged in his coat for his pipe and drew it out.

"They are allies of convenience, I think everyone agrees, Monsieur Norton. In the North Pacific, each has acknowledged its inability to keep out the other—they satisfy themselves by declaring their intention to keep out others, such as my own country."

"Yes, well," Norton said, pulling out his tobacco pouch. "They've done a pretty damn fine job of that so far, wouldn't you say?"

"No. I would not."

"I see no fleur-de-lys banner waving in the wind. I'd say that they've done well enough so far."

"How . . . quaint." Damon waved his hand, dismissively. One of the seamen set to guard him let his hand stray near his cutlass. Damon noticed it and looked down at the sword belt and then at the man, who was burly and muscled and could not have been more than twenty. "If that is the criterion you use, then I should agree with you. But we do not need to plant our flag here in order to *be* here."

He waved his hand again toward the long dock that jutted out into the bay. On it, Norton could clearly see a colorful entourage: four or five soldiers or guards in some elaborate uniform, with a gentleman in a formal morning suit and top hat in their midst. Norton couldn't identify the uniforms: they weren't Russian, surely, and were far too elaborate and gaudy to be British.

He glanced from the dock to Damon, who was grinning, as if he expected this outcome all along.

"The French consul keeps a fine house up the coast at Ka'anapalli," Damon said. "I shall make sure that you are furnished an invitation during your stay."

CHAPTER 4

A cool spring evening. It had rained, but the storm seemed to have tired of the game and moved on. New Englanders settled in Saint Helena were accustomed to changeable weather, but the Russians never seemed to get used to it: winter and summer were distinct things, while spring and autumn seemed inconvenient and unpredictable.

The ladies and gentlemen arrived just the same at the Caspian Sea Rooms, liveried servants waiting to hand them down from their carriages and protect their evening dress from the drizzle. The exclusive club had been a fixture of Saint Helena society for nearly twenty years: in its earlier days, the Princess Doroteja fen Lieven herself had been one of the Lady Patronesses, the governing body of the club whose word was law and whose disapproval—often represented by no more than the slight raising of one elegant eyebrow—could ban a man for life, his name stricken from the books.

In the 1840s, when Her Serene Highness had made her home here, there were few other entertainments or civilized diversions in this outpost of the Russian Empire. There were others now, but none so particular in their membership. Recognized members had no difficulty making their way past the elegantly-dressed hostess who stood just within the porticoed door, whose lectern with the members' book governed the admission or rejection of petitioners . . . others, whose names had not (*yet*, they hoped) been inscribed in that volume, were compelled to wait and be subjected to inquiry and examination. Some were admitted.

Gregori Andreivich Gyazin and his lovely Andrea, of course, were admitted, even being granted the slightest of bows by the doorkeeper. He expected no less, standing as he did forty-first (or forty-second, or forty-third) in line for the crown and throne of the tsar. The expectation of deference came naturally to him.

Past the paneled hallway, a servant took his hat and stick as well as Andrea's wrap. In the soft, buttery light of a hundred candles in wall sconces and crystal chandeliers, he marveled at his wife's exquisite beauty.

"You are staring, Grisha," she whispered. "People will talk."

"Let them," he said. "We do not do this often enough."

"The children . . ."

"Are in good hands, my dear." Gregori smiled. "Tonight we shall spend time in the company of friends."

Andrea looked around the entry hall; it was only half-full, though there were faint sounds of music and conversation drifting down the grand stairway from above.

"I do not know *anyone* here, Grisha. What on earth will they think of me?"

"They will bask in the glow of your beauty," Gregori answered. He offered his wife his arm, and she wrapped her gloved fingers around it, almost tentatively. It was true that she had rarely ventured into society in the time they had been here in Saint Helena: there had been dinner-parties, of course, and they had been received by the Governor-General at the Presidio upon their arrival—but Andrea had been content to remain off-stage.

That is about to change, Gregori thought as he walked slowly up the stairs, his wife on his arm. Indeed, as she had said, people were talking: the arrival of the handsome young nobleman in his guards uniform, his wife on his arm, turned every head.

Let them stare, he thought. *Let them enjoy the view . . . but I am the lady's escort.*

* * *

Andrea was a superb dancer; she moved past the first tentative steps and permitted herself to enjoy the evening. After a few dances, Gregori allowed an older nobleman—whose wife sat near the French doors in animated conversation with two other ladies—to cut in and take a turn with his wife. He walked across the dance floor to a sideboard, where he was offered a crystal goblet filled with a pale-colored punch.

"You should take care. That old *boyar* will sweep her off her feet."

Grigori turned at the comment. If it had been most people making the observation, he might have felt the need for a sharp reply: but John Jacob Astor, III, was not most people. Stocky and imposing, affecting a wide, drooping mustache of which (Grigori was sure) his father, William Astor, would surely disapprove, the chief factor of the great British corporation was an imposing figure in any setting; here in the Caspian Sea Rooms, a member of the elite in a gathering of his peers, it was even more the case.

"Is that why you never bring Charlotte here, Vanya?"

John Astor did not accept the Russian diminutive from most people, but Grigori enjoyed watching others react when he used it. "I do not bring her," Astor said quietly, leaning close, "because she would find this a frightful bore."

"She told you this herself."

"I assured her it would be the case. Mrs. Astor dislikes this sort of thing."

Grigori knew that Vanya—John—found whatever excuse was necessary to separate himself from his wife, who (unlike the family into which she had married) was from a southern colony: one of the Carolinas, he recalled, or perhaps Georgia—there were far too many to keep straight. She disliked New York, and disliked Saint Helena even more. Like his father, though, John had been assigned to this most important outpost of the Astor empire, and she would have to deal with the circumstances as best she could.

But not, apparently, at the Caspian Sea Rooms.

"It is not for everyone."

"Andrea is enjoying it," Astor said gruffly, gesturing toward the Dance floor with his half-filled goblet.

"Mrs. Gyazin—gospozha Gyazin—likes this sort of thing. She gives herself few opportunities."

"Better to make the best of them. Would you care to join me on the balcony for a cigar?"

"I should tell Andrea—"

"I wouldn't worry too much about that," Astor said. "That old fossil will take good care of her, and there are any number of young bravos who will defend her honor if he does not."

Cuban tobacco was not common in Saint Helena even with the railroad, but nothing less would be acceptable to the House of Astor. Grigori accepted the small, tightly-wrapped cigar and the light that John Astor offered him. For a few moments they stood apart, inhaling the fragrant smoke and letting it drift off the balcony; smoking was not permitted within the ballroom, but even the Lady Patronesses could not prevent the practice entirely.

"I have noticed," Astor said after a few moments, "that your real estate man has been very active."

"'My' real estate man? You mean Norton? He's not 'my real estate man.' He provides services to me from time to time, but . . ." Grigori let the sentence trail off into the night.

"I trust we know each other well enough for you to avoid dissembling with me," Astor said. "You protest too much. You've got him looking at lots north of the Battery—there must be something of interest there."

"And if there is?"

"The House of Astor is interested."

"I am merely following advice from my consigliere. Some of my countrymen prefer to squander their money on lavish entertainments and wild speculations. I have other ideas." He turned away from the Englishman and looked through the open balcony doors; the dance had ended, and the older man was offering his arm to Andrea to escort her to the refreshment table.

For just a moment his wife caught his eye, or so he thought: she looked flushed, excited and—somehow—suddenly vulnerable.

"Completely understandable, Excellency. We, too, wish to bet on opportunities that promise good return."

"Of course. Your mercantile house has always been most insightful."

The cigar was a very fine one, and Grigori enjoyed it for a little while before John Astor ventured a further comment.

"Surely your consigliere must have something in mind, to have you speculating in land at this time, in that particular place."

"What do you want from me, Vanya? Surely you are not stooping to discuss business here at the Caspian Sea Rooms. You know that the Lady Patronesses frown upon that sort of thing."

Astor didn't respond to Grigori's obvious provocation except to scowl and pull at his cigar. In the dim light of the shrouded moon and the slight glow from his cigar-end, Grigori could see the famous Astor scowl, at the sight of which lesser employees were said to quail.

"Excellency," Astor said at last, his voice low and ominous, "I realize that this all seems to be a game to you. But I assure you that it is not. Not to the House of Astor; and not to others."

"Others?"

"Such as the gentleman who presently engages gospodzha Gyazin's attention," he added quietly, gesturing with the dimly-burning tip of his cigar.

Gregori looked back into the ballroom. A few feet from the refreshment table, a different man was speaking with Andrea. He was tall and handsome, his evening dress turned out in the most exact fashion, his hair pomaded and his moustaches carefully trimmed. He wore no beard, but did have a pair of Oxford glasses balanced carefully on his nose. Over his left breast he wore some sort of decoration, suspended from a fleur-de-lys ribbon.

Gregori took two steps forward, but Astor touched his sleeve and he stopped.

"You know who that is."

"Enlighten me," Grigori said. His first reaction was to say, *unhand me*, and he expected that his father—or his uncle—or any

number of other, older members of his family would already have a sword in his hand at this point.

"His name is Étienne-Louis Gros," Astor said. "His father is Baron Jean Baptiste-Louis Gros, who is presently installed here in Saint Helena as consul for His Most Christian Majesty Philippe IX. He is his father's . . . what would you call him? Stalking-horse, I suppose."

"What does he want with Andrea?"

"Other than to admire her beauty, Excellency, nothing at all, I trust. It is *you* he wants to learn about. Your lovely wife is merely a means to an end."

Gyazin shrugged off Astor's arm and walked back through the French doors into the ballroom, dropping his still-lit cigar on a servant's tray as he walked by. For his part, Astor came to the doorway and watched, unmoving and silent, as if he wanted to see the scene play out.

By the time he crossed to where Andrea was standing, the young Frenchman had faded into the crowd. Gregori looked around for him but couldn't catch a sign.

"Is something wrong, Grisha?" she asked. "I saw you go out to talk to John Astor—"

"Was that man bothering you, my dear?"

"Which man?"

"The one you were just talking to," Gregori answered, his voice on edge.

Andrea looked alarmed, as if she were just realizing her husband's mood. "You mean the young Frenchman. No, not at all: he was very solicitous, very complimentary. He told me my French was exquisite."

"And so it is. Did he ask you any questions?"

"What is wrong?" she said, touching Gregori's sleeve. She drew him off, a few feet away from the press at the refreshment table. "Is something upsetting you, Grisha?"

"I wish you would not call me that in public."

She arched her eyebrows at him. "You didn't mind it a few minutes ago. Did Astor tell you something to upset you?"

"Do you know who that 'young Frenchman' is?"

"Yes, of course. He introduced himself." She reached inside the top of her left opera-glove and produced a calling card, which she handed to Gregori. "His name is Gros. Étienne-Louis Gros. His father is the chargé d'affaires, and—"

"I know exactly who he is."

"Then you should be content that he is a man above reproach and a gentleman. His father is a baron, a peer of the Kingdom of France. I believe we were introduced to *Monsieur le Baron* last year—a middle-aged gentleman, somewhat stocky with side-whiskers and no beard. He has a hobby . . . let me see . . . oh, yes. Daguerreotypes. He makes daguerreotypes."

"I don't see—"

"Grisha. Gregori, my heart," she corrected herself. "We do not keep secrets from each other. If I was offended or affronted by this Étienne-Louis Gros, I should have already told you, and you would have already caused a most unseemly incident."

"I would not."

"You most certainly would, and I in turn would be disappointed if you did not. But you do not need to do so." She adjusted her gloves, smoothing down where the calling-card had been. "Monsieur Gros was kind and polite, and extended an invitation to us to come to tea at the consulate."

"Tea," Gregori said. "Both of us."

"But of course. I would not go unescorted." Andrea smiled. "And you would not be invited except to escort me."

"Is that all he wanted? Is that all he asked?"

"I told you that it was." Andrea looked as though she might poke further fun at her husband—his pride, his jealousy, or his desire to be protective—but she appeared to think better of it. "He asked if Mr. Astor was a particular friend. I told him that I had no idea—"

"He would know otherwise."

"I *told* him, Grisha," she said in a whisper, "that I had no idea whom you considered a particular friend, but that Prince Gyazin was well known to all in Saint Helena society, and, of course, you would be acquainted with the gentleman. If you chose to give him some of your valuable time, it was not my place and none of his business to inquire."

Gregori began to answer, but took a moment to look at his wife. Andrea was not merely a beautiful ornament, though of course she *was* that: she was his friend and helpmate, his confidant. He did not keep secrets from her.

She had said just the right thing to this inquisitive Frenchman.

It angered him to think that Astor had pulled him out of the ballroom and forced his lady to deal with the foreigner on her own—but he had, and she had.

"So, we are invited to the French consulate for tea," Gregori said at last, softening his expression. "Indeed. Well, my heart, we shall have to make sure we oblige him."

From where they stood, the next dance beginning to form in the ballroom, Gregori could see John Astor, III, still standing in the doorway, watching, watching.

What do you know? Gregori thought. *And what do you want to know?*

CHAPTER 5

A soft summer evening. Steady rain struck the roughly cobbled pavement on the street below; whale-oil lamps burned steadily, turning back the night.

Norton's Russian was certainly good enough to conduct business in Saint Helena or most anywhere else in Novaya Rossiya, but he could not keep pace with Captain Sharovsky's angry monologue. The captain was upset at having been forced to release the Frenchman into the hands of his country's representative at dockside earlier in the day, and angrier still at receiving no satisfaction from the consul, who sat calmly in his padded armchair, his hands folded across his lap, listening to Sharovsky's complaints.

It occurred to Norton that if the consul were less patient, he might not be willing to tolerate the extent of Sharovsky's ire . . . but it might mean something else: that the captain of *Nevsky* was more, and more important, than he seemed.

Finally, the consul held up his hand, stood and walked to a side table, where there was a flask of liquor and four glasses. He unstoppered the flask and poured two drinks—and then, after a moment's hesitation and a glance back at Norton, poured a third. He placed them on a lacquered tray and brought them to where Sharovsky and Norton still stood. The captain took his glass, as did Norton; the consul took the third.

He said something in Russian, and then for Norton's benefit added what he assumed was the translation: "God is far up high, the tsar is far away." Then he tossed back the drink.

Sharovsky followed suit, and Norton did as well. It was vodka, and a fine example of that most Russian of spirits.

After setting the glass carefully back on the tray, Sharovsky said, "So you intend to do nothing."

"I do not say that it is nothing, Kapitan, but you may think it so. It is out of my hands and out of yours. But I will tell you that I was not surprised that things happened as they did."

"Did you know that I had a stowaway?"

The consul did not answer, but looked stonily at Captain Sharovsky. He took the lacquered tray with the three empty glasses to the side table and set it down.

"You will be in Lahaina for a few days, da?"

"We must take on the assigned cargo . . . and do other business."

"Then you should go and do your business," the consul said. "And you should not dwell on this anymore. It is out of my hands. It is out of your hands."

He took a long look at Norton and said nothing: it was as if he was saying, *gospodin, it was never in your hands.*

"But—"

"But, but, but. The tsar is far away, Kapitan," he said, without looking away from Norton. "But the Secret Chancellery is not. You are in beautiful Lahaina. Enjoy it . . . but speak no more of this."

✷ ✷ ✷

Sharovsky parted company with him in front of the consul's residence on his own business, leaving him on his own. The rain was accompanied by low-lying fog that hugged the ground as Norton walked along Front Street toward the lights of taverns and ordinaries that lined it. They all did a brisk business: Lahaina was the center of the whaling trade in the North Pacific, and as he ambled along the causeway he could hear fragments of half a dozen languages: English, Russian, French, Filipino, Chinese (he supposed: it had no syllable or phrase he could make out). Whale-oil lamps with coated-paper shades to protect them from the rain gave a colored tint to the fog.

He had just about decided that he would patronize a nicely decorated place called the Pale Rose when he heard his name spoken, and a figure loomed out of the fog to the right and in front of him.

He was on his guard at once: anyone who knew his name these days was one more person who could use him for his own purposes. He made sure his hands were free, one resting on his left pocket where he kept a small knife. It wasn't much, but it was all he had.

"No need for that," the figure said, and made a gesture that Norton immediately recognized. More at ease, he allowed himself to be steered under an awning, off the causeway, and out of the rain.

"Who are you?"

The man was wearing an oilcloth coat with a hood. He pulled it back to show a middle-aged face, with a trimmed beard and deep-set eyes.

"A brother and a friend," he answered. "And word has reached us of your difficulties. We offer our help—and advice, if you're interested."

Norton looked around. There were not too many people walking abroad at the moment: a pair of Chinese men in pigtails and quilted jackets; a small group of Russian sailors looking for another place to spend their roubles. A lad of twelve or thirteen went sprinting by, barefoot, heedless of the rain and of the water he splashed on those he passed.

"I'm listening."

"I am from *Le Progres de l'Oceanie*," the man said. Norton knew that name: it was the Masonic lodge in Honolulu. "I was sent here to warn you that you are being used by your current employer."

"I am not surprised," Norton answered. "I don't see as I have any choice, given the ruin of my situation back in Saint Helena."

"You may have more friends there than you realize."

"I scarcely need one hand to count them," Norton said, a trace of bitterness in his voice. "My business partner betrayed me, my patrons abandoned me —"

"Peace," the man said. "There was a stowaway aboard the ship that brought you to the Islands, correct?"

"Yes. Everyone seems to know this, and some people knew it in advance. Only Captain Sharovsky and I seem to have been caught by surprise."

"The . . . your employer expected it to happen. You are aware of the current situation here?"

"Only a bit, and I do not see what it has to do with me."

"Everything, brother. Everything. For the last dozen years Imperial Russia and the British Empire have maintained treaty ports in the Sandwich Islands: the Russians here in Lahaina, the British in Honolulu. Each has sought favor with King Kamehameha, offering concessions and help and technology. There was a smallpox outbreak on Oahu in the spring that ended almost as soon as it began because of British doctors performing variolation on those coming into contact with the infected.

"Each empire hopes to obtain a favorable alliance with the Kingdom of Hawai'i as a result of this largesse. As for the king, he finds it to his advantage to nod courteously to each while committing to neither. But he, and the two European powers, face one significant threat: a third power that has thus far been kept out of the North Pacific."

"France."

"That's right. The French sent a naval expedition to Honolulu a few years ago—a 'reconnaisance in force'—seeking to establish its own concession. Fortunately, the Pacific Squadron of the Royal Navy was on hand to replenish its stores. They sent the French on their way without a cannon being fired, but it has made the British even more wary of French intentions. Sooner or later this will lead to war."

"There hasn't been war since the Peace of Ghent forty years ago," Norton said. "This is all—what do they call it?—the Great Game. The British and French play it in India, in Asia, in Africa. All very
romantic. The French have their Spanish ally, weak as it is. The British have the Russians as friends. To go to war as they did last
century would be the ruin of both empires."

"You may scoff if you wish, Brother Norton. I would not tell you this if it was not true—and if it was not important that you know it."

"I still don't see what it has to do with me."

"Do you know what cargo *Nevsky* is transporting back to Saint Helena?"

"I have no idea. We're loading in Honolulu, but I'm not the cargo master. I'm . . ."

"Yes? What exactly is your role aboard the Russian freighter?"

Norton did not answer; he knew, and suspected that his new-found acquaintance knew, that there was no real answer to that question. He had been told to accompany *Nevsky* to the Sandwich Islands as a means to recover his financial situation. He had found no alternative but to comply.

"What cargo will *Nevsky* load here in Lahaina?"

"Whale oil, I believe, and sandalwood."

"And what will it load in Honolulu?"

"The Frenchman wanted to know that as well. I have no idea, though I assume it is some part of the grand scheme that ensnares me. Do you know?"

"I have information I believe to be correct, but I have to admit that it makes no sense."

"I am intrigued," Norton said. "Tell me."

"The Russian is going to transship a large cargo of pineapples from Honolulu to Saint Helena."

"Pineapples? The . . . sweet fruit?"

"Yes. They grow in profusion in the Islands, and are apparently much in demand on the tables of idle Russian noblemen—or their wives. Apparently that includes your patron Prince Gyazin."

"Grigori Gyazin wants me to . . . escort *pineapples* to Saint Helena? I am aboard *Nevsky* for . . . you're right, Brother. It makes no sense."

"As I said."

"The Frenchman has offered me an opportunity to benefit by providing him with information. At first, I had no intention of even speaking with him again: but now I am not sure where I stand."

"You must be careful, Brother Norton. If you are, you may learn something from the exchange. Now I must go, but remember that you have friends. Here and elsewhere."

Norton did not know what to say, so he merely grasped the other's hand, with a friendly and brotherly grip. The stranger, who had never given his name, melted into the shadows, gone as quickly as he had appeared.

He stood under the awning for several moments, watching the rain assault the cobblestones. The humid, sultry air seemed chillier.

Pineapples, he thought.

CHAPTER 6

The weather was always variable on the Saint Helena side of the bay, but sometimes the clouds parted and granted a perfect, crisp spring day. He was at the office off Alexander Square early, but Thorne was earlier: the great oak door was open, and workmen were affixing something above the brass plaque that bore the name Norton, Thorne, and Company; the Connecticut man was observing closely, as if he was suspicious that it could be done properly without his supervision.

"Zachariah," Norton said, pointing toward the door with his umbrella as he opened the street-side brass gate and closed it behind him, walking the half-dozen steps to the three stairs leading to their front door. "What is this about?"

"A bit of decoration," Thorne said, without looking away. He gestured to the door: there was a wooden object about six inches high, three-dimensional, centered above the plaque. "I am told it is most compelling."

The object was oval with a sort of bloom at the top, with a crosshatch pattern.

"What is it?"

"A pineapple. The fruit we enjoyed at Lord Gyazin's hunting lodge. It is evidently a sign of prosperity, as it indicates far travel. I thought it appropriate, and so I have obtained one for our door."

Thorne stepped around the workman and into their offices. Norton followed him, hanging up his hat on the coat-rack and setting his walking-stick in the stand.

Norton, Thorne had obtained a fine accommodation for its office: through the broad window one was afforded a beautiful view. From Alexander Square, Romanov Street sloped quickly down toward the

Embarcadero, and beyond was the bay, sparkling in the bright sunny morning.

The first piece of furniture they had ever obtained was in the great first floor room: a huge octagonal table, made from the timbers of a wrecked China clipper. It was covered with a large, carefully annotated survey map of Saint Helena; two brass paperweights held it down at the near corners, with stacks of bound documents at each of the other ones.

"So: have you gotten a look at the tracts Gyazin wants us to obtain?" Thorne asked, scowling through his spectacles at some part of the map that seemed to have offended him.

"I took a ride up there yesterday."

"Not much to them."

"Well, Zachariah, I think he wants the land not for what it is, but rather for *where* it is."

"Meaning?"

"Well, it's the closest ferry point to the east bay."

"He already owns the company that handles the ferry. Clearly he doesn't need the other lots. He'd have to clear out the squatters—"

"I don't think that matters." Norton leaned over the map and traced the line of the bay with his finger. "This isn't particularly good land, and you're right—even if he was looking to enlarge the ferry landing Gyazin wouldn't need all the land he's looking to have us buy. I think there's something more to it."

"Such as?"

"I looked into the survey records. All of the deeds and titles were investigated and perfected about ten years ago, along with a detailed survey that was done across the bay and upcountry in what became the gold fields. It was all paid for by the House of Astor: they hired a real estate attorney from New York, a man named Van Buren. His affidavits and research notes are all recorded along with the documents."

"Astor?"

"Yes. Not John Astor, but his father William, who was the principal of the company back then before his father died and left him in charge of the whole estate. Apparently—and this is what I understand from people who were here at the time—the Astors were looking to secure title to all of the land where gold was, or would be, discovered, and they used this Van Buren to do the legwork in order to avoid suspicion."

"But everyone knew about the gold right after it was discovered."

"Not *right* after. It actually took several months. But the Secret Chancellery learned of it, and there was a plan to pull the rug out from under Astor. But apparently the old man had made provision."

"That still doesn't explain interest in the land on this side of the bay. Surely they didn't think there was gold here as well?"

"No, and they didn't look to gain title to it either. But they did do an extensive job at surveying and recording it, and Van Buren did some of that, too. The House of Astor was quite interested in all of it."

"Any idea why?"

"I have my suspicions."

Thorne leaned over the map, his hands flat on the table; he looked across it at Norton. "Well?"

"They built a railroad across all of British North America, then through and across the mountains all the way to the terminus at Archangel across the bay. Wouldn't they like to bring it all the way to Saint Helena?"

"Across the bay? That's absurd. How could they even do it?"

"There's a bridge across the Thames. There is talk of a bridge across the Mississippi."

"A river is not an inland bay. It's impossible—it's far too deep, the current is far too swift."

"Ten years ago no one believed that it was possible to build a rail line through the Sierras—but the Astors did it, with help from Chinese engineers and a hell of a lot of brute force labor. Maybe this is just as possible."

"A bridge across the bay."

"Yes. I think that's exactly what they have in mind. I don't know how, but I can certainly see why."

✳ ✳ ✳

The Consulate-General of the Kingdom of France was located on Rezanov Prospekt, uphill and somewhat inland from the eastern edge of Saint Helena. Even from the street, there was a nice view of Telegraph Hill; as he disembarked from his carriage and handed down Andrea,

Grigori's glance was drawn that way. He wondered what the French consul must think when he looked out at the great cathedral—or whether he chose to situate his office so that he did not need to do so.

In any case, Gyazin had always thought that the French favored style over substance. The average Russian was proud—justifiably proud—of the rodina, of the deeds of its greatest citizens, of the might and majesty of the tsar . . . while the French were eager to preserve the appearance of power, its trappings and the stylistic presentation of their country's relationships. The French Consulate was a reflection of that modus operandi: a section of the solid, stolid Russian street was interrupted by gilt doors, and once inside the excessively ornate and elaborate Empire furnishings, from the burgundy pile carpets to the exquisitely-tooled and ornately-painted tin ceilings proclaimed: "France is a great nation: trouble yourself with no other."

Grigori Gyazin was having none of it; he affected an air of annoyed indifference as they were left to wait in the front sitting room for their host to appear. Andrea busied herself with the examination of an exquisite set of ceramic miniatures on display in a grand glass-fronted cabinet.

"Aren't these beautiful," she said, without turning.

Grigori didn't answer, lost in his thoughts, until she said, "Grisha, did you hear me?"

"I thought I asked you— "

"Oh, my dear, don't be such a sourpuss." She turned from the cabinet and walked to take his arm, smiling so sweetly that it banished his scowl. "You will behave yourself with Monsieur Gros, I trust."

He did not look away from the grand portrait that hung above the fireplace, commanding his attention, but said, "Yes, of course, I shall. My French may not be up to the task, but I will be the *parfait gentilhomme*." The French words embedded in the Russian sentence seemed_like a foreign invasion.

"This is not a campaign of war, my sweetest."

"They are not our friends, dear heart. They are without doubt listening to this very conversation for later consideration, but I am not afraid to say that I believe us to be standing on enemy soil."

"A shame," she said airily. "I so adore the furnishings."

Before he could frame a reply to her comment, the doors opened, and a liveried footman bowed Étienne-Louis Gros into the room. Andrea disengaged herself from Grigori's arm and smiled, offering a hand to the young man as he approached. Grigori stood stiffly, smiling, inclining his head very slightly.

Étienne-Louis took Andrea's hand and gently touched it with his lips, and then gave a courteous handshake to Grigori. "Prince and Princess Gyazin," he said, stepping back, "it is a decided and genuine pleasure to have you here in our sovereign territory." Grigori tensed for a moment, which Andrea did not—or chose not to—notice.

"I was admiring your appointments," Grigori said. He gestured toward the gilt-framed portrait over the mantel. "Who is this impressive gentleman?"

"One of our great national heroes," Étienne-Louis said. "His Grace Marie-Joseph Paul Yves Roch Gilbert du Motier, the Duc de Lafayette. He was His Majesty's chief minister for nearly two decades, during the great rivalry with the English."

"Lafayette. Of course." If there was one name known—and generally reviled—in British America, it was the Marquis—later the Duke—de Lafayette. He grew up during the period between the Twelve Years' War—which British Americans called the French and Indian War—and the French invasion in 1777. Lord Burgoyne earned his peerage at the great British victories at Saratoga and Charleston, and then the two sides fought each other to exhaustion: in the end it was the purse and not the sword that brought about peace. France was nearly bankrupt when King Louis XVI turned to the young upstarts, led by the brilliant Lafayette, to reform the wrecked French economy and return the nation to its former glory.

"Of course."

"And do you light a candle in reverence?"

"Grigori," Andrea said.

At least she didn't call me Grisha, he thought. "I apologize, Monsieur Gros," Grigori said. "I know you hold the Duc de Lafayette in high esteem . . . but surely your quarrel with the British is long since healed?"

"Our king cultivates the virtues of courtesy and mercy," the Frenchman answered. "Yet while he forgives, he commands us to never forget."

"You sound like a true Russian."

"I take it that is meant as a compliment, Highness."

"It was intended as such, Monsieur."

The Frenchman did not hesitate for a moment to offer a sincere smile, which Grigori found disarmingly charming. For the first time since setting foot in the consulate, he felt genuinely at ease.

"I have had luncheon set out on the terrace," Gros said. "The weather is lovely, and the view superb. If that meets with your approval, all is in readiness."

"Please," Grigori said. "Lead the way."

The cuisine was exquisite and the service was courteous and attentive, as good as any establishment in Saint Helena. Indeed, it could have been a supper-club in London or Paris, and was superior to anything he had visited in Saint Petersburg.

Grigori's French was practiced and careful, but did not permit much in the way of innnovation. He yielded to his wife—whose French was, indeed, superb; she alternately charmed and sparred with Gros, making him eager to please his guests and voluble in his conversation.

In the space of an hour, Grigori felt that he learned more than a Secret Chancellery interrogator might have obtained from a willing captive. It was difficult to determine whether the young Frenchman was prepared to give out information of the sort he provided, or whether he was overly susceptible to Andrea's considerable charms; but if it was an act, it was a decidedly good one.

As he sat and listened, Grigori determined several important things.

First: the French were interested—*very* interested—in what went on in Saint Helena. It was by far the best natural Pacific harbor in North America, with the inner bay easily navigable and sheltered from ocean storms. There was no French window on the Pacific: New France did not extend past the great mountain range that divided British and French North America from Novaya Rossiya.

Second: His Majesty Philippe IX was eager to establish a trading post and treaty port in the Sandwich Islands, similar to the British one in Honolulu and the Russian one in Lahaina. The north shore of the largest island was under discussion, but the king of the island chain had simply not made up his mind—perhaps because it was clear that his British and Russian friends would not take it kindly.

Third: Monsieur Gros' father, the Baron, had an ever-expanding staff and an ever-increasing budget for the consulate here in Saint Helena— and the younger Gros hinted that there was considerable interest in expanding the friendly relationship with Russia here on the Pacific rim. In short, France would be eager to establish a strong diplomatic relationship with Russia . . . perhaps in order to drive a wedge between the tsar and the Queen.

Andrea did her best to affect complete indifference to political matters about which Gros seemed more than willing to talk. Very little of this was directed to Grigori; Gros seemed more interested in flattering, and flirting with, his wife—enough so that under other circumstances, he might feel as if he was being slighted at least and cuckolded at worst. But he understood his wife completely—all this flattery was means to an end.

After the luncheon, Grigori and Andrea took a pleasant carriage ride along the shore, following the road that fronted the east bay. Once beyond the ferry landing and the market, it was quiet and desolate; the Archangel shore was cloaked in fog so that the smaller city could not even be seen; it was a striking contrast to the bright sunlight on their side of the bay. At a command, the coach driver halted near the place where the road turned west: a high bluff, flat and grassy, where there was a stone embrasure that had once held a cannon.

Andrea took his arm, and the two of the walked to the vantage, where they sat on the flat area, which was large enough to accommodate them both and low enough that their shoes rested on the ground. The coach driver remained with the carriage, offering them some amount of privacy.

"That wasn't so bad, now was it, Grisha?"

"It was really quite enjoyable," he agreed. "And you were magnificent, my dear. You kept him talking."

"He was very inquisitive."

"It is so with that sort of person."

"Diplomats?"

"Frenchmen."

She laughed. The wind tried its best to tousle her hair, but the bonnet she wore was expertly pinned; only a few stray strands made their way out, and she gently brushed them aside.

"You are such a . . . a *Russian*."

"And you are not?"

"Of course I am. But I am also a citizen of the world, my dear Grisha. As our children shall be."

"But Russians first."

"Yes, yes, of course. But did we not learn from Pyotr Alexeivich that in order for our country to survive, we must become . . . what is the word? Cosmopolitan." The Russian word, *kosmopolitichesky*, was an awkward one, but it sounded like poetry coming from Andrea.

"Peter the Great is a fine model to follow, my dear. It is why we have a bust of him over our mantel. So much more admirable than Lafayette, whatever Monsieur Gros says.

"Still, he seemed quite well-informed about my business dealings. He had many questions regarding things which are decidedly not his business."

"And you answered nearly none of them. But tell me, Grisha . . . have you been buying parcels of land?"

"Yes. Yes, I have, through intermediaries. Joshua Norton has been handling all of that for me. In fact," he said, standing and looking out across the fog-shrouded bay, "you are standing in one of them at this moment."

"You . . . *own* this barren place?"

"Yes. Or I soon shall."

"But why?"

"Come here," he said. She stood and came to stand next to him; he put his arm around her shoulders and pointed across the water. "Do you see that promontory, just there?"

"Yes."

"That is, in fact, an island. And the distance from where we stand to that island is a bit under half a mile. It is possible—it *will* be possible—to build a bridge to connect them; and then another bridge to cross to the other side. It means that someday, not too long from now, it will be possible to board a train in Boston or New York and ride it all the way to Saint Helena instead of stopping at Archangel."

"By crossing the bridge."

"Yes. I do not know if we will be able to obtain an elephant."

"What?"

Grigori smiled. "There is an old tradition that says that an elephant will not step where there is danger. If we could find an elephant, we could cause it to cross the finished bridge and assure everyone that it is safe."

"It seems like a great deal of trouble."

"If there is one thing of which I am sure, my sweet, is that when it comes to reassuring the common person it is always worth the trouble. Many people will need to use this bridge—and they must be satisfied that it will not hurl them to their death in the bay."

"I imagine that bringing an elephant here would cost a great deal—several years of Mischka's private schooling at least."

Grigori took his arm from Andrea's shoulder, and gently turned her to face him. He took her hands in his and looked into her eyes.

"My dear," he said, "if this project is carried to completion, we will never have to worry about money again."

CHAPTER 7

An overcast morning with too great a share of tropical humidity.
Honolulu was, altogether, a much more sophisticated place than Lahaina; but the British were more devoted to the idea of bringing a part of their home abroad with them. The Russians had left the old capital on Maui much as they found it: pastoral, dusty (or muddy, if it was raining), with no real division between natives and Europeans.

Honolulu, on the other hand, was an outpost of Britain; the Union Jack flew in the breeze, the streets had been macadamized or cobbled at least along the quay at Pearl Harbor and into the British Town between the harbor and the great cliff side called Diamond Head; and there was an air of get-to-it and no-time-for-slackers that smacked of the industrial and commercial might of the greatest country in the world.

We are here, it all said. *And we are here to stay.*

Honolulu was scarcely bigger than a provincial town, more the size of Archangel than of Saint Helena. It reminded Norton of Cape Town—yet it was unquestionably cosmopolitan: like Lahaina there were flags of many lands on display and snatches of many languages among those who walked about and did business at Pearl Harbor. But the common pidgin was sprinkled with English idiom.

While *Nevsky* offloaded its cargo and prepared to take on the crates that it would be transporting to Saint Helena—pineapples, according to everyone that Norton had spoken with: he had no reason to believe otherwise—he went for a stroll through Kamehameha's royal city.

And almost at once, he realized that he was being followed.

Joshua Norton did not pride himself either as a soldier or a spy: he had not been trained in either profession's methods. However, he had enough native guile to know when someone was shadowing his movements.

The city was not that big, and his shadow was not that clever, for Norton to overlook it even in his distracted state.

There were only two alternatives—try to lose the tail, or to find a way to confront it. Since he had no specific objective, and since he was likely presumed to have arrived aboard *Nevsky*—the only Russian-flagged ship presently in the harbor—there was no real point in slipping away. The pursuer only need to wait for Norton to appear dockside prior to re-boarding the ship. On the other hand, the idea of teasing out a single additional thread of the mystery intrigued him.

In the instance, it was actually not difficult to trap the tail; all he had to do was act in the way that he was expected to do.

Much of what comprised the Hawai'ian royal capital had been built in the last ten years, since King Kamehameha had moved it here from Lahaina and the British had established their settlement. Queen Street was the principal thoroughfare, leading away from the harbor; Norton made his way up the street, considering where he might be expected to engage in . . . *espionage,* he supposed: the person following him must assume that he was in the Sandwich Islands for a reason, rather than just being a pawn in some Secret Chancellery game.

At the corner of Queen and Fort Streets, he came upon a dry-goods store: H. Hackfeld and Company. If nothing else, it was an opportunity to get out of the heat, which had already become oppressive.

Within, it was dim compared to the brightness outside; it took a few moments for Norton to accustom himself to it. There were a few people there, examining all manner of goods: crockery, bolts of various sorts of cloth, open crates of hardware, even small sheets of window glass. It was a remarkable inventory, considering just how far away the Sandwich Islands were from everywhere else in the world.

He made his way into the back of the store, where there were unopened crates and barrels. One barrel had been rolled to the front but not yet opened; a copy of the *Polynesian,* Honolulu's weekly newspaper, lay folded on top. A pencil lay next to it.

Suddenly, he had an idea. He took the newspaper, unfolded it, and with the pencil he carefully and deliberately marked several words on the front page. He chose them completely at random: it didn't matter—there was no code he was following . . . but his pursuer couldn't know that.

When he was done, he looked around as furtively as he could manage, then went to a shelf filled with small boxes and tucked the newspaper carefully between two stacks.

Then he did his best to conceal himself in the shadows of the room.

Shortly, his patience was rewarded. A man came back into the rear area; he too looked around carefully, as if to see if anyone was watching, and went directly to the shelf and withdrew the newspaper. He opened it out and looked at it, frowning.

"Now," Norton said, his pen-knife placed carefully near the man's neck as he stepped up behind him, "let's have a wee talk."

As expected, the man reacted suddenly, dropping the paper and trying to whirl around to face Norton, who had managed to get the drop on him; but Norton was ready for it, and knocked his feet out from under him so that he fell to the floor. Norton's knife nicked him slightly on the ear as he went by.

Joshua Norton had not managed to become successful in rough-and-tumble Saint Helena without having a few tricks ready; there was a stepladder nearby, and he dropped it behind where the man had fallen to the floor, making it difficult for him to scuttle away. He held his hand to his ear, which was bleeding.

"It's just you and me for a few moments, friend," Norton said. "I would guess that Herr Hackfeld won't want blood mixing in with his nice clean sawdust, but I'm willing to take that chance. How about you tell me why you've been following me."

"Look," the man said. "I am just the hired man. I am not looking to trouble you."

He spoke English with a decided accent: French, Norton guessed—but not exactly *haute Parisienne*. It reminded him of the traders from the French colonies of Senegal and Côte d'Ivoire who sometimes turned up in Cape Town.

"Who hired you?"

"Dillon. Monsieur Dillon. He just told me to keep track of your movements."

"To what end?"

"He wants to know . . . where you go, who you meet. He wants to know what *Nevsky* carries."

At that moment, a heavy-set, moustachioed man wearing a long apron appeared, frowning. Norton slipped the pen-knife into his sleeve, and reached a hand out to help the fallen man.

"What is this?" he asked, in thick German-accented English. "What is happening?"

"My friend tripped on the stepladder," Norton said. "I think he cut himself, but he's all right, aren't you, Jean?"

The storekeeper scowled at Norton and the other man, who accepted Norton's assistance in standing. After a moment, the German sighed. "My clerk assistant did not put it away, I would guess. Can I help you find a thing?"

"No," Norton said. "Just looking around."

After one more scowl, he turned and went back toward the front of the store.

Norton firmly took hold of the man's arm. "Let's go for a little walk, and maybe this can end well for you."

His pursuer, who was happy to remain "Jean," was eager to get away; Norton really had no reason to hold him, and didn't think that Sharovsky did either.

He did learn who he was working for: William Patrice, Baron de Dillon, His Majesty Philippe IX's consul to the Kingdom of Hawai'i.

Pineapples, Norton said. He can find that out without cloak and dagger. Nevsky is carrying pineapples to Saint Helena.

Then why are you here? "Jean" had asked. Why do they need you, a prosperous man of business in Saint Helena, to escort fruit across the Pacific Ocean?

He refused to answer that question; the Baron de Dillon could try and figure it out for himself.

Then, perhaps, he could present his compliments to Norton and explain the reason . . . because Norton himself still wasn't sure.

✳ ✳ ✳

Sharovsky left him standing and didn't offer him a glass from the flask on his desk.

"He gave you Dillon's name."

"Yes. He's the consul—"

"I know who he is, gospodin Norton."

"You know a lot more than that, don't you, Captain? More than you're saying."

"We all know more than we're saying."

Norton reached for the flask and the glass. Before Sharovsky could stop him, Norton poured himself a shot of the vodka and downed it, then placed both back in front of the captain of *Nevsky* and leaned over toward him.

"I'm tired of not knowing what is going on, Captain Sharovsky. The fellow who followed me here in Honolulu asked me a leading question: why I would be needed to escort a cargo of pineapples from Honolulu to Saint Helena. I want to know that too: why, at the moment at which Zachariah Thorne hung me out like wash on a line so that I would be ruined, a member of state security—an agent of the Secret Chancellery—would offer to make my debts whole if I was willing to travel aboard your ship.

"And what happens? We catch a spy that we have to let go. I am kept in the dark about all of this mystery. And now . . . we ship fruit back to Saint Helena? What are we really carrying, gospodin Captain? What is being loaded into your hold?"

"Fruit."

"And?"

"And more fruit. What do you think we are carrying, Norton? Weapons? Subversive tracts? Russian language pornographic books? We are carrying fruit—mangoes, taro, pineapples. Delicacies for the tables of the Russian aristocrats in Saint Helena and elsewhere—people like your friend Lord Gyazin."

"Who could not be bothered to help me out of my difficulty—even though I was working for him at the time."

"Perhaps he had other reasons."

"Or perhaps he decided that he could not be bothered." Norton reached for the flask again, but the Russian captain clamped his hand down on it.

"You do not know the whole situation."

"Do you?"

"*Nyet.* No one does—outside of the Secret Chancellery. All I can tell you, *gospodin*, is that this runs deeper than you know, and if you understood it you would be less angry with your . . . friend."

"He is not my friend. Perhaps he never was."

Sharovsky leaned back in his chair, still holding the flask in his hand, as if to keep it away from Norton.

"Such as they live in their own world, *tovaritch*. You and I are men of business, not men of title. There is a great unbridgeable gap in between: so it has always been and always will be. There is no society in the world that has crossed it.

"I am sorry to say I do not think any ever will. It is the way of the world, and we must do the best we can."

"It still doesn't explain why I am here."

"For the same reason I am," Sharovsky said. "Because they need us for something."

He took a long, searching look at Norton, then placed the flask back on the table, and reached without looking for a small door on the shelves above. He opened it and removed a second glass, similar to the one on the table. After rubbing the inside of it with the tail of his shirt, he opened the flask and poured vodka into both glasses.

He beckoned to Norton to take one, and he took the other and raised it.

"To always being useful," he said, and drank it off.

CHAPTER 8

An unseasonably warm morning, with a gentle breeze coming through the open bay doors of the Governor-General's reception room.

Grigori Gyazin was neither accustomed to being summoned nor being required to wait—and yet the former had come, and the latter was ongoing.

The summons had arrived just as he and Andrea and the children were settling down to breakfast. It was the only meal they always shared. Whatever other privations might exist in Saint Helena, so far from the Imperial Court, breakfast was always a pleasure; their cook had been provided with the means to make sourdough bread, Grigori's particular favorite, and it appeared fresh-baked every morning.

He had just spread a warm slice with butter when a footman appeared and presented him a card on a silver tray. He customarily forbade interruptions at family breakfasts unless it was vitally important; Andrea's face held the slightest hint of annoyance, but as soon as her husband picked up the card her mood changed to concern.

Grigori stood, wiping his mouth with his napkin, apologized and left the room without explanation.

Now he was at the Governor-General's office, waiting for the man who had sent his card to Odessa Street. He was someone not to be trifled with, even if one was forty-first (or forty-second, or forty-third) in line for the throne. His name was Alexey Fyodorovich Orlov, and he was head of the Third Section—the Secret Chancellery—the tsar's secret police.

Count Orlov was very close to Tsar Nicholas, and when he went abroad it was customarily as a high-ranking diplomat. The very last place

Grigori would have expected to encounter him was Saint Helena, ten thousand miles away from Saint Petersburg.

It was a mark of particular interest by the tsar himself . . . or it meant that something, or someone, was under suspicion.

The idea that it was him gave him pause: another man might have been filled with dread, but he refused to do so. Count Orlov was just a man, a servant and subject of the Great Autocrat as he was. There was some explanation for his presence in Saint Helena, and for summoning Prince Grigori Gyazin to attend him (which, if it were merely a matter of rank, would have been tantamount to an insult.)

The real question was why it was taking so long. It was, no doubt, to unnerve him.

Just as he thought of this and was considering the extent of his annoyance, a door opened and Orlov appeared. He was an older man, going quite bald, with a heavy moustache and no beard. He wore a Life Guards uniform—a bit out of style—and the cross and sash of the Order of Saint George, First Class, awarded to him after the war against the Turks a dozen years earlier. He walked and looked like a soldier even now, and his stern gaze took in Grigori Gyazin from head to toe; it was as if he was evaluating a cavalry mount.

"Count Orlov," Grigori said, clicking his heels and bowing very slightly. "It is an honor to have you in Saint Helena."

"Hmm," Orlov said. "I am not here for honor, Prince Gyazin. But I thank you for your courtesy. I . . . apologize for being abrupt, but it was vitally necessary that I speak with you."

"I am at your service."

Orlov gestured toward two overstuffed chairs, and settled himself into one of them. Grigori sat in the other.

"You are engaged in certain transactions of land," he began without preface. "This has come to the attention of numerous persons."

"I have done nothing illegal."

"I do not believe that I have said otherwise."

"No. Of course you have not," Grigori said. He felt that he had replied a bit too eagerly. "I merely wish to suggest that there is nothing particularly unusual about the purchases."

"You have used an intermediary."

"Of course."

"Of course," Orlov repeated. "It would be unseemly for a Prince of the Empire to be engaging in land speculation of his own accord. The arrangements have all been made through a man of business, a certain Norton."

"Joshua Norton. That's right."

"A Briton. And a Jew."

"I don't see how that bears on the question, but yes, Joshua is a Jew who came here a few years ago from South Africa. I count him a friend."

"Your Highness is too trusting," the spymaster said. "Such persons should not rise to the rank of friends." He tinged both *person* and *friend* with an air of faint disgust. "He has your commission to act on your behalf?"

"Yes."

"But you have not yet furnished him with the funds to complete the transactions."

"He has not requested it, but I intend to do so at the appropriate time."

"No," Orlov said. "You will do nothing of the sort."

"I beg your pardon?"

"Norton will undertake these transactions for you. But when it comes time to pay for them, you will not do so."

"I am—no. No, that would be completely dishonorable. Even if I were to consider such a course, it would be highly damaging to Joshua Norton's business. Such a considerable outlay—he would be ruined."

"That is correct, Prince Gyazin. But it is ordered that you do so, and it is precisely this outcome that is desired. When combined with the betrayal by his business partner, Norton will be desperate."

"Betrayal?"

"By Zachariah Thorne, yes. He has already planned to abscond with a considerable sum in company funds."

"Why would he do that?"

Orlov allowed himself a fierce little smile. "He is a closet Catholic, Prince Gyazin, and is more than happy to aid the cause of a Catholic country. He has taken money from the French, who are eager to thwart this plan of yours."

"Zachariah Thorne is a canting dissenter from some British

Atlantic plantation. I don't even remember the name—"

"Connecticut."

"Yes. That's the one. A Catholic? That's absurd."

"Third Section confirms it," Orlov said quietly. "And he has already made arrangements to withdraw all of the firm's cash. Without it, and without your financial backing, Norton will be exactly where we want him."

"This is a heinous plan. Why do you wish to ruin my . . . man of business?"

"We don't. We simply want him beholden to the Chancellery. You see, Prince, the real villain is the scheming French. They have suborned Thorne, and they believe that they can thus stop your ambitious plan. But their ambitions extend far beyond Saint Helena: they want to interfere all over the Pacific. They are an existential threat to the Russian Empire, and they must be stopped."

"Then stop them."

Orlov sighed. "Prince Gyazin. I ask your patience as I explain this to you.

"The greatest naval power in the world is not France; it is not Russia. It is the Kingdom of Great Britain, which the tsar counts as his ally. But Her Majesty's government does not see the Kingdom of France as a threat—to Russia or to itself. In order to obtain the help of Britain in stopping the French, a task that you toss off as lightly as you might order dinner, it will be necessary to get them to show their intentions.

"To do this will require your man of business, this Joshua Norton, to be vulnerable enough to act on our behalf. In exchange for his help, we shall offer to make his debts whole. The French will be exposed as aggressors; the Jew will have his money; and all will be well."

"Except that I shall appear as an ungrateful and dishonest man."

"I think that it is of little moment," Orlov said. "At least when compared to the national security of the rodina."

* * *

When he returned to his home, Andrea could see that Grigori was troubled. She followed him into the library: usually a sanctum where neither she nor the children visited, she knew that she was invading his privacy.

Some Russian aristocrats would respond angrily or even violently to such assertiveness, but that was not Grigori—and Andrea was someone he trusted implicitly. He explained to her what the tsar's spymaster had ordered him to do.

"I do not know why the tsar would elevate such a one to high rank," she said at last.

"He may be made a prince."

"He would demean that title as well."

"I am not the tsar, my dear," Grigori said. "But I am a loyal servant. He has ordered me to do this—"

"This Count Orlov has ordered you, Grisha. *Ordered* you! Are you sure that this comes from the highest authority?"

"Do you mean, is he acting on his own? I doubt it." Grigori had settled himself at his writing-desk, and he stood and pulled another chair alongside. After Andrea sat down he took her hands in his. "I regret to say that it sounds like exactly the sort of thing that would come from the highest authority.

"If you were to walk through the Summer Palace and ask ten noblemen which was the greatest empire on Earth, they would to a man say 'Russia.' But they are wrong: the greatest empire is Britain, and it is getting stronger while we are getting weaker.

"There are times that I think that we exist only at the sufferance of the British—that without that alliance, we should be cast adrift like the Spanish, carved up like a roast at a feast by its hungry neighbors. Orlov, on the tsar's orders, seeks to use our allies to protect Russian interests—but also to show that it is we whom they need, and not the French or the Spanish or anyone else. Britain could throw us over and find another partner, and this interview made clear to me that he is terrified of that possibility."

"Another partner? Who?"

"I don't know. Prussia, perhaps. Or Austria."

"Prussia?" Andrea laughed. "You can't be serious. What could the British find of interest in that piddling little country of toy soldiers and sausage makers?"

"There is an old family connection. The Dukes of Hannover are cousins."

"Queen Victoria is cousin to every crowned head in Europe. This grubby policeman has filled your head with nonsense."

"It is not nonsense," he answered. "There is talk of emancipating the serfs, and while men such as Orlov and Dolgorukov scoff at such a thing it must surely happen, just as the English have freed their slaves, even the ones in America. The world is changing and Russia must change with it or be left behind . . . if that has not already happened. I think that in order for the rodina to survive, we will have to give up our pretensions to nobility and generosity."

Andrea carefully disengaged her hands from those of her husband and laid them flat on her skirts. Grigori could see anger in her eyes, but it was not directed at him—but rather at the words he had just spoken.

"This is not what it means for the rodina to survive, my dear Grisha. Norton is already caught in their web, but there is no reason for you to believe that you are trapped as well."

"I cannot do other than what I have been told."

"I would not say otherwise, my heart. But you do not have to act exactly as they have told you."

"What do you mean?"

"You must let Norton know that you have not abandoned him—but when he approaches you personally, you must be away."

"Away?"

"You have promised the children that we will go across the bay and visit the great tall trees. It is time to take that trip, Grisha, so that we are not in Saint Helena when the—unpleasantness—takes place."

"I hope that Norton does not do anything out of desperation. A man facing ruin can be . . . rash."

"He is very strong, my dear. He has survived other things—he will survive this."

"Betrayal by his partner, and by his patron?"

"You will *not* betray him, Grisha. Not in the end. You are true to the standards of nobility, and ultimately loyal to your friends—no matter what such as this Count Orlov may say."

"How can you be so sure?"

"Because I know the man I married." She took his hands again. "Even if you are not sure, I am."

CHAPTER 9

An overcast night on the Pacific. *Nevsky* cut through the waves; but the fog isolated the ship—it could have been the only one in the world.

Sharovsky found Norton on the foredeck, smoking his pipe and looking out across the ocean.

"Can't you sleep?" he asked.

"I sleep too much," Norton answered. "I had the strangest dream, and after that I had to get some air."

"My grandmother used to tell me that the best way to dispel a nightmare is to share it." Sharovsky leaned on the rail next to Norton. "What did you dream?"

"I was in Saint Helena," Norton said. "Though it wasn't really Saint Helena—it wasn't Russian. It was British, I think—everyone spoke English. I was walking through the town and everyone seemed to know me. I was walking my dogs."

"You have dogs?"

"I did in this dream. And I was wearing a uniform of some kind: it was fancy, but it was more like a costume than clothing—as if I were pretending to be a general or an admiral or something similar. Yet I was greeted with the greatest respect. They called me 'Emperor.' But behind my back they were laughing at me."

"Emperor?" Sharovsky chuckled. "Emperor Norton. I cannot lie, gospodin: I would laugh at you too. I cannot imagine you in a uniform."

"It was frightening, Captain. I was not myself. I was a madman, or a simpleton. In the dream . . . they called me emperor, and I think I believed it was true."

Sharovsky reached into his coat for his own pipe and drew it out.

"Dreams are strange things, gospodin Norton. Sometimes they are just hopes or fears, but . . . sometimes they might be other things: windows into places that never were, or other worlds like our own but not quite the same. Maybe in that world you are an emperor, a clown in uniform. And when that figure dreams . . . he is on the foredeck of *Nevsky,* wondering what kind of world this is."

"What kind of world is this, Captain?"

"We have had this conversation, Norton. You know what kind of world we live in: where the decisions are made by others."

"But what are the decisions? What is the point of all this?"

"It will all become clear, *gospodin.*"

"When?"

Sharovsky looked up at the topmast and then back at Norton. "If I am not mistaken . . . it will be soon."

"What does that mean?"

There was a shout from the crow's nest. Sharovsky shouted back: the fog had lifted enough for a ship to be sighted.

"What's happening?" Norton asked, as men began to come on deck.

Captain Sharovsky had tucked away his pipe and was walking quickly toward the chart room, but stopped and turned to look at Norton.

"This is the point at which it becomes clear."

"You were expecting this?"

"Yes. Of course. This would be the French. They will be boarding us now, I expect."

"Why?"

"It's not because they are looking for the Emperor, gospodin," he answered. "I expect . . . they want to look at our pineapples."

* * *

Nevsky was not a ship of war. *La Poursuivante,* however, most certainly was: with its guns trained on the Russian trader, there was no alternative but to heave to. The seas were calm, and *Nevsky* cast its sea anchor.

Presently a boat bearing French soldiers and a trio of officers rowed over from *La Poursuivante*. A rope ladder was lowered for them, and they came up on deck, where Sharovsky was waiting. Norton had begun to go below, but the Russian captain indicated that he should remain.

The chief officer was an older man, dressed in a gaudy uniform festooned with medals and decorations. He wore a red riband over his right shoulder and a prominent medal with a croix-pattée on his left breast.

"You are the captain of this vessel?" he asked of Sharovsky in passable Russian.

"I have that honor," Sharovsky said. He was not given to ceremony, but had located a service cap that Norton had never seen him wear. "I am Georgy Sharovsky, and I presume you have some reason to intercept an unarmed merchantman of a foreign country with which you are not at war?"

"It will all become clear. Allow me to introduce myself: I am Louis-François de Tromelin, Admiral in His Most Catholic Majesty's service."

"Your king sent an admiral to intercept a Russian merchantman," Sharovsky answered. "A crowning act of honor to cap a brilliant career, I have no doubt."

"You make light of this, Captain Sharovsky. You are a brave man to make jests while under the guns of an armed ship."

"Should I be afraid?"

"Are you not?"

"No. I do not believe that the French have turned pirate, especially when commanded by an admiral bearing the sash and medal of the Order of St. Louis. I have nothing you want—unless you are particularly fond of pineapple."

"You are carrying more than pineapples."

"Of course. Pitch and tar, whale oil, coils of rope; a brace of chickens, various other supplies—"

"Enough," Tromelin said, cutting him off with a wave of his hand. "This is no joking matter. You will show me these—these pineapples, and I will see for myself."

✳ ✳ ✳

159

Admiral de Tromelin was beside himself with anger.

They had opened several crates, and a number of the fragrant,
sweet fruits had been cut open to examine them. In the swaying
lantern light of *Nevsky*'s hold, Louis-François du Tromelin was beginning
to realize that Georgy Sharovsky was telling the truth.

It was only then that word reached him that three British men of
war were on the scene.

✳ ✳ ✳

Joshua Norton's homecoming in Saint Helena took place on an
overcast morning. It reminded him of the day he had first arrived
four years earlier, with little to his name other than the clothes on his
back and a small carpetbag in his hand.

If he was going to be honest with himself, it might be true now.

The firm's offices and possessions had likely been seized; his partner
had fled—to Veracruz, if the spy Damon was to be believed.

And his patron . . . he could hardly have expected Gregori Gyazin to
meet him on the Embarcadero after abandoning him to financial ruin. He
did not truly expect anyone to be there to meet him when he walked
down the gangplank of *Nevsky*. He stood on the dockside looking up
toward Telegraph Hill, mostly shrouded in fog.

He heard a throat being cleared, and turned to see a young man
dressed in the elaborate uniform of a customs gendarme.

"I have nothing to declare," Norton said. "You can search my bag if
you like."

"Your pardon," the man said. "You are Norton, yes?"

"You know who I am already. What do you want?"

"Your presence is requested," he said, and gestured toward a coach
parked at the foot of the street.

"Who requests it?"

The young man did not reply, but gestured again; he seemed
insistent. Clearly this was someone of importance, who didn't care to
show himself in the sunlight.

He was not going to get any further answer: it would obviously be
necessary to find out for himself. He nodded and followed the man

across the busy Embarcadero to the waiting carriage. The door was opened for him, and he stepped inside.

To his surprise, he found himself sitting opposite Grigori Gyazin and another man whom he did not know—an older nobleman, who seemed almost as ill at ease as his former patron.

"I had just told myself," Norton said, as the carriage began to move, "that the last thing I should expect is Prince Gyazin come to meet me at dockside."

"I owe you an apology, Joshua," Gyazin said. The other man, who had not been introduced, scowled at this, but Gyazin continued, "but this was all necessary."

"Your concern and your apology is several weeks too late for me, I fear, Highness. Perhaps I should put on a uniform and parade."

"I'm sorry, I don't—"

"Nothing." Norton closed his eyes and pinched his nose. "It is nothing. To what do I owe the honor?"

"You should consider yourself lucky, Norton," the other man said. "For some reason I fail to understand, you have a loyal friend."

"Do I really." Norton opened his eyes and let his hand fall to his lap. "And who might that be?"

"Me. Actually, Andrea: she gave me a severe tongue-lashing about this, and told me that I shall make good all that you have lost."

"Your Highness should not trouble himself," Norton said. "The Secret Chancellery has offered to do so. While you were—out of town— they made me an offer I could not refuse. Of course, I have no particular reason to believe that they will honor their commitments."

He looked pointedly at the other man.

"Your race has a habit of making itself unloved," he said. "I should remind you that you are beholden—"

"To what? To you, for sending me off as . . . as bait for the French, to provoke an international incident? Very well. I would be beholden to you, my lord, whoever you are, if I felt that I had anything left to lose.

"You see, on the last leg of my journey, after the British squadron intercepted Admiral du Tromelin's ship, I realized that if your ministry chose not to do as it promised and left me broken and ruined, it would mean that you had no more hold on me. I arrived here in Novaya Rossiya with almost nothing and built up a fortune; I can do it again, here or elsewhere, with or without your help. Or yours, Highness," he added to Gyazin.

"You accuse us of betraying our commitments?" the older man said. "And you spurn the help of a prince?"

"I accuse you of nothing," Norton said. "Except of using me, of manipulating me against my will. I am sure you found it easy to do. As for the help of my . . . friend . . . he owes me nothing."

Gyazin appeared to be ready to reply, but the other man placed a hand on his sleeve.

"You are a man of some principle," he said. "As for the prince, here . . . he is rather quaintly attached to his personal honor. The world we live in is one that suffers from a lack of that particular characteristic; it is not what drives me, nor is it of any help when dealing with matters of national security. But—" he shrugged, as if it was something of no importance.

In my dream I was Emperor, Norton thought. *A madman or a fool . . . but everyone knew me and they were courteous, even if they laughed at me.*

And no one made me their pawn.

No one had spoken for some time. They had ridden along the shore, toward the empty stretches of land that Norton had intended to buy for Gyazin.

The prince rapped on the roof of the carriage with his walking-stick and it stopped. He moved to get out, while the other man remained sitting. Norton did not know whether to stay or go, but Gyazin beckoned to him, and he climbed down and followed.

Gyazin walked up to the stone embrasure, just as he had done with Andrea weeks ago, before everything had happened. Archangel was clearly visible: the other side of the bay was brightly dappled with sunlight.

"Your guess was a good one, Joshua."

"About the Secret Chancellery? He represents them, doesn't he? And he is higher ranking than the man who promised to save me from creditors."

"He *is* the Secret Chancellery. That is Count Orlov."

"I've heard of him. What is he doing here?"

"This."

"He came all the way out to Saint Helena to ruin my life and remake it? I should be honored."

"You should shut up and be courteous to him, Joshua. Everything can be made as it was—it is up to him. He holds your fate in his hands."

"No," Norton said. "He doesn't. Any more than you do, Highness, or the tsar, or the Queen of England. If this little adventure taught me anything, it is that my life is my own, to make of what I wish."

"So you are rejecting my help."

"I didn't say that. I'm not rejecting his help either. But I fear that there will be strings attached in each case. If things had gone wrong, if I had been killed during this little adventure, neither you nor Orlov would have given me a second thought."

"That is decidedly not true in my case at least. Do you doubt my friendship?"

"I am not of your station, Highness. We both know that. In another world, where we met as equals, perhaps . . . but not in this one. Even Thorne understood that. I should have realized it long ago."

"I still want to build this bridge."

"I believe that you can. Perhaps I will stay and help you—or not. I'm not sure what I'm going to do."

"Your debts and obligations will be addressed."

"I am grateful. Please forgive me for making you think otherwise. I . . . am simply not sure what to make of it."

Gyazin did not have an answer. The two men stood there for a long time looking across the bay, trying to see the future.

INTERLUDE:
ANDREA'S GARDEN

1856-1857

When Grisha told her that as Governor-General of Novaya Rossiya he was expected to reside at the Presidio, Andrea was upset. Their comfortable house on Odessa Street had been a perfect home for their growing family ever since they had come out to Saint Helena; she had done her best to make it as welcoming as possible, a refuge from all that went on outside. The children's rooms, the small but beautifully-appointed drawing room, the secluded garden and their private balcony that overlooked the bay—she did not want to give it up. Of course, Grisha assured her that Mikhail and his wife would take good care of it while they settled into the official residence in what had begun as a Spanish fort when there was nothing in Saint Helena but a Catholic mission.

She had visited the Presidio, of course, both when it was the Spanish ambassador's residence, and then when it had been turned over to the provincial government of Novaya Rossiya four years earlier. For official receptions it had been gaily turned out, made to look far less rustic and unwelcoming than it might have otherwise seemed. But when they toured it the first time after the old governor-general and his staff had vacated the place, it drove her to tears: the rough, grimy walled fort surrounding a handful of wooden and adobe buildings might as well have been a Cossack camp at the edge of the great steppe. It was no fit place for a prince, a man in the line of succession to be tsar, to sleep even for one night, much less *live*. But Grisha was not moved by her protests or her outburst. What was to be, was to be, and she would have to try to make the best of it.

Would there be funds at her disposal? *Certainly,* he had answered. *Whatever is required.*

She scarcely knew where to begin.

The Presidio was at the top of a long, sloping hill that descended to marshy ground, where there was a native village: Ohlone Indians, who had lived there long before any Europeans came to the shore. They had been tolerated by the Spanish and largely ignored by the Russians, even when they came up the little muddy creek to a sacred place just outside the gates of the fort itself. Between the marsh and the fort was nothing but sand dunes, whipped up by the incessant breezes from the bay, with nothing to shield them. No one had ever thought to plant anything there—or if they did, it had met with no success. There were no trees to break up the sight lines: perhaps it was to prevent attack from the sea, an existential threat that had never existed—or perhaps it was because there was nothing anyone knew of that would grow in the sandy soil.

A few years earlier, at a dinner party she and Grisha had hosted, there had been an unusual visitor: Ilya Gavrilovich Voznesensky, a member of the Russian Academy of Sciences, who was on an extended trip through Novaya Rossiya to collect plant and animal species to be shipped back to the Zoological Museum in Saint Petersburg. He was an interesting man, very self-absorbed and fussy, but extremely intelligent; he had been solicitous, and when Andrea showed him her little garden, he had been thrilled to find one or two native flowers that he had not previously catalogued. Over the past few years, they had exchanged several small packages, as she sent him cuttings from her garden, and he wrote back with advice on cultivation and fertilization.

A week after Grisha advised her that they would be moving to the Presidio, she wrote to Voznesensky, inviting him ("inviting" was too polite a term, though it stopped just short of "summoning" . . . but she showed the letter to Grisha, who applied his own seal to the outside of the envelope) to come to Saint Helena to advise her on how best to proceed.

As it happened, the letter crossed paths with him in Vladivostok, where he had been commissioned to give a series of lectures on behalf of the Geographical Society. Her invitation implied that no expense would be spared; within a month he had presented himself, and Princess Gyazin and Ilya Voznesensky went to work, identifying plants that might have a chance of growing in the sandy soil below the Presidio. A week or so into the project, Voznesensky began to consult with an Ohlone medicine man who called himself Water Carrier. The naturalist developed an easy relationship with the native, though he hesitated to mention it to Andrea, perhaps fearing her disapproval: but Andrea Gyazin was focused on the goal, and took no issue with the means. Soon her head gardener, despite his reluctance, took on the Ohlone as his deputy—insisting, however, that Water Carrier made some attempt to dress properly.

It took a few months for any progress to be visible. Voznesensky first planted hardy grasses—some took to the soil, and some did not. Grisha was able to arrange for a team of engineers to take time away from work on the Saint Helena sewer system to excavate and widen the muddy stream to help irrigate the barren landscape, dredging the swampy land near the ocean; the Ohlone objected, but were mollified when Andrea went personally to their village to assure them that their sacred place would not be disturbed. Even when the Metropolitan of Saint Helena came down to consecrate the chapel, and made disparaging remarks, she stood her ground: the Ohlone tribe, such as it was, came under her personal protection and she was not to be gainsaid.

Despite the conflict, despite the expense, Grigori Gyazin stood by and approved all that his wife did. *A fierce woman,* he told the Metropolitan in private. *Your Grace does well not to force the issue: I know this from experience.*

By late summer, when Voznesensky took his leave after four months on retainer, the dunes had gradually been transformed into grassland, and tree saplings stood in a proud line along the western flank of the great hill. Some did not survive the harsh autumn storms, but the hardiest ones did; and by the following spring, the much more verdant land, sheltered somewhat from the ocean breezes, was ready to be transformed.

It would be a few years before the gardens she had imagined that first year would emerge, a pale shadow of the ones that graced palaces in Europe; but as she put her hand and heart to the work of transforming the Presidio, the staff and the natives in their little village began to call the lands *Andrea's Garden*.

HIDDEN PROPHET

1861

CHAPTER 1

With a final chuff of steam, the locomotive ground to a halt. The midnight train that arrived at Archangel—the last passenger train of the day, and far less fashionable (or comfortable) than the transcontinental ones that arrived in the morning or late afternoon—deposited travelers from Denver or Zion City or far-off Franklin on an often cold and deserted platform. From there they would have to make their way to lodgings, or the last ferry to Saint Helena (at 12:30, mind you, and God forbid the train should be late; the ferrymen were not in the habit of waiting) or make themselves as comfortable as they could in the vast, largely empty railroad depot until morning crept over the hills of the city by the bay.

Tonight, someone was waiting on the platform to meet a disembarking passenger. It was a chilly, early-spring night, and Joshua Norton wondered why he had let himself be talked into this, when he'd rather be at home, enjoying a good book.

". . .I have very few men so trustworthy in my employ," Gyazin had told him. "This is important, and needs to be kept very secret."

"What about Mikhail?" Norton had asked him. "Surely you trust him now that he's a grown man."

"Of course," Gyazin replied. "But he will attract far more attention than you because—"

"Because?"

"Because he is my *son*," Gyazin had said. "The son of the Governor-General meeting a midnight train at Archangel? People would talk."

Norton doubted whether people were actually taking notice of who might be getting off a train on the other side of the bay in the middle of the night, but he trusted Grigori Gyazin—the thirty-first (or thirty-second, or thirty-third) in line for the throne of the Tsar of all the Russias—to know what he was about. Mikhail was waiting at Gyazin's hunting lodge, where Norton would escort the special guest after his arrival. He had a coach and a trusted man as driver.

It took a few minutes for the passengers to disembark. His man was in the first-class carriage; only three emerged from there: an elderly woman and her companion and a stocky, bearded man carrying a carpetbag. He climbed down, following the two ladies, and seemed to take stock of everything around him.

As Norton approached, the man turned his attention to him. Even in the gaslight it was clear that he was no one ordinary, but rather a man accustomed to giving orders: he fixed Norton with a fierce scowl, as if expecting an argument.

"Do you have any luggage, sir?"

"None. I have traveled only with what I carry." His was an English accent, to be sure, but there was an unusual quality to the speech.

"I have a carriage waiting."

"Are we under observation?"

"Not that I know."

The man looked up and down the platform. "I assume we are. But there is nothing for it. Please lead on."

* * *

There was scarcely a word said as they traveled to the hunting lodge. Norton was not a gregarious man by nature, but the man he escorted had nothing at all to say: he rode in silence, clutching his carpetbag, looking straight ahead. It was a relief to reach the remote lodge and disembark.

Mikhail had opened up the lodge for the new arrivals. Norton had not been there in years, and he knew that the older Gyazin hardly used it anymore—the business of being Governor-General, and the demands of his wife and ever-growing family, made it difficult to make time.

"Gospodin Norton," Mikhail said, as they stepped inside the building. Mikhail Gyazin was seventeen, but was already a tall young man; he was a member of the guard regiment stationed at Saint Helena, and was wearing his uniform *sans* cravat and jacket, his sleeves rolled up.

There were no servants about: Mikhail had laid the fire and uncovered the furniture himself.

"Good evening," Norton said. "You've been busy."

"Father's orders. Welcome, Governor. I hope you will find this comfortable."

"Governor?" Norton managed, a bit surprised. Gyazin hadn't told him who the man was.

Mikhail didn't speak for a moment, wondering if he'd said something he shouldn't have. Fortunately, the silence was broken by an opening door from the pantry, and Grigori Gyazin himself stepped into the common room.

"It's all right, Mischa. Joshua, thank you for your help in escorting our guest from the train. Permit me to introduce Governor Brigham Young of the British colony of Deseret. Governor, this is my man of business, Joshua Norton. The soul of discretion."

"I should hope so," Young growled. "If word of my presence here was revealed—"

"Everything has been done to prevent it," the elder Gyazin said. "It is why I chose to meet you here. As my son says, I hope you will find it comfortable."

Young looked around, neither confirming nor contradicting Gyazin's hope.

"Are we expecting anyone else?"

"Other than myself, my son, Mr. Norton, his driver, and two of my best men outside, we are quite on our own." Gyazin settled himself into a comfortable armchair near the fire. "I'd offer you a drink, but I know you do not partake."

"Certainly not."

"Then perhaps we can begin."

* * *

For his part, Norton would have been willing to simply withdraw, but Gyazin gestured for him to remain as Brigham Young, the leader of the unusual community that called itself "latter-day saints," described the reason for his visit to Novaya Rossiya—and under the cover of night with more than the usual cloak-and-dagger.

"You know our history, Lord Gyazin," Young said. "Thirty years ago, our brother Joseph Smith received his divine revelation that created our society. Unwilling—or unable—to accept the truth, our enemies drove us from our original dwellings, ultimately causing us to make our great trek to our land of Zion in Deseret. There we have lived in relative peace for fifteen years."

"Without your original leader."

"Murdered," Young said. "By a jealous mob, near the town of Franklin. Our community scarcely escaped with our lives. That was three years before we crossed the wilderness."

"But from all I've heard," Gyazin said, "you have lived in peace since then. Whitehall and the British Governor-General have been very tolerant of your . . . divergent beliefs."

"That has been true for some time, yes. Lord Scott appointed me Governor of Deseret Colony six years ago: a fig leaf to reassure Her Majesty's Government that we were comfortably within the Empire."

"And are you? Are you 'comfortably within the Empire,' Mr. Young? Because—not to put too fine a point on it, as the English so quaintly say—" he exchanged a knowing glance with Norton "—you are *here*, and this is hardly a state visit."

Young scowled at the Governor-General of Novaya Rossiya, who returned the look with polite equanimity. Evidently whatever the power of Young's gaze with his regular constituency, it had little effect on the Russian nobleman who sat opposite.

"I suppose," Young said at last, "the situation was inevitable. You must realize, Lord Gyazin, that the frontier is growing smaller—and civilization is growing ever closer to our Zion. When we began to build Zion City in 1849, the settled lands of British North America were very distant. The transcontinental rail line was still under construction—and even when it was built, it scarcely affected us. But a decade has made a great deal of difference.

"Lord Scott is elderly and will soon step down. All that we have heard from Philadelphia is that the next Governor-General will have no interest in respecting our differences. Anglican missionaries and English tax-collectors will tread a path to our land, and there is talk of reform and conformity. We will have none of it: our culture is our own, and we deliberately separated ourselves to create it."

"What do you expect the outcome to be?"

"In a word? War."

"That is a very drastic conclusion to reach, Governor. Do you truly think the threat is that great, and the solution that dire?"

"Yes."

"You were very quick with that answer."

"I had a long train ride to think about it, Lord Gyazin. It is not what we want—but I believe it *is* what Philadelphia will want, and what the Empire will want."

"And what do *you* want?"

"To be left in peace."

Gyazin leaned back in his chair and folded his hands in his lap. "You misunderstand my question, sir. What I want to know is . . . what do you want from *me*?"

CHAPTER 2

Even though his fortunes had been restored by the assistance of Gregori Gyazin and the Russian government, Norton had not wanted to remain in the offices at Alexander Square he had shared with Zachariah Thorne. There were too many unhealed wounds and unpleasant memories. Instead, he had found a place more convenient at the lower end of Market Street at Mission Bay; someday, he hoped, there would be a bridge from there across to Archangel: he might well be located directly opposite a railroad depot, which would be even better for business.

The new offices (he'd been there eight years and still thought of them that way) were up two flights of stairs in a fairly new and airy building, with large windows that overlooked the bay. On a clear day he could see Archangel in the distance, with the small island between in the foreground.

When he walked in, though, he found someone else enjoying the view. His clerk Sergei, who was familiar with Norton's orders not to admit anyone when he was not in the office, looked on helplessly, as if something had induced him to violate the rule.

Norton didn't want to spend any effort reproaching the young man, who was rarely in need of such treatment: in any case, he would not do so in front of a stranger.

"I generally do not receive visitors in the morning," Norton said, handing his hat and umbrella to Sergei and nodding for him to close the door.

"You must forgive me," the man replied. "It was a matter of some urgency—and some delicacy."

"I also don't handle matters of delicacy in the morning."

The man—an Englishman from his voice, but with a peculiar accent that Norton could not readily place—was of late middle age, thinning hair giving way to baldness, but clearly in good physical condition. The visitor's glance was all-encompassing, as if he was operating an accurate and efficient camera.

"I hope you will make an exception."

"We shall see." Norton gestured to a chair set before his desk; he walked over to sit behind it, settling into his comfortable armchair. His visitor moved with a lithe grace, like a hunting cat, which put Norton slightly on edge.

As he took his seat, Norton said, "Let us begin with your name."

"My name is John Sherwood," the man said.

"I confess that the name means nothing to me. Should it?"

"I have only recently returned to Saint Helena after a long absence. I was last here before you came to Novaya Rossiya, Mr. Norton."

"You are . . . a student of my whereabouts?"

"More a careful observer, I should say. You are a very interesting man, Mr. Norton, very interesting indeed. And quite loyal."

"Perhaps you should come to the point, Mr. Sherwood. I have a very busy day ahead."

"But not a busy morning."

"I will ask you once more, sir: what is your business with me?"

"You are a *man* of business, Mr. Norton. I have a business proposition for you—you have something I want, and I have something to offer in return."

"What do you want?"

"Who did you meet at the midnight train last night?"

"Why do you want to know? Indeed, why is it you know I met someone—are you following me?"

Sherwood spread his hands and smiled. "You know how it is."

"I confess that I do not."

"Oh, of course you do, Mr. Norton. There was that affair with the French a few years ago . . ."

Norton stood up abruptly. "I don't require someone to spy on me. Good day, sir."

Sherwood hadn't moved; he remained sitting opposite, the same slight smile on his face.

"I said—"

"I heard what you said, Mr. Norton. I thought that before dismissing me, you might be interested in hearing what I have to offer."

"You haven't answered my question."

"Which one?"

"Why you want to know?"

"I am not at liberty to say, Mr. Norton. But let me assure you that I mean no harm to you . . . or to your employer, for whom I assume you were at Archangel Union Station a handful of hours ago, waiting for someone to disembark. I simply wish to know who that was. And in return . . ."

"What, exactly?"

"The whereabouts of a person. You would very much like to know where he is—because he, too, has returned to Saint Helena after some time away."

"You mean . . ."

"Your former business partner left a few loose threads when he departed Saint Helena in such great haste. He arrived at the port of Saint Helena yesterday morning, under a false identity. He will be here two days, and then will return to his home in San Diego, where he enjoys the protection of the Viceroy of New Spain."

Norton carefully resumed his seat. He kept his voice level and said, "I don't care about Zachariah Thorne, Mr. Sherwood. He means nothing to me."

"He helped ruin you, sir, and but for the intervention of a wealthy patron, you would remain ruined. Surely there is some small desire for revenge."

"There is no profit in revenge."

"There is no satisfaction in the world like it, Mr. Norton, and you know it."

"I gave up the desire for it a long time ago, Mr. Sherwood. Good day, sir: I have already dismissed you from my office once, and I have concluded the interview a second time. If I have to do so once more, it will be by physical force. Do I make myself clear?"

Sherwood did not react for a moment except to smile, as if to suggest that he found the idea amusing.

At last, however, he stood up and offered Norton a slight bow. "I will leave my card with your assistant. If you change your mind—"

"I will not."

"In case you do, I will be happy to engage in a transaction with you. Nothing personal, Mr. Norton: this is strictly business."

Norton didn't answer, placing his hands face-down on the desk in front of him. Sherwood turned and walked out of the office, not looking back.

* * *

"Yes, I know who he is." Gyazin sipped his tea and reached for a biscuit. Andrea gave him a sharp look, and he slowly withdrew his hand.

Norton smiled at the exchange. Almost defiantly he picked another sugar-cube from the bowl and dropped it into his teacup.

"She doesn't want you to get fat."

"People like a stout governor," Gyazin said. "It's a sign of a happy marriage."

Andrea chuckled and walked away, leaving the sunroom.

"So this John Sherwood . . ."

"A mercenary. He had some dealings with the Secret Chancellery fifteen or twenty years ago, but there was some incident that made him leave Saint Helena in a hurry. I wouldn't concern yourself with him, Joshua."

"Does he concern *you*?"

"A little, I confess."

"In my limited experience, very few things happen in isolation. Sherwood struck me as a professional; he knew exactly what to say, which lever to turn."

"You mean mentioning Thorne."

"He seemed well-informed. I told him I didn't give a damn about Zachariah after all this time: it was a lie, of course: naturally I'd like to wring his neck for all the trouble he caused me."

"But not in exchange for betraying a confidence. I appreciate your loyalty, Joshua, considering all the trouble *I* caused you."

"That was a long time ago." Norton sipped his tea; it was a strong, dark Russian blend, decanted directly from a samovar Gyazin had brought with him when he came from the home country a dozen years earlier. "I know who my friends are."

"So do I."

"Thank you."

"What I don't understand is Sherwood's motivation. Who is he working for? Did he give you any indication?"

"None at all. He had some motivation, some desired outcome. But it didn't give me any idea who his master might be."

"I have some ideas. There have been some disturbing rumors coming from the rodina. Since the *Krestyanskaya Reforma*, the freeing of the peasants, there has been an angry reaction among the nobility. Any time there is disaffection among powerful men, there are provocateurs looking to gain advantage."

"I don't see how that affects Saint Helena, or you, or me."

Gyazin picked up his teacup, then set it down again. "What concerns me is that Sherwood appears just as these things are happening back home. He is not acting alone—someone has sent him, just as someone sent him years ago."

"He mentioned that he had not been in Saint Helena for some time."

"And a good thing: he was involved in an affair that nearly upset relations between our Empire and the British. It had to do with the discovery of gold—"

"Perhaps he is working for the Astors," Norton said.

"Vanya is not interested in politics." Gyazin smiled as he thought of John Astor, who despised—but tolerated—the Russian diminutive.

Norton did not answer; Gyazin and Astor—the head of the immensely wealthy family's operations on North America's west coast— were friends, and he did not wish to antagonize his patron. But the idea that John Astor was not interested in politics was, if nothing else, naïve.

"You seem thoughtful, Joshua."

"There is always the possibility that this Sherwood is not involved with the Russian intelligence agencies at all," he said. "Perhaps he is working for the British."

Gyazin's smile disappeared.

"I hadn't even considered that, Joshua," Gyazin said, tracing a line in the pattern of the table-cloth in front of him. "If that were true . . . it would explain why he might be interested in our guest and his identity."

"Unless he already knows it."

"Meaning . . ."

"That his . . . offer to me was no more than a confirmation. Or a loyalty test, to see if I would take the bait. It would give Sherwood's master an informant close to *you*, my lord, with the price supposedly being the whereabouts of my old business partner."

"Do you think Thorne is actually in Saint Helena, then?"

"Oh, I expect so. I even think that Sherwood would be willing to turn him over to me. What I don't understand is why Zachariah would ever consent to show his face in Saint Helena again. What 'business matters' could possibly draw him back here?"

CHAPTER 3

The ferry ride across the choppy waters of the bay the following morning gave Norton a chance to think. There were too many loose ends: a Mormon leader coming to ask for help from Grigori Gyazin against the encroachments of the British government; an espionage operative making him an offer he might not refuse; Gyazin's offhand remark about troubles in the mother country; the impending change as Lord Scott retired after more than twenty years in the Governor-General's chair . . . it was all too much, a jumble that seemed to ebb and flow like the tides that rolled beneath the ferry-boat.

When he reached the Archangel dock, however, there was a crowd gathered—it was more like a scarcely polite mob. They were pushing and trying to get copies of newspapers that were being hawked at various locations along the promenade. Norton was able to get one, and almost dropped it when he saw the front page.

VIOLENT DEATH IN SAINT PETERSBURG
Three Anarchists With Bombs Captured; Second Bomber Slays Tsar
Zemlya I Volya Suspected

Sir Winfield Scott, Governor-General of British North America, had made an announcement at Continental Hall in Philadelphia shortly after receiving the telegraph message of the event; it had traveled across the country, and was just reaching Saint Helena. Norton turned away from the crowd, still holding the newspaper, and made his way toward the railroad station, where his man was waiting to take him to the hunting lodge.

* * *

Norton found Brigham Young sitting in the arbor outside the house, a book in his hand, the morning light through the trees painting him in light and shadow.

Without a word he took the newspaper—which he had read thoroughly during the carriage ride—and handed it to the Mormon governor, who carefully placed his book aside and spread the paper on his lap.

Young looked at it, then up at Norton. His expression had not changed during the few moments he examined the paper.

"I would like to think that you have no prior knowledge of this event," Norton said. "Assure me of that, if you please."

"I am not accustomed to insolence in servants."

Norton wanted to respond with the back of his hand, but held back. "I am not a servant; I am Lord Gyazin's man of business. He will ask you the same questions; he may reach the same conclusions. Did you know that the Tsar of all the Russias was going to be assassinated by nationalist thugs?"

"There were rumors."

"More specific."

Young laid the paper beside his book, making sure not to cover it. He stood, straightening his coat and adjusting his sleeves. "It continues to amaze me," he said, "how men like your master view the world. A hundred years ago there was war and turmoil, and now things have settled down into power blocs—what some English wag calls "'the Great Game'. On the one hand you have the British Empire, the greatest in the world, straddling every continent from Europe to Australia and dominating all the oceans—and its loyal inferior partner Russia, a great old Empire that struggles to catch up with the modern nineteenth century. On the other hand you have the French Empire and its lackey the Spanish. Each have their minor allies: France has Austria and the

Italian states, Britain has Prussia and Bavaria, and all around the world they play little chess games for the scraps. It's a beautiful picture, in which every corner of the globe belongs to one alliance or the other.

"But out of sight of the Great Game there are many other people and places—like Deseret, and like these anarchists in Russia. The game has always been about them—us—in a way, but the great powers have never looked down and taken notice. Things like this, terrible things, force them to do so."

"Is that what you are trying to do, Governor? Make a great power take notice?"

"Not in the same way."

"Two nights ago you told us that your people expected that there would be war. Three men—not an entire community, not people as numerous as your Mormons—committed an act of war, slaying the tsar who just a few months earlier freed the serfs. He was a friend of the people—"

"You will do me the favor of sparing me such cant," Young interrupted. "Freeing the serfs? What makes you think that their lot will be any better as 'free' peasants than as men and women tied to the land? They are still numerous, they are still poor, and they are still chained to an ancient system and a corrupt, tainted religion. They are not free, Mr. Norton. They will *never* be free—not in a world of empires and kingdoms."

Norton felt the anger from the prophet of the Latter Day Saints— along with a raw, visceral disdain for all of the great powers of the world: the French king, the Queen of England, the Tsar of Russia—not co-religionists, none of them sharing the worldview of his people.

He feels no grief for the tsar, Norton thought. *He might even be glad of it.*

"Those three men think they have struck a blow for freedom with their violence," Norton said. "But there will be a tremendous backlash. Many people will go to prison, or into exile, or simply be killed as a result."

"It depends on whether you believe that they acted alone."

"Meaning?"

"Most such men are not 'lone wolves,' sir. They serve a cause—or a foreign government."

"What government would want the tsar assassinated?"

"Name a government that would not."

"Russia."

"Nonsense. Most of the *boyar* nobility are no doubt enthralled with the idea that the 'liberator tsar' is dead."

"Great Britain."

"The Russian Empire has been an unfortunate albatross around Britain's neck for decades. When Admiral Lord Dewey 'opened' Japan a few years ago, it was an opportunity for Britain to exploit the resources of the Far East. That is not in Russia's interests. And the British crown has been connected with certain states in the Holy Roman Empire since the late seventeenth century. Strengthening them will weaken Russia as well."

"And I do not need to be convinced that King Louis XIX would like to see a rival in turmoil."

"Just so."

"But how could such an act possibly benefit *you,* Governor? Surely without orders from Saint Petersburg, Lord Gyazin could not possibly do what you ask—take Deseret's side against Russia's ally, the British Empire."

"Without orders—isn't that the point? No one will be giving any sort of orders in the near term. Your master is *on his own,* Mr. Norton. He can do what he pleases, and claim that it is in Russia's best interest. Surely the new tsar will thank him for it."

"I doubt Lord Gyazin will see it that way."

"It is up to him to decide."

"Of course it is. But tell me something, Governor; you arrived here in secret, and you told me you were being watched. Do you know by whom?"

"How would I know that?"

"It is merely an idle question. Let me ask another. Do you know a man named John Sherwood?"

"I have never heard the name."

Norton considered himself a good judge of character, and he watched carefully as Young answered the question. When he spoke, he might have betrayed the slightest hesitation—or Norton could have simply imagined it. He wasn't sure, and he wasn't sure what he would tell Gyazin.

The tsar is dead, he thought. *And Young might be right: Lord Gyazin is on his own.*

*   *   *

Being in the governor's employ only afforded so much deference; it took until the early afternoon for Norton to make his way back to Saint Helena. The streets were crowded with people who seemed to have nothing better to do than to talk about the murder of the tsar; flags had been lowered to half-staff all along the pier and half-mast aboard ships in the harbor (including the ferry-boat that had at last deposited him on the Saint Helena side of the bay).

At his office, he collected the card that John Sherwood had left with his clerk and made his way to the address given, which turned out to be a small hotel that catered to English guests. Sherwood himself was not difficult to find: he was in the parlor on the ground floor, casually perusing the special afternoon edition of the Saint Helena *Examiner*, the best English-language newspaper in the city—and a better source of actual news than the Russian-language *Chronika*.

If he saw Norton approaching he gave no sign, and continued to read until Norton settled into a chair opposite. Then, as if he was in no hurry—and was unaffected by the crowds within and outside the hotel— he lowered the paper to his lap, and presented Norton with a smile.

"You have changed your mind, Mr. Norton."

"I require some answers."

"And what do you have to offer in return?"

"How do you feel about spending some time in the prison on the island in the bay? I'm sure Lord Gyazin could arrange it. Consider that as an alternative to your comfortable circumstances."

"I really don't think that's a prudent threat," Sherwood said, not appearing to be bothered by it in the least. "My patron—"

"Lord Scott is far away," Norton interrupted.

Without missing a beat, Sherwood said, "Yes, and he is old and soon to retire. Viscount Palmerston is said to prefer a Southerner for his successor. So." Sherwood folded his hands in his lap atop the newspaper.

"I rather think I'm a bit old for prison in any case. What can I do for you?"

"The tsar has been murdered by anarchists. Tell me what you know about that."

"Very little," Sherwood said. "Except that they're not anarchists: they are *nationalists,* members of a group that thinks that they are a few bombs away from disposing of the Russian imperial system. As if somehow with a wave of the hand—" he waved his hand—"hundreds of years of tsarist rule over an impoverished people in an enormous, largely empty country could be dispensed with.

"They seized their opportunity, but if they had not done it, the nobility would have, just as they did with Karl half a century ago. Russians in general have very little stomach for change."

"And you had nothing to do with it."

"Certainly not. A bit out of my range of speciality."

"Still, you seem to be singularly well informed."

"There is no profit in ignorance, as I am sure you are aware, Mr. Norton. Best to be informed on as many things as possible."

"All right," Norton said. There was a sudden noise outside the hotel; both men turned and saw some sort of altercation along Market Street, struggling and shouting. After a moment, Norton continued, "I would like to know why you are here in Saint Helena, *coincidentally* when the Tsar of all the Russias is assassinated. You knew this was coming."

"I suspected."

"I'll assume that's a distinction without a difference. Please answer the question."

"Certainly," Sherwood said. "Let's be forthright and honest. Your governor is secretly entertaining Governor Brigham Young of Deseret Colony, who arrived a few nights ago by train. It is to be assumed that Governor Young is soliciting assistance from the Russian Empire, which is duplicitous at least and treasonous at worst."

"So you already knew the identity of the passenger when you came to my office to ask the question."

"More or less. Your information would have further confirmed it."

"And Thorne—"

"Thorne is of no consequence. It took remarkably little to convince him to turn up here; Lord Scott doesn't care if you have him in your custody or not."

"So what do you intend to do?"

"With regard to Thorne, or Young?"

"Young."

"I am directed to convey a warning. Nothing should be asked of Lord Gyazin, and nothing expected. The next British American Governor-General will allow a certain amount of autonomy to the cult out in the desert; but if they wish to practice treason, they should expect to be prosecuted with the full force of Her Majesty's law. Nothing need be said, now or in the future, regarding this little unofficial embassy—as long as it is brought to a conclusion in short order."

"I don't think Lord Gyazin likes threats."

"The threat is directly aimed at Brigham Young and his lunatics in Deseret, Mr. Norton."

"I don't think Lord Gyazin likes threats," Norton repeated, standing. "I think it's time for you to absent yourself from Saint Helena."

He walked away from Sherwood, but stopped and turned around. "And tell Zachariah Thorne that he should leave the city as well, with positive assurance that should I find him I won't have him arrested: I'll simply have him shot."

CHAPTER 4

At his office in Mission Bay, there was a carriage waiting for him with Gyazin's livery, and a note from Sergei indicating that he'd closed up for the day. Norton climbed into the carriage, which moved off—slowly—through the still-gathering crowds.

Mikhail Gyazin was inside, and he was in full uniform, including saber and pistols. He looked worried.

"What's all this about?"

"My father wanted you to come to the house. You'll be safer there."

"I'm in no danger."

"My father disagrees. There's a nasty rumor that the tsar's assassins were all Jews, and he was worried that you might be a target for the mob."

"It's not a mob."

Mikhail parted the curtain very slightly; Norton could see that the streets were full of people—angry people. Somewhere in the distance he heard the sound of breaking glass.

"Yes, it is."

"Nothing the gendarmerie can't handle."

"They've become very angry, Mr. Norton," Mikhail said. He didn't just call Norton by his last name, as so many of the elite of Saint Helena were fond of doing; *he had been taught well*, Norton thought. "The gendarmerie will control them, eventually, but people will die tonight. My father wanted to make sure you weren't a casualty."

* * *

At the house on Odessa Street, a half-dozen gendarmes were on duty, and he was escorted—*hustled,* he thought—quickly from the portico into the house. Gyazin was in the drawing room; he had two glasses in his hand, and held one out to Norton.

"This is needless precaution, my Lord, though I appreciate the sentiment."

"*Nasdarovje,*" Gyazin said, and raised his glass, drinking it down in one gulp. Norton obligingly followed. It was a superior vodka; his sinuses immediately became astoundingly clear.

He waited for Gyazin to speak, and after a moment the Russian said, "I understand that Sherwood issued a threat."

"He was rather forthright."

"I don't like being threatened, and I don't like my people being threatened."

"I think that his intended target was Governor Young."

"Or my guests," Gyazin said. "But it's being dealt with. When the situation settles down, I will arrange for our visiting prophet to be escorted aboard his rail carriage and he can return to his Zion in the desert."

"He wanted you to help," Norton said. "And he thought that the death of the tsar would make it easier."

"I know. It probably makes it harder; the tsar's son has no stomach for reform, and no interest in angering the British. We are facing a time of turmoil, Joshua, and I don't know what is ahead.

"But, as I say, it's being dealt with."

"Young—"

"And Sherwood as well. He might want to try something against Governor Young; he'll not get the chance."

"Meaning?"

"I think you know exactly what it means," Gyazin said coldly. "It is remarkable what can happen in a situation that gets out of control."

Gyazin looked past Norton at his seventeen-year-old son, who stood in the doorway, listening to the exchange. The young man looked very slightly pale—but he knew what it meant, too.

I don't think Lord Gyazin likes threats, Norton thought. *No: I'm sure of it.*

INNOCENCE ABROAD

1878

CHAPTER 1

"I have decided that I shall call you 'Harris'."

Reverend Joseph Hopkins Twichell did not reply at first; he looked out the window at the bay, which was spread out like a picture-postcard; from the train, on the bridge, it was one of the most beautiful views he—or his traveling companion—had ever seen.

"That's a bit stuffy, don't you think, Sam?"

"It's a perfectly good name. Wasn't there a divine in Boston named Harris?"

"Thaddeus Mason Harris. Yes. Most of a century ago, and he as much as *defined* stuffy."

"I like it."

"Of course you do. So I shall be Harris, Mark Twain's sturdy, and stuffy, traveling companion. His foil."

"You don't like the role, Joe?" Samuel Clemens leaned back in his seat, his hands behind his head, his legs stretched out. First class accommodations on the Crown Pacific Railroad had their advantages.

"I like it fine. I suppose I'd rather be a part of the joke than the butt of it." Twichell placed his hands on his thighs, sweeping away a few flecks of soot that had come in through the window. "I imagine it will all make for good reading."

"If I can manage it."

"You will. You always do."

"Like hell I do—"

"Sam—"

"All right. I *don't* always manage it. Sometimes it comes quickly, words fly off the page, ideas present themselves so fast that I can hardly keep up. And other times . . . other times it's what the Germans call *treppenwitz:* you meet someone on the stair as you're going up and they're going down, and they say something that begs for a snappy comeback . . . except you think of it when you're two flights further on."

"'The Awful English Language.'"

"Oh, very good, very good, Reverend. I shall be sure not to use that in the book."

"Harris gets no snappy retorts, only . . .'"

"Only *treppenwitze.*"

"Capital," Thacher said. "Absolutely capital. Very well: I look forward to what Mark Twain does to me."

✳ ✳ ✳

They had been underway for seven days, the first week of a round-the-world tour that had taken a few months to plan; most of the engagements had been arranged by others. It was up to Sam to appear at the proper time and put on his now-familiar guise of Mark Twain, to step onto the stage and do what he did best: tell amusing stories to eager audiences that didn't know quite *when* they'd laugh, but were mighty sure that it would happen regularly.

It was a matter of giving them what they wanted in spades. The rest was food and drink and good cigars and all the sights one could see.

They'd started in Boston. They hated him in Boston: at least the stuffy tea-drinking Brahmins on Beacon Hill and along Queen Street hated him—they banned his books and called them trash and unfit refuse and all kinds of unkind things. But he'd packed the Melodeon on Marlborough Street for two nights—there probably weren't too many Brahmins in that audience, but shillings from Her Majesty's most common subjects weighed just the same as the ones paid by baronets and his hand grew sore from signing his name.

He'd spoken the next day at a luncheon in Springfield, and then there had been a black-tie event in Albany, the Burgoyne Dinner, where he'd done his duty, lampooning the great Governor-General and his trusty American sidekick General Arnold, as well as some very satisfactory jabs at the Marquis de Montcalm. The Battle of Saratoga was always a good subject in the Colony of New York.

A few days later they'd been in Franklin, where the great fire of 1871 had evolved from a tragedy into a punch line. Franklin was a bona fide city now, one of the greatest in British North America, and full of contention of all kinds.

Then began their great trek across the Plains. British settlements grew up wherever the rails ran; they had changed trains in St. Louis from the Vandalia and Ohio to the Crown Pacific, a marked step up. The Astors knew how to run a railroad, and how to treat a celebrity.

In Denver, his venue had been the ballroom at the Inter Ocean Hotel, where he regaled the audience with his tales of the Comstock Lode and his travels in the Sandwich Islands, with the highlight of the night a re-telling of the story of the Jumping Frog. Even Joe Twichell, who had heard it a thousand times, was beside himself with laughter. Sam told him that based on the sights and the food—Delmonico's, Cella's, even Ford's People's Restaurant—he could as well abandon the rest of the trip and do pieces for the *Rocky Mountain News* and the *Tribune*; but that was not to be.

There was a stop in Zion City, but Mark Twain was, if not *persona non grata* in Deseret, at the very least *persona incognita,* and it was best left that way.

And now: Saint Helena, the metropolis of the Pacific, the heart of Novaya Rossiya. It was most of twenty years since his last trip, and so much had changed. Archangel wasn't even the end of the line anymore: the Crown Pacific ran all the way to a terminal on the east side of the Peninsula, crossing a brand-new bridge, the Tsarevich Nikolas, more than two miles of Carnegie steel stretched across the choppy waters of the bay. (Except none of the locals used that name: it was apparently called the "Norton Bridge." Sam wondered why, and was eager to find out.)

When he'd come to Saint Helena in 1864, a newspaperman because, as he told himself, he couldn't get honest work; it was a world away, before all of the success, before Livy, before poor Langdon and his dear girls, before Tom and Huck . . .

Now here he was, celebrated humorist and novelist and whatever-else-ist, the conquering hero returned.

Joe Twichell must have known *exactly* why he was smiling.

* * *

Celebrities did not handle their own luggage; both Clemens and Twichell had no more than their portmanteaus as they stepped off the train onto the platform, bustling with more people than all those who were living in Saint Helena when he was last there. Inasmuch as he was something of a public figure, Clemens knew that he was recognized; he was scheduled to speak at Egyptian Hall, and the advance man was sure to have provided some publicity.

What he was not expecting, however, was a certain sense of hostility.

As he stood there, waiting for his bags to be unloaded and transported to the Saint Ekaterina Hotel down town, he was approached by a man in a rather impressive powder-blue uniform with gold and crimson edging at collar, wrists, and epaulets; he wore highly-polished knee-high boots, a neat cap with a little brush standing straight up in the front, and had a sword and holstered pistol at his belt. A white satin sash completed the outfit.

"Are you to be arrested, Sam?"

"If so, it is more entertainment than I had planned."

The man stopped in front of him, came to attention, and offered a polite bow, then extended his hand.

"Mr. Clemens?" he said in perfect English.

"My secret is out, General—"

"Major. Major Mikhail Gyazin, Mr. Clemens. Let me welcome you to Saint Helena."

"I wasn't expecting a full dress welcome."

Gyazin smiled. "This is a good way from full dress, Mr. Clemens. As for the welcome: my father thought it would be best for you to be properly received."

Clemens thought for a moment. "Your father . . . that would be Prince Grigori?"

"Yes, sir."

"Then this is an honor. Allow me to present my friend and traveling companion, Reverend Joseph Twichell. We are staying at—"

"The Saint Ekaterina. The finest hotel in all of Saint Helena, even though its proprietor is English." He smiled even more broadly.

"I will try not to hold that against him."

Gyazin did not answer immediately, as if he was trying to decide what he thought of the comment.

"Is anything wrong?"

"Wrong? No . . . no. It is nothing. We should talk—but not here. The saloon at the Saint Ekaterina is much more amenable to polite discussion."

"Do they serve spirits?"

"Mr. Clemens. Reverend Twichell. This is a *Russian* city, even if it is an English hotel. Of course they do."

"Then lead on, man. By all means."

✳ ✳ ✳

Major Mikhail Gyazin was apparently a figure of some authority; he was able to obtain private seating in a secluded part of the dining room of the Saint Ekaterina, away from the prying eyes of the general public. Clemens noted that a junior customs officer was posted at the doorway—the sort of thing that drew attention rather than diverting it, but no matter: if there was a celebrity inside, no one was going to see who it was.

"This is a fine way to publicize your visit to Saint Helena, Sam," Twichell said, looking around at the empty room.

"We can just stand at the bar," Clemens said. "Joe's right: I don't understand all this cloak and dagger."

Gyazin produced a portfolio, and drew out several newspapers. "Perhaps you will understand the matter more clearly after looking at these."

Clemens took the papers, setting aside the ones in Russian—though he did notice that a good likeness of him appeared below the fold on each of them. The Saint Helena *Examiner,* one of the widest-circulating dailies in the city, had a feature article to go with it; Gyazin poked it with a finger.

"Read it, Mr. Clemens."

By Walter H. Hunt

ENGLISH WIT TO APPEAR AT EGYPTIAN HALL
Are Other Motives Involved?

The well-known writer and raconteur, Samuel Clemens, is scheduled to appear at Egyptian Hall this coming Wednesday through Friday, in his renowned persona of "Mark Twain." This visit to our city is a part of a worldwide tour to promote his latest work.

It has been widely rumored that Mr. Clemens has close ties to the Governor-General of British North America and has been provided with special diplomatic credentials for his travel through Novaya Rossiya. This newspaper has obtained information to suggest that Mr. Clemens's visit is for something other than mere entertainment . . .

There were a few more paragraphs of the same.

Clemens looked at Gyazin, then sidelong at Twichell—and then burst into a guffaw. He patted his jacket and drew out a cigar.

"Major," he said, "after years in the newspaper business, I can tell you that this is nothing but a hook at the end of a long pole. This fella is just out fishin'."

"I would agree with you, sir," Gyazin said. "Except that it's in the *Chronicle,* and the *Mirror,* and in all the Russian-language papers as well. It is not some intrepid reporter at the *Examiner,* Mr. Clemens. It is either someone with a serious intent to make you look like a spy, or . . ."

Clemens stuck the cigar between his lips. "Or?"

"Or, sir, the story is true."

CHAPTER 2

Sam had the audience in the palm of his hand all night Wednesday. Evidently rumors of his career in espionage were somewhat exaggerated: there had been a little bit of hooting and jeering at the start, but once he was well into the Tom Sawyer part of his presentation they were rapt, laughing at all the right places for all the right reasons.

He never read directly from written work. There were plenty of writers who did: the great Dickens had always done so, practicing his gestures and intonation in front of a hotel room mirror. But Sam just spoke from memory, telling stories, his eyes on the people in front of him rather than some open book on a lectern. He gave them two hours of it, interspersing his tales with comments on current events, though he stayed clear of anything that might give credence to the rumors.

When he was done and back in his dressing room, jacket tossed on a chair and tie loosened, he let himself enjoy a good cigar. It would have been the end of the night, except for a knock at the door.

"Joe, I told you I'd see you back at the Saint Ekaterina—"

The door opened and two men in evening dress stepped into the small room: one was an elderly, distinguished Russian, and the other was a shorter, stout man with darker skin. Sam stood up, setting his cigar in a ashtray.

"Can I help you gentlemen?"

"Forgive the intrusion, Mr. Clemens. My companion was very eager to meet you."

"I'm always glad to greet a member of the public eager to meet me, especially after I've inflicted myself on him for two hours. I'm afraid . . ." Sam squinted at the Russian. "I'm afraid I do not know you, sir, though you look familiar."

"Ah. Yes, of course. I am well known here in Saint Helena, but you are, of course, not from here. Allow me to present myself: I am Gregori Andreivich Gyazin. I believe you have made the acquaintance of my oldest son Mischa on your arrival."

"Major Gyazin. Yes, of course. A great pleasure, Excellency. I had no idea you were in the audience."

"And my companion is David Kalakaua, an admirer of yours. He and his lovely wife Kapiolani are on a state visit to Saint Helena, and he was thrilled to hear that you were to speak."

"State visit . . ." Sam prided himself on maintaining his equanimity in the presence of everyone of every class, but he was taken a little aback. "Your Highness," he said. "I'm honored."

"It is I who should be honored," King David said. "I have read all of your writing about the Sandwich Islands, as well as your wonderful fiction. I could scarcely remain in my seat while you spoke."

"I'm glad you enjoyed it." He looked around, wondering if he should put his tie in place or pull on his jacket. "But . . . surely you are here for more than polite courtesies. What can I do for you, sirs?"

"I am here on behalf of my wife," Gyazin said. "With an invitation."

"The formidable Princess Andrea," the king said, smiling. "She wants to meet you."

"I am relieved," Sam said. "For a moment, I thought you might be inviting me to the Caspian Sea Rooms. Imagine what that would do for the reputation of a rascal such as myself."

"I'm sure you would be welcome," Gyazin said. "They could hardly turn you down."

"I've been turned down by better establishments than that," Sam answered, smiling. "But I appreciate Your Excellency's high opinion of me."

"It is very high indeed, as is my wife's. Which returns me to my original intent—to invite you to the Presidio for an afternoon luncheon on Saturday. I understand you will be here in Saint Helena through Sunday when your steamer departs, so I hope you could make time for it."

"Your Excellency is very well informed about my itinerary."

"As the Governor-General for the Great Autocrat, it is my business to know everything that goes on here in Novaya Rossiya. It was not always the case, of course. But it does have its privileges."

"Such as residence in the Presidio."

"Andrea would rather we remained in our house in Odessa Street—"

"Which you outgrew years ago," Kalakaua said. "Six children, and a dozen grandchildren—"

Gyazin smiled. "God has graced us with a healthy family. I realize that your schedule is busy, sir, but would you consider my request?"

Sounds more like a command, Sam thought. But it was hardly an invitation he could pass up; not too many steamboat pilots and ne'er-do-wells got an invitation to luncheon at the Presidio. "Excellency, it would be my pleasure to perform for your wife's pleasure."

"Perform? Oh, goodness no. You misapprehend me, Mr. Clemens. I would not presume to ask you to add a performance to your schedule. I merely ask for you to come and give us your company. A pleasant luncheon, a bit of give and take. His Highness and Queen Kapiolani will be joining us."

Give and take, Sam thought. "Yes, of course. I would be honored."

"Excellent," Gyazin said. "Then it's settled." He reached his hand out and gave Sam a firm handshake. Kalakaua did so as well, though a trifle more tentatively. His two visitors then took their leave, shutting the dressing room door behind them.

Sam settled back into his chair and picked up his cigar, which had gone out during the visit. After a moment, however, he set it down and stood up, allowing himself to pace a bit within the narrow confines of the small room.

What was that about? He asked himself. *It could be exactly what it seemed: the tsar's governor and a visiting prince were so taken with me that they want me to come to lunch for some . . .*

Well, not a performance. He stooped and squinted in the mirror, smoothing down his bushy moustaches. *Except that it's all a performance, isn't it? They're not interested in Sam Clemens—it's Mark Twain they want to have to lunch.*

When combined with the brief conversation with Prince Gyazin's son, Major Gyazin, it felt very much like a trap—a sandbar that was invisible from the pilot house, but upon which a less-observant pilot would run the boat aground.

They want something, Sam concluded. *But what?*

* * *

There was even less hooting and jeering on Thursday and Friday. Egyptian Hall was packed to the limits: the first show had been promoted by word of mouth—or, Sam mused, possibly by the good offices of Prince Gregori Andreivich Gyazin. If he had been less of a cynic he would have been grateful for the providential assistance—but it made him wonder if he was being set up in some way.

Joe said all the right things, and chatted up the arts reporters from the *Chronicle* and the other newspapers—English-language, Russian-language, and even the one Spanish-language daily (*El Diario de California*—small-circulation, but eagerly read, or so he was told: and who would lie to a man of the cloth?). He dispelled the repeated rumor that Sam was here for some nefarious purpose: "He's far too busy making you folks laugh—and think," he told them.

After Thursday's entertainment Sam told him about his invitation to the governor's palace on Saturday.

"I know," Joe Twichell said. "I am cordially invited to take a tour of the cathedral of St. Helena. For my sins, Helena—Prince Gyazin's oldest daughter, as you may know—and her husband, Captain Nikolai Sharovsky, are to take me on a stroll up the three hundred odd steps from the base of Telegraph Hill to the summit, where we will view the vaulted interiors."

"Charming."

"Diversionary, I should say. They seem to want to talk to you alone, Sam."

"I talk a lot to people on my own," he said.

"You talk *a lot*," Twichell responded. "I keep tossing it off as the silliest thing imaginable, but people keep asking about how close you are with Lord Lee."

"I talk to a lot of people, and in front of a lot of people. The General and I are old friends, and I covered some of his campaigns during the War of Texian Annexation. I've performed in every colony –"

"I know, I know. I'm your *soi-disant* press agent, remember? But they still ask."

"Sir Robert is a friend of mine, and that's an end to it."

"Sam, they're going to ask you the same questions. You know that this Prince Gyazin has been here in Saint Helena for most of three decades? And he has all kinds of friends back in the motherland. I was told that he is very close to the Secret Chancellery."

"My, that sounds very conspiratorial."

"That's the secret service, Sam. I'd think twice before mocking them. They became much more powerful after the Russians assassinated their tsar. It only takes a glance to put a man in prison."

"I'm not a Russian citizen, Joe, and if they haven't arrested me yet, they're unlikely to."

"Laugh while you can, Sam, but for God's sake be careful what you say."

"You worry too much."

"And you, my friend, worry too little."

✳ ✳ ✳

On Friday night, it rained like a second Flood was coming. Sam was at the top of his powers—there were no empty seats for the performance.

He emerged from the stage door, looking for the carriage to take him back to the hotel, and found it waiting directly opposite. Two steps drenched him but he pulled open the door and climbed inside, taking off his hat and shaking the water off.

"Joe, have you ever seen—"

But it was not Joe Twichell sitting opposite him. He couldn't make out the figure, but it reached up with an ornate walking-stick and rapped the ceiling and the carriage began to move.

"I beg your pardon," Sam said. "I think I got into the wrong carriage."

"No, Mr. Clemens," the figure said in heavily Russian-accented English. "You are in the correct place."

"I don't like the sound of that."

The figure leaned forward into the spare light from the dim street-lamps coming in through the half-curtained window. It was a heavy-set man with a close-cropped haircut and a large, bushy moustache.

"You will indulge me with a few minutes of your time, sir, and then you will come safely to your hotel."

Sam considered the alternatives: it was probably a bad idea to try and jump out of a moving carriage in a heavy rainstorm in the dark.

"All right, then," he said. "You've got an exclusive. What do you want?"

"Not to interview you for a newspaper," the man said. "But I do have some questions."

"And to whom do I have the pleasure of speaking?"

"My name is Drenteln. General Alexander Drenteln. But I suspect mine is not a name you know."

"Can't say that I do."

"I report directly to His Majesty the Tsar, Mr. Clemens. He has asked me to investigate certain matters here in Novaya Rossiya, and in Saint Helena in particular."

"I'm just passing through here."

"You are here long enough to be of interest."

"I'm a storyteller, not a spy, if that's what you're getting at. You can tell the tsar that I stay away from politics, because it's likely to leave stains on my white suit."

"That," General Drenteln answered, "is exactly what a spy would say."

"And that is exactly what a—what, a secret policeman would say. General, if you want to do something to me, why don't you go ahead and do it. Otherwise, I will just get out and walk."

"In this downpour?" The moustaches drooped downward, accompanied by an ample frown.

"I've seen worse." Sam leaned forward to open the carriage door.

"Wait."

He stopped, letting his hand remain extended, short of the handle.

"Mr. Clemens," General Drenteln said, "this does not need to be so awkward. There is a rumor—too persistent and too prevalent to ignore—that you are here in Saint Helena with secret instructions from your Queen."

"What sort of instructions?"

"Nothing more sinister than to evaluate the settlement, and what would be required to take it by military action."

"I assure you, General, that this is nothing more than a rumor. I have no instructions, and I'm nowhere near the right person to make such an evaluation."

"But your companion—"

"Reverend Twichell?"

"He was in the armed forces, was he not?"

"He was a *chaplain*. He ministered to Her Majesty's Seventh regiment of cavalry during the Indian wars fifteen or twenty years ago. He wasn't a commander, or a military planner. He's not even very handy with a rifle."

Drenteln seemed to ponder this for several moments, his face half in shadow. There was no sound but for the rain and the steady sound of the horses.

"So neither you nor—Reverend—Twichell are here for military reconnaissance."

"I am here," Sam said, "to tell stories and entertain, to help sell my work. You should take in my performances; I am told that I am quite funny."

"Oh, wait: tonight was the last show. I'm sorry, General; perhaps you'll be interested in coming to hear me in Manila or Yokohama."

At the name of the Japanese city, Drenteln seemed to become angry. Sam wasn't sure what to make of that at the time.

"I do not like to be mocked, Mr. Clemens."

"No one does, General. And no one likes to be threatened either. Is the interview over?"

Drenteln held Sam's gaze for a long time. The sound of the rain continued, but the clip-clop of the carriage horses had stopped.

"We have reached your hotel, sir. So I believe the answer to your question is 'yes'."

CHAPTER 3

On Saturday morning, a barouche with the Gyazin arms was waiting at eleven o'clock in front of the Saint Ekaterina Hotel in Union Square. A liveried footman clicked his bootheels together and stood at rigid attention as Sam Clemens climbed up into the carriage; it attracted a considerable amount of attention from passers-by.

When he had himself seated, Sam looked around at the audience that had seemed to form of its own accord; he was dressed in his best white suit, which he'd had specially cleaned and pressed for the occasion. Normally it would be just a matter of *famous writer* waving to *devoted admirers* . . . but he couldn't get the idea out of his mind that some of those *devoted admirers* might well be the tsar's spies, looking to see if he was passing some sort of secret information to English *agents provocateurs*.

Any spy-watchers would have to conclude that Sam Clemens would be remarkably bad at it. They'd scribble down in their little notebook: *Mark Twain knows nothing.* That was certainly true enough, especially in Russian.

* * *

The barouche was expertly designed for Saint Helena's hills, but even so, Sam found the journey somewhat hair-raising—on the upward inclines he wondered if he might fall out, and on the downward ones he feared that the carriage would be catapulted over the heads of the draft horses that pulled it.

The famous cable cars might have been a safer, if possibly less dignified, way to traverse the distance between Union Square and the great park that surrounded the governor's mansion; but he was not about to disappoint his hosts by arriving other than in state. By the time the carriage reached the relatively flat promenade of Sankt-Petersburg-Prospekt, where new buildings were going up, he had quite recovered his aplomb and sat upright, doing what he enjoyed best: watching people.

About forty minutes after departing he arrived at the portico of the Presidio, where another stiff footman assisted him in climbing down from the barouche, and an elegantly-dressed butler waited to take his hat and stick.

The Presidio had been built in the last century as a barracks and military base by the Spanish, and had been refurbished in the 1820s as the home of the Spanish ambassador; by the time it was converted for use by the Russian Governor-General, it was in poor shape. But the work of Andrea Gyazin had made it a showpiece, decorated inside in a distinctively Russian style.

In the reception hall, Sam found the lady of the house unexpectedly waiting for him. He had been prepared for a series of servants or family members, but Princess Andrea Gyazin was apparently having none of that.

"Mr. Clemens," she said, and offered her hand, which Sam bowed over and kissed. "I cannot tell you how glad I am that you can join us."

"I could hardly stay away," he managed.

"You are too kind, sir."

Andrea Gyazin was a truly beautiful woman in middle age. She had been Grigori's wife for more than thirty years, and had given him six children; still, she looked as if she could play a symphony, ride a steeplechase, direct a kitchen, or deliver a stump speech—all without missing a step.

For the first time in many years, Sam Clemens was close to speechless.

But close only counts in horseshoes, he reminded himself.

"I am nothing of the sort," he answered, and offered Andrea his arm. She took it, and led him from the hall into a bright, airy reception room that overlooked a small pond that was dappled with sunlight. Beyond he could make out a part of the bay, partially shrouded in fog. There, Grigori Gyazin and two of his sons—Mikhail and one other he had not met—as well as the king and queen of the Sandwich Islands stood, glasses in hand, waiting to greet him.

"My son Mikhail, whom you have met," Andrea said, "and Konstantin, whom you have not. The governor," she smiled at her husband "—gave him leave from his post at the harbor to be with us this afternoon."

"Always good to have friends in high places," Sam said, shaking the young man's hand.

A servant hovered nearby, and Sam took a delicate flute of something with a smile and a nod.

"I was telling my wife that you had asked if you were coming here to perform," David Kalakaua said. "I am glad you have a bit of a respite from that."

"Well," Sam answered, "it's something I enjoy. If it isn't fun, why do it."

"We all have our serious responsibilities," Grigori said. "But you have . . . shall we say . . . a different lifestyle."

"An understatement, sir," Sam said. He glanced around him. "I would not mind the style to which *you* have become accustomed."

"This is relatively recent. Antonin Karelevich Nyazov, my predecessor, lived here until he was called home."

"Home, as in . . ."

"Saint Petersburg. There are commands that cannot be refused. In the meanwhile—" Grigori raised his glass; Sam saw that Andrea, too, had taken one of her own. "'God is up in Heaven, and the tsar is far away.'" He drank deeply, draining the glass; Sam did the same, and found the liquor sweet—and potent.

"Let us sit," his hostess said, and directed them to a comfortable set of couches. Andrea sat next to the Hawai'ian queen and her husband; Sam somehow found himself at the center of the grouping.

❋ ❋ ❋

This wasn't supposed to be a performance, Sam told himself. *Except that it always is.*

The conversation was brilliant. Sam was at his best; he was witty and urbane, topical, clever to a fault. But it was clear that this was no simple society party—an opportunity to swap *bons mots* with a celebrity. The king and queen were charming; the two young sons said very little, deferring to their parents. Andrea Gyazin was brilliant, keeping everyone at ease while providing her husband with the opportunity to lead the conversation—before, during, and after the exquisite lunch served on the patio.

It was the *after* that was the key, of course.

* * *

"My wife still wishes we were living in our house on Odessa Street," Gyazin said as they strolled through the gardens. "We moved in there just after we came to Saint Helena a quarter century ago. We were so young . . ."

"We were all younger a quarter century ago, Excellency."

"Grigori, please."

"Grigori." Sam smiled. "I appreciate the informality."

"I appreciate being off the stage, Mr. Clemens."

"Sam."

Grigori Gyazin stopped walking at a small statue—an exquisite bronze dancing girl. It caught the afternoon light on its burnished surface. He reached his hand out and ran a finger along the left arm, extended ending in a palm-up gesture.

"I'm curious," Grigori said. "How well do you know your Governor-General?"

"Lord Lee? Well enough. I've had the pleasure of visiting Stratford House several times, and I was a featured speaker at a couple of Jackson Day banquets."

"What's he like?"

"Sir Robert is just about the epitome of a Virginia nobleman and gentleman. His family is one of the oldest in the Old Dominion."

"Old Dominion?"

"Virginia. The First Colony makes a great show of it, and there is no name that carries as much weight as Lee. And there's no Lee who fits the mold better than him. Why do you ask?"

"I'm curious."

"There's more to it than that, Grigori: you spent all of lunch dancing around it, and now you're giving me the third degree. And forgive me, sir, but I know what this is about—it's this poppycock about my reasons for being in Saint Helena: that I'm a spy for Her Majesty's Government."

"I don't believe that, Sam, and I didn't invite you to lunch to confirm my suspicions."

"Then why did you?"

"Because my dear Andrea wanted to meet you. No more and no less. My wife is a formidable woman, I count a crowned monarch among my friends . . ."

"Your Excellency—"

"Grigori."

"*Your Excellency,*" Sam repeated, "you may want to have me escorted off the reservation once I say this, but you are a terrible, terrible liar. I should know."

"You're accusing me of lying about my intentions?"

Sam brushed a speck of dirt from the cuff of his jacket and scratched his chin. "Yes."

Grigori Gyazin walked along the path to a bench and sat, gesturing for Sam to sit with him.

"Andrea tells me that too. Though I think she views it more as a virtue than as a fault. I should have known that a man of the world such as yourself would not be easily fooled."

Sam sighed. "I suppose I'll be having supper with the secret police then. After last night's interview, I shouldn't be surprised."

Grigori was surprised. "The secret police? And . . . last night?"

"General Drentln."

"I don't understand."

Sam described his brief carriage ride the previous night with the man he took to be a secret policeman.

Grigori Gyazin appeared quite surprised and even more angry. And this time, Sam was fairly sure that he wasn't lying.

"I was not aware that General Drentln was in Saint Helena, Sam. Please accept my apologies. The Secret Chancellery and I are not on particularly good terms. I have not discussed you with them, and have no intention of doing so."

"Who is this general?"

"He is the head of Third Section. They are the agents of the tsar particularly responsible for rooting out espionage and treason. After Tsar Alexander II was assassinated, they were given wide authority to find enemies of the State . . ."

"Or invent them."

"Just so. Alexander II is rightly called 'the Liberator': he ended serfdom in the Empire, and encouraged participation by his subjects. His son is . . . less forthcoming. He sees enemies everywhere and fears that he will suffer the same fate as his father. Which might happen: he took the throne when he was only twenty-one, and is not well liked in the rodina or out here in the colonies. The outlying peoples—the Finns, the Poles, the Bulgars, the Aleuts, the californios—either hate him or simply feel no allegiance."

"Then what is this general's motivation? If, as you say, he is operating without your authority or knowledge, what's he after?"

"He, or our tsar, is afraid of something."

"Such as . . ."

"Great Britain."

"Our Empire has been your Empire's ally for a hundred years or more. What is there to fear? And if you're not a party to this—investigation—why are you asking all these questions about Bobby Lee?"

"Sam. Mr. Clemens. I know this isn't your first visit to Saint Helena, but I suspect that you don't really know too much about it. This city is built around a settlement that was established in 1816. It was essentially given to the tsar by the King of England.

"On several occasions during the last sixty years, Saint Helena—indeed, Novaya Rossiya—has been threatened by one or another enemy, and each time it has been saved by the King—or the Queen—of England."

"Russia and Britain have been allies for a long time, Grigori."

"Yes, that's true. Except that twenty-odd years ago Baron Perry forced Japan to open to the world—and since then your country has done anything and everything to bring that nation into alliance."

"Japan—"

"Japan is not Russia's ally, Sam. Japan is Russia's *rival.* It might someday be her enemy. When that day comes, your country will discard its *old* friend in favor of its *new* friend—and that will be the end of Russia. That is what our tsar suspects will happen, and he appears to have sent the general here to do what he can to stop it."

"And what could be more high-profile than making it look like I was a spy for Her Majesty Queen Victoria."

Sam looked off into the distance, at the vague outline of the far shore.

"But that sounds cold-blooded, Grigori. It doesn't sound like our Queen. I've met her, and she would never turn her back on a friend, not in the way you say."

"Perhaps not. But it will come, Sam. When Britain and Russia first became allies most of a century ago, there were many powerful nations in the world. Now there are only two: yours, and the French Empire. Louis XIX rules a third of the Earth; Victoria rules a third.

"And the rest of us, including my sovereign lord the Great Autocrat and Tsar of all the Russias, must be content to hold what we can of the rest. This—dalliance—with the Empire of Japan may not bring about the end of Russia in my lifetime, or yours, or Her Imperial Majesty's . . . but I fear that, eventually, it will.

"I want to believe that all of this"—he spread his hands expansively—"and, for that matter, my friend King David Kalakaua's beautiful little realm—land in safe hands."

"I'm not sure quite what you're saying, and I have no idea what I have to do with it."

"I believe that the Secret Chancellery has spread the rumors of your supposed . . . espionage. It isn't the imagining of some newspaperman: it's directly from Third Section . . . but the fact is that if you were here to intrigue on behalf of your Queen, it might be the best thing that could happen to Novaya Rossiya."

"I don't think Her Majesty, or Lord Lee, has any designs on Novaya Rossiya, Grigori."

"No," he answered. "But I think they should."

CHAPTER 4

"After everything else, Joe, I guess I'm not surprised."

"It was probably goons working for that general you met. The governor invited you—and me—to be out of the way." Joe Twichell picked up his valise, then set it down again. "Probably enjoyed giving that order."

"He says that he and the Secret Chancellery aren't getting along."

"You believe him? Russians are—"

"Russians are what?"

"Well, you know. *Russian.*"

"I don't think it's quite that simple," Sam said.

"While you were out eating canapés, or whatever you were doing out at the Presidio, I was wearing out shoe leather in the company of a very—*very*—energetic young Russian woman, who had no pity for an old man." Sam snorted and Joe looked affronted, but he continued. "She kept me plenty long enough for those lead-foots to ransack our rooms."

"They didn't *ransack* our rooms. Things were mostly put back where they were supposed to be."

"*Mostly.*"

"What is the problem, Joe? They did just what we might expect. Is anything missing?"

"Not so far as I can tell."

"Then let it go. We board *Star of the Ocean* in four hours and we'll leave Saint Helena behind."

Sam went to the window and looked out at the Russian city laid out before him like a lithograph. He wasn't sure what to think: Drenteln had menaced him—seemingly for no purpose; Gyazin had been frank about the future he saw, almost disarmingly so.

The cities on North America's west coast were largely small ones. The Spanish capital, San Diego, was a pretty little place, about what Saint Helena might have been in the Spanish had stayed. But the Russians had changed all that.

Except that wasn't really true: the Russian Empire had done a great deal to build what was here, but the railroad had done a lot more, as had the Astor Company. It might be a Russian city, but the Empire of Great Britain had really built Saint Helena. Why wouldn't Queen Victoria want to make it part of the Empire in fact as well as in principle?

But that begged the question of why the bloody hell it was Sam Clemens's job to make that happen.

It wasn't. It never was. Gyazin must know that: Sam was no spy, and he sure as hell was no diplomat. . . not that they needed one: what they needed was a *lifeline*. They might not even realize that off in St. Petersburg, ten thousand miles away. The future, in Grigori Gyazin's view, was an end to Russian America, maybe even an end to Russia itself. . . except that was foolish, too—Spain had been in decline since Lord Schuylkill's day and it was still here. The Viceroys of New Spain and New Granada might as well be kings themselves, but they *did* still bend a knee to Queen Isabella in Madrid. Form was still important.

"Sam."

"Let's get out of here, Joe. I may not be quite tired of this place yet, but I'm pretty sure it's tired of *me*."

✳ ✳ ✳

On the foredeck of *Star of the Ocean* Sam watched the cigar smoke gently waft away in the light of the setting sun. He had put the envelope with Gyazin's letters away in his pocket to be passed to Her Majesty's consul in Manila: a diplomatic pouch would take it back to London bearing the prince's compliments to Queen Victoria, thus taking it out of his hands. There might even be some sort of reward for him, not that it really mattered.

The other letter had been a personal one from Grigori and Andrea Gyazin, thanking him for coming to the Presidio and apologizing for any indignities he might have suffered while in their city. It seemed heartfelt—he let his cynicism recede into the background enough to be touched by the gesture. Still, it cost the prince and princess nothing to exercise magnanimity, and it cost him nothing to appreciate it. In the end, Saint Helena had been the place he'd been accused of intrigue and almost drawn into it. That didn't go with a successful literary career, that was for damn sure.

Later he would write about Saint Helena—the quaint, authentically Russian city perched on the edge of the continent. The people, the food, the customs would all be subjected to Mark Twain's unique perspective. Everything he wrote was with an eye to the future but clearly was a window into the past—when some unknown reader might come across it.

Ultimately, Sam thought, that would be enough.

WATER OF LIFE

1893

CHAPTER 1

"Father! What a surprise." Julius Norton rose from his desk and stepped around to embrace his father. It was a sunny day in early June, the clouds scattered across the sky, the bay beautiful from his window, and Julius was in an excellent mood. "You're not here to check up on me, I trust."

Joshua Norton was in excellent shape for a man of seventy-five. He was more than forty years older than his son, to whom he had left much of the day-to-day operation of his business a few years earlier. He returned the embrace, setting his cane next to his hat on a side table. He walked over to the window and looked out across the water.

The office still had many objects from Joshua's time—a diagram for the proposed bridge across the East Bay to Archangel, completed fifteen years ago; three handsome prints of everyday life in the Sandwich Islands; a collection of signed copies of Mark Twain books neatly arranged on a shelf. But Julius had added touches of his own. A small stock ticker chattered from time to time, reporting transactions on the Royal Exchanges in New York, New Orleans, and Franklin; beautifully-illustrated volumes of Lope de Vega (Julius's Spanish was excellent); a glass jar with the small, exquisite, foil-wrapped Ghirardelli chocolates that both Nortons liked.

"No, nothing like that."

"You miss it, don't you?"

"Miss it?" Joshua turned to see his son impishly grinning. "No. I don't, not really. I enjoy my days and my diversions. Your mother would have loved to see all this, but . . ." He spread his hands. "The Lord is just."

Joshua's wife, Julius's mother, had passed from cancer a few years earlier. Thanks to Norton's many business connections, and long-time friendship with the Gyazin family, most of Saint Helena had turned out for the funeral.

Neither man spoke for a time, then Julius asked his father, "Then what can I do for you?"

They settled into chairs, father in front and son behind the neatly-arranged desk.

"Some years ago we took a position in a company that grows produce in the valley of the Saint Cyril River. It was bankrolled by some *boyar* in the home country, I don't remember his name. Some of the best oranges and peaches in Saint Helena markets are grown there."

"Of course, yes. Their reports are impeccable. We've made a fair amount from them."

"I have received word that the farm manager has left without warning. He took a small amount of the operating funds, but certainly not all: enough for a passage to the Sandwich Islands or French Polynesia."

"*I* hadn't heard of this."

"Diversions," Joshua said, smiling. "Not more than half a dozen people know, though obviously word will spread quickly."

"I assume there's more to this than that."

"I don't know why he left, or in such a hurry. But it makes me wonder. It is also the case—I heard from the same source—that the workforce has declined in number. Not catastrophically: just gradually. None of this has apparently made it into stock-holder reports."

"Declined? As in—"

"As in *died*, yes. If this were construction or mining, the number might be easily discounted. But other than falling off a ladder . . . onto an upturned pitchfork . . . there just aren't too many ways to die in an orchard. So it makes me wonder."

"Do you think we should divest ourselves?"

"If I said 'yes,' would you do it?"

"Not without investigating. But I would consider your information and advice when making the decision."

"Good man." Joshua smiled. "You don't need an old man around to tell you what decisions to make."

"Apparently I *do* need one around to bring me rumors." The two men laughed. "How long before this becomes public knowledge?"

"Oh, a few days, I'd expect. Enough time for someone to go out and visit and return. The farm is about a third of the way between the delta and the headwaters. Most of the workers are Khazaks and Uzbeks, on three- or five-year indentures, and the overseers are mostly from New Granada. The indentures that make it through their term are paid off and either come here or find work in the mines further upriver."

"Indentures?"

"It's a hell of a lot better than spending your life scrabbling for wheat or raising scrawny cattle and sheep out on the steppes. This must seem like Paradise to them."

"But they're dying."

"A *few* are dying. Not in mass numbers, but more than you'd expect. It's worth looking into. You could send someone—Kirov, or perhaps young Rosinsky—"

"Kirov has left to go run a factory in Archangel, Father. And I can make my own personnel decisions. But this sort of thing sounds like something I should look at with my own eyes."

"Can the business survive without you for a few days?"

"If it can't," Julius said, "I'm in the wrong business. And if some old man comes in to bother the staff, they'll have orders to send him off at once." He rang a little handbell and an assistant opened the door, surprised to see his boss and an elderly visitor laughing uproariously.

*　*　*

To travel from Saint Helena to the Saint Stanislaus Valley required a train trip to New Odessa.

It was a town that was gradually becoming a city, where the river emptied into the bay through a lowland delta. In recent years, it had become the home to a few thousand Japanese, who at first had been largely in the fishing and fish-processing business, but were gradually moving into more lucrative pursuits. There was a rumor that the government of the tsar was considering a proposal to have them deported due to tensions between Russia and Japan in the Far East: but they were there at the moment.

Julius decided against Rosinsky: he liked the young man, but he had a habit of nattering on about his primary hobby—he was a birdwatcher, and was constantly on the lookout for a red-feathered crested something or other. A few days of that would make Julius want to decamp for the Sandwich Islands as well. Instead he chose Lisimov, a dour, precise Ukranian. He was a perfect traveling companion: careful with his toilet, taciturn, and trustworthy.

The train ride to New Odessa was completely routine. The train between Archangel and New Odessa ran four times a day; the second-class coach was crowded but comfortable, and it took a full day to travel up through the hills and down into the fertile river valley around the growing city. Factories belched smoke into the deep blue sky: all part of the scenery of a prosperous place.

He and Lisimov took a carriage from the railway station to the Delta Astor, the best hotel in New Odessa. Julius was willing to forego first class rail travel, but when it came to hotels it was a different matter. The further he went from Saint Helena, the more important it was to make sure he had a good night's rest before a business day.

As they entered the well-appointed lobby, Julius noted a group of Asian businessmen crowded at the registration desk. There appeared to be some sort of heated discussion between a harried-looking clerk and several of the men, which was growing progressively more heated.

"I'm going to see what I can do to help," Julius said to Lisimov, but the Ukranian put his hand on his superior's sleeve. He stopped and looked at the other.

"You speak Japanese, Mr. Norton?"

"Not a word."

"I would think that your involvement would only make it worse."

Julius was about to reply, but Lisimov gestured toward the desk. A young Asian dressed in the uniform of a hotel clerk emerged through a door next to the pigeon holes for guest mail and approached the desk.

A rapid exchange ensued, including words and gestures and a few bows. The clerk in charge stepped back and let the clerk take charge, but did little to hide his annoyance—possibly even disgust—with the situation. After a moment, the potential guests formed a quiet and orderly queue to sign the guestbook and receive their room keys.

Lisimov let his hand fall to his side. Julius and Lisimov walked over to join the queue, but another clerk gestured to them to come directly to the desk. As they approached, the Asian men began to murmur among themselves.

"Welcome to the Astor, sir."

"Norton," Julius said. "Two rooms; I sent you a telegram yesterday."

The clerk looked down at his book perfunctorily, running his finger down a column of entries. "Yes, of course. Your rooms are ready, sir." He turned and took down two keys, each attached to a wooden fob bearing the Astor arms. He slapped the bell to summon a porter, which set off an additional round of comments from the Asians. Julius turned slightly to look at them, and they looked away as a group.

"Thank you," Julius said.

"I must apologize for the disturbance, sir. These . . . guests speak no English and very little Russian. And they all seem to want to speak at once."

"They are Japanese?"

"Yes, sir. Businessmen. They are apparently here because of the new factory. Something to do with removing salt from water."

"A desalination plant."

"Just so, sir." The clerk looked as if he was filing the word away for future reference. "Is that your business as well, may I ask?"

"No, no. Import and export. We're going up river tomorrow. My Baedeker says that the train to Saint Stanislaus leaves the central station at 9 a.m.?"

"I can confirm that for you, Mr. Norton. I can have a cab waiting at eight-thirty. Our breakfast parlor opens at six, so if you are an early riser, sir, it should not be an inconvenience."

"Unless all the Japanese gentlemen have to get to the train at the same time."

The clerk pursed his lips and said quietly, "But of course your request has already been made, Mr. Norton. . . the same will be true if you choose to dine with us this evening. Would you care to make a reservation for the dining room?"

CHAPTER 2

The train from New Odessa to Saint Stanislaus was hardly up to Crown Pacific standards, but it was reliable and moderately comfortable: another well-run, well-maintained Astor concern. The wealthiest corporate entity in British North America had its hands in everything in Novaya Rossiya, and always had; Julius had wondered once to his father why Saint Helena and the surrounding land hadn't simply been annexed into the British Empire, and Joshua had laconically replied, "Because they don't have to." There was some truth in that.

Outside the car windows, Julius and Lisimov could see planted fields out to the horizon, as well as vines and trees and all manner of growing things. It was a Garden of Eden covering tens of thousands of square miles, divided up into huge plots devoted to agriculture of all kinds. Draft animals and laborers were visible as well, and the latter sometimes paused in their work to look up at the train as it passed along the river, on its way to another city. Also, from time to time, they spied small oil derricks slowly pumping petroleum in among the vast farms.

When they reached Saint Stanislaus, a carriage was waiting to take them up to *Raiskiy Dvorik*, the great plantation in which Norton and Company held a partial stake.

As the carriage lumbered along the road, Julius noticed amusement on the face of his traveling companion.

"Care to share the joke?"

Lisimov snorted. "It's the first I've heard of the name of this farm, Mr. Norton."

"Raiskiy Dvorik. I assumed it was someone's name."

"Not hardly," Lisimov said. "'Heaven's Backyard.' Seems like a boast."

"Well," Julius said, gesturing outside the carriage. "It seems fairly heaven-like."

"Except that people are dying. Now, it's true that people die: and these *rabotniki* that have come over from the rodina to work here are no less mortal than anyone else. But I'm sure they don't find it very . . . heavenly."

"Compared to the steppes?"

"You've been on the steppes, I suppose?"

"I've crossed this country on the railroad. I assume the steppes are the Great Plains drawn large."

Lisimov snorted again, enough to make his point but stopping short of being derisive: the man was aware of his standing in the company, but seemed honest to a fault.

"To compare some of the native tribes to the steppe horseman is not unreasonable—the Apache and the Comanche and the Lakota seem like they're born on horseback, and they range widely—but the Russian and Central Asian steppe is more like an ocean than a sea. An ocean of grassland. It has swallowed up every invader from Ancient Rome to the present. They say that the men of the steppe have the wind of the open plain flowing with every breath. I would choose Novaya Rossiya, but steppe men . . . I wonder if this is the dvorik of raiska—heaven—or anywhere else."

"Then why did they come?"

"What drives any man?" He rubbed his thumb and index finger together in an age-old gesture. "Gold."

His expression was passive and polite, but there was something in it that said, *I would have thought you would know that.*

✳ ✳ ✳

The great house of Raiskiy Dvorik was located at the crest of a hill, overlooking cultivated fields and neatly planted orchards. As they rode up the hill they were accompanied by a rough-looking man on horseback, wearing a large floppy canvas hat and long, shaggy moustachios. He was a Spaniard from the look of him; that was confirmed for Julius when he heard the escort engage in a shouted exchange in Spanish that, if Julius had been an angrier man, he might have had words with him; instead he pretended he didn't understand the language, exchanging a shrug with Lisimov.

"He insulted your parents, didn't he?" Lisimov said.

"To say the least," Julius answered.

"Why are there Spaniards here?"

"They probably know the business better than Uzbeks or Khazaks."

"I don't like the look of this Cossack."

"He's not a Cossack. Not anything like. He's a—what is the Spanish term? *Gaucho*. Down in Patagonia, in New Granada, they herd animals on the plains. According to what I have read, they serve as overseers for the manager."

"I don't like the look of this gaucho, then."

They had reached the house, and prepared to step down from the carriage. "Indeed. Neither do I."

✳ ✳ ✳

The new manager of Raiskiy Dvorik was an officious little man with a perfectly-trimmed turned up moustache. His name was Schönberg: he was a Prussian, hired by the plantation owner to direct the day-to-day affairs of the place. He looked as out of place as Julius could imagine, but he welcomed them cordially, making no mention of the sudden departure of his predecessor.

"Can I offer you some refreshment? Perhaps some fresh-squeezed orange juice?"

"Orange juice?" Lisimov said.

"Oh, yes indeed. Direct from our orchards. By all means." He gestured them toward a rear veranda. The house was very well appointed: it would not look out of place in the best residential neighborhood in Saint Helena or, indeed, in Franklin or New York. The view from the porch was exquisite, with the sun streaming down and a gentle breeze wafting past, a world away from the changeable weather of Saint Helena.

A glass was placed in front of each of them, and Schönberg lifted his with the word "Prosit." They drank: to Julius it was one of the most delicious things he had ever consumed—like a glass of liquid sunshine.

"So," the Prussian said. "To what do I owe the honor, Herr Norton? You are welcome to visit any time, of course, but most of our investors don't take the time."

"I think more of them should come down here and see what you've done."

"I shall take that as a compliment," Schönberg answered with a tight smile. "We pride ourselves on our produce."

"Actually," Julius said, "I am curious about a report that has come to our office concerning the health of your workers."

A flicker of—something—came across Schönberg's face, but it vanished immediately. "I'm not sure what you mean."

"You have lost some of your staff, from what I understand."

"The *kholopy*? Well, yes, they're used to a different environment. It's really nothing to be worried about."

"The death of one's *employees* is a matter of some concern, da?" Lisimov said. His emphasis was deliberate, Julius knew; they'd both noted that the manager used the term kholop and not rabotnik—kholop was a bit more pejorative, conveying more a sense that the workers were chattel.

"Herr Lisimov," Schönberg said, "they come here by the hundreds. If they don't adapt to the climate—" he spread his hands, as if to say, *what can you do?* "In any case, they are eminently replaceable. There has been no interruption in production or delivery."

"No, indeed," Julius said. "There has not."

✳ ✳ ✳

Schönberg summoned one of the overseers to show them around the grounds. Sometime before the end of their interview with the Prussian, Lisimov excused himself to attend to personal needs, and he had not returned by the time the overseer had arrived.

Schönberg engaged in a quick exchange in Spanish with the overseer; Julius understood the entire conversation, but affected indifference as he listened.

"Where is the Ukranian?" Schönberg asked.

"I have not seen him, Señor."

"Find him. Detain him, as politely as you can. We'll not have someone snooping around."

The Spaniard left, returning after a few moments—evidently the direction had been given.

The Prussian then smiled, his carefully-waxed moustaches lifting upward. Julius smiled in return, as if nothing had happened.

"Your colleague," Schönberg said. "Do you know where he went?"

"To the . . . necessary, I assume. Is there a problem?"

"No, not at all. I thought he wanted to see the grounds."

"I'm sure he can catch up with us."

"Yes, of course," Schönberg said, smiling again.

* * *

They walked through the orchards, which extended over a large area. They heard numerous dialects, some Russian and some not. Julius affected the air of an uninformed investor, a businessman from Saint Helena who didn't get much sun. Schönberg retained his business suit but affected a rather unfashionable straw hat. As they walked along Julius was quite at his ease, but the Prussian seemed quite on edge—and Julius knew why: he wanted to know where Lisimov had gone.

Everything was beautiful and scenic; even the small oil derricks in the distance had a certain mechanical attractiveness, bobbing up and down regularly. The air was tinged with the soft odors of growing fruit, with only a distant tang of earth and oil—but it was still there in the background.

"The oil rigs are rather close," Julius said, when they had stopped walking and stood under the shade of a rather large peach tree. He removed his hat and wiped his forehead with his sleeve.

"To what?"

"To the orchards and fields," he said. "And . . . what waters them."

"The residue flows downstream. It doesn't affect the plants."

"It can't be healthy for the *rabotniki*."

"They are healthy enough," Schönberg said, shrugging. "If there are health issues, it is due to the climate. They are simply used to a harsher environment; this may be too warm for them."

The idea struck Julius as absurd: but it was clear that Schönberg had no interest in his workers' wellbeing. At this moment, he seemed to be disinterested in everything other than whatever was distracting him as he looked around.

"Is something wrong, sir?"

"I am concerned about your subordinate, Herr Norton. I fear something may have befallen him."

"I assume he has just gone for a stroll, Mr. Schönberg. Surely there's nothing wrong with that?"

We'll not have someone snooping around, Julius thought, remembering the exchange at the plantation house. *There's something he doesn't want us to see.*

"Of course not," the Prussian answered, still glancing away. "I am just concerned for his wellbeing."

"My wellbeing is perfectly fine."

Lisimov had approached quietly enough that Schönberg had not noticed him. He whirled around to come face to face with the Ukranian, who had taken out a handkerchief to mop his brow.

"How was your walk?"

"Most refreshing," Lisimov said. "And most informative. Thank you, Mr. Schönberg, for your solicitous care for my health. It is much appreciated: but as you can see, I merely took a few moments for some fresh air."

The Prussian recovered his equanimity after a moment, adjusting his straw hat and then his Oxford glasses.

"Very well, then," he said. "Perhaps I can show you the sorting and canning facilities."

✳ ✳ ✳

There was a smaller guest house on site, which had once been a part of an adjacent, more modest farm. Schönberg lodged them in the house, which was staffed by three Russians—a maid, a footman and a handyman. It was small, but comfortable, and after a late-afternoon rest, Julius and Lisimov went for a short walk on the grounds.

"There is a part of the farm that seems unused," Lisimov said. "Where it extends to that hill." He gestured toward a low ridge, perhaps a quarter of a mile from the farmhouse. "It's not under cultivation, and the trees there are not pruned. They just grow wild. But I saw a small party of *robotniki*, with their gaucho escorts, going up that way with a cart. It was well out of sight of the main house."

"A burial party."

"I think so. I suspect that if we tried to look closer we would be prevented by the ever-watchful Spaniards."

"We still don't know what is affecting them."

"Ah. *That.*" Lisimov gestured toward the river. "The plantation house gets its water from a well nearby. The staff drink water drawn from the river—which contains all the runoff from the farm and from the wells. I would not let my dogs drink that water."

"Are they being poisoned?"

Lisimov stopped walking, and Julius looked at the Ukranian; normally diffident, he had a pained look on his face. "Worse, I think. The water is spreading cholera."

"And Schönberg is aware of this, I assume."

"It is certainly nothing he cares to discuss, but I cannot imagine he is ignorant of it."

✱ ✱ ✱

Schönberg set a fine table; he was unmarried, but had a couple that worked at the farm as bookkeeper and accountant who joined him for formal meals. The meal was sumptuous even by Saint Helena standards, and afterward in the vanishing daylight the little house's handyman drove them back for the night. No mention was made of Lisimov's constitutional; it was unclear whether he had seen anything that he had not been meant to see.

As they approached their night's residence, without speaking, Lisimov gestured toward a pair of gauchos not far from the house who seemed to be keeping a close eye on the place.

And yet, sometime after dark as the two men sat in the house's drawing room enjoying a late cigar, the housekeeper interrupted them. She had with her another man who, from his appearance, was a laborer. Both he and the housekeeper looked nervous; as he stood in the doorway, his hat held tightly in his hands, she crossed the room and lowered the window-shades, presumably concealing the inside from the outside.

"Who do we have here?" Julius asked, setting his cigar aside.

"I am Istvan Rakov, if it please you, gospodin," the man said in clear but unaccented Russian. He and the housekeeper exchanged glances; she shrugged and took her leave.

"You might have offended her," Julius said. "I think she expected to introduce you."

"She knows who I am."

"But I do not. What business do I have with you, gospodin Rakov?"

"I understand you are here to inspect the premises?"

"My colleague and I are employed by an investment firm in Saint Helena. We are here to examine our interests."

"Ah." He glanced from Julius to Lisimov and back. "I am sure that the head man told you that all is well and his employees—his kholopy; did he call us that?—are healthy and happy."

"He said that some of you had trouble adjusting to a climate so different from your home."

"It is what he says."

"Is it true?" Lisimov said.

"It is different," Rakov said. "But, gospodin, it is indeed Raiskiy Dvorik: Heaven's Backyard. We are having trouble adjusting, but not because the weather is fine. We are . . ."

Julius waited; the man had conveyed a sense of confidence, perhaps even arrogance—but it began to fall away, like a mask dropping to the floor and shattering. There was some pain that had not been obvious, and now had come to the fore.

"We are *dying*, gospodin. And it is not the weather. It is the water."

Julius looked at Lisimov, who spread his hands.

"How many have died?"

"I am not sure."

"Twenty? Thirty? Fifty?"

Rakov laughed—suddenly, bitterly. "This *month*? Less than fifty, I think. But overall? Hundreds. Perhaps a thousand. The manager does not care—when our people fell sick he simply said that he could bring in more. He said it when my . . . when my wife Yelena fell sick."

"Did she recover?"

"She did not, gospodin. She—she did not."

Julius thought of reaching for his cigar, but decided to let it lie. The room was quiet for several moments, as the thought of a thousand deaths began to sink in.

"Can you prove this, gospodin Rakov?"

The man seemed suddenly taken aback by being addressed as gospodin, but recovered his composure.

"If you would accompany me this night, I can show you personally."

"This is why you are here," Lisimov said quietly and levelly, meeting the man's eye. Julius watched carefully: Rakov did not look away. "To offer this invitation: this is why you have come to us tonight."

Rakov nodded, still not giving up Lisimov's gaze.

"What do you think, Lisimov?"

"I think," he answered, "that there is some chance that Herr Schönberg has sent this man to entrap us. But he could indeed be telling the truth."

"Those are very different choices with wildly divergent outcomes, my friend. It doesn't seem that you are offering much in the way of advice."

"You did not ask for advice. You asked me what I thought."

"A fair point. So what do you think?"

"Oh, I think we should see what he has to show us. It seems like a fine night for a walk."

$$* * *$$

Rakov led them down the stairs into the building's cellar. He held a bullseye lantern that cast light only forward; it was immediately obvious that this had been his route to enter the building. In the cellar, which contained barrels and crates, Rakov moved quickly to a particular wall; he ran his hand along a wood frame just above his head, and pulled open a door.

"Gospodin," he said, gesturing.

"Lead the way," Lisimov said, gesturing for Julius to go ahead of him.

By Walter H. Hunt

The door opened on a short passageway that led upward to a bulkhead. At the end, Rakov held up the lantern to his face and gestured for quiet. He carefully lifted the bulkhead door, which admitted gentle moonlight; after a moment he climbed three stone steps and gestured for the two others to follow him.

They walked through a small grove of uncultivated trees for a few minutes before Rakov spoke.

"The overseers are keeping a close eye," he said quietly. "They were not happy that you walked out on your own, gospodin," he added to Lisimov.

"I sorrow for them," Lisimov answered dryly. "If you are telling the truth, there is much they would not want me to see."

"How far is this burial place?"

"Not far," Rakov answered. "At first they were placed in an unused field, but now our burials are in caves in the hill. They think it makes it harder for us to count our losses. They are wrong," he added, after a pause.

They made their way up the hill in the moonlight; on three different occasions Rakov halted their progress and hushed the two men from Saint Helena, hearing or seeing something they did not; and then, just as abruptly, beckoned them to continue.

At last they reached the summit. Skirting it to a place out of sight of both their farmhouse and the plantation house there was a large cave entrance that gaped black against the hillside. Rakov extended his lantern, casting a beam into it, and strode forward, the other two men behind.

Just within the cave was a pathway made of rough planks, leading into the interior and inclining downward. It bore evidence of many feet having trod it; after perhaps thirty yards it passed under an archway and into a large cavern that was too vast for Rakov's small lantern to fully illuminate. Everywhere in sight were small wooden or stone markers—some carved with symbols scarcely visible in the lantern light, others bearing crosses or other emblems.

The cavern smelled of dust and quicklime.

Rakov, without speaking, stepped off the path and down a row until he was almost at the limit of the feeble light. Julius thought he saw him kneel and touch one and then two other stones; after a moment he rose and returned. There were tears at the corners of Rakov's weathered face.

"Here is your evidence," he said. "We can all be replaced, gospodin. For the masters of this plantation, it is merely a matter of signing a few papers."

CHAPTER 3

It was an act of will to speak politely to the Prussian manager the next morning as breakfast was served. He provided them with printed statements regarding the production quotas and efficiency of the plantation to take back to Saint Helena; it was unclear to Julius if Schönberg was aware of their night-time expedition to the graveyard and did not care, or was simply oblivious.

The carriage-ride to the train station was tense; they waited for something to happen with the Spaniards that rode alongside, but the trip was without incident.

They waited until they were safely aboard the train at Saint Stanislaus to converse—and even then, it was in quiet tones. Julius wasn't sure whether Schönberg might have threatened or actually done violence to them, but he felt relieved when the train was speeding along through the countryside, putting miles between them and the plantation.

"That was unexpectedly morbid," Julius said, stretching his legs in front of him.

"I think you should divest yourself from that company, sir," Lisimov answered.

"Divest?"

"Yes. It is clearly a poor investment, inefficiently run."

"People are dying."

"Just so," Lisimov answered dryly. "A waste of resources."

"A *criminal* waste of resources. People are *dying*," he repeated. "Most likely cholera. Don't you think this is a matter for the Governor-General?"

"And what will he do? Send the poor bastards back to the steppe? They'll die there anyway. He has no authority, and even less interest, to tell a private company how to regulate its drinking water. He could prevent them from bringing in any more—"

"Victims."

"If you please. That would destroy their business, and relatively quickly, I should think. Best that you be rid of the investment before that happens."

"Your lack of empathy is striking, Lisimov."

"I am sympathetic to poor Rakov, sir. But I met him personally: he is a man, not some item on a ledger. I am touched by his loss and his predicament.

"If I may be so forward, Mr. Norton, I think you are losing perspective."

"Perspective?"

"As a businessman. Your concerns are merely humanitarian."

"Merely—"

Lisimov looked out the window: Julius' anger was palpable, but Lisimov was unprepared—or perhaps merely uninterested—in facing it.

"This is not about business."

"Really, sir. Then what is it about? What is any of this about? You are not a crusading humanitarian, at least not by profession; would you go to the tsar and demand that he do something about all of the peasants out on the steppe, starving when the harvest is bad? Will you demand that the rich empires seek out and cure cholera and typhoid and yellow fever, that they empty the prisons of all the miscreants that suffer there?

"This is business, Mr. Norton. Nothing but business, and it is a bad one. Your company should not be involved with it a moment longer than it needs to be. And that should be the end of it."

Julius did not reply; and when Lisimov next looked at him, his superior had taken out his notebook and was scribbling something down in it.

When they reached Saint Stanislaus and were waiting for the train that would take them back to New Odessa and home, he left Lisimov with the luggage and strode across the busy terminal to the telegraph office. When he returned, he had a determined look on his face, but said no more.

When they reached New Odessa, Lisimov learned what had happened.

* * *

A telegram was waiting for them at the Delta Astor, which was thankfully devoid of Japanese businessmen queuing to register. Julius opened it, scanned it briefly, and turned to Lisimov with a satisfied expression.

"Ivan Kyrilovich," he said as they crossed the lobby with the porter, "I have a special assignment for you. How soon can you be free of personal and business commitments?"

"A few days, Mr. Norton. What sort of assignment?"

"I wish to put you in charge of something."

"I appreciate your confidence. What is it?"

Julius smiled. "Raiskiy Dvorik."

Lisimov stopped in his tracks. "I'm sorry . . . what?"

"Raiskiy Dvorik. I propose to replace that Prussian martinet with you. You may fire whomever you wish, beginning with him, and possibly including every one of those Spaniard toughs. You may hire whomever you wish, but I hope you will find a position for gospodin Rakov."

"But how—"

"I bought it. The farm. I have liquidated a modest amount of capital to buy a majority position, and over the next few weeks I will obtain title to the entire property; the first thing I intend to do is to clean up that river. It's the nineteenth century, Lisimov, almost the twentieth. There is no need for cholera to be an issue—not here, not anymore.

"Now please understand: anyone who takes over management of Raiskiy Dvorik will be expected to meet or exceed the production quotas previously established. That person will need to find a way to do that, short of poisoning the workers or working them to death. Now, if you don't think you are equal to the task—"

"I didn't say that," he interrupted. "It might take a little time for those quotas to be met, but I have some ideas. I—I'd welcome the opportunity, Mr. Norton."

"The sooner the better, I would think."

"Yes, sir. The sooner the better."

* * *

A few months afterward, Julius was working his way through a stack of quarterly reports when Rosinsky knocked and entered his office. He was carrying a small wooden crate bearing the familiar logo of Raiskiy Dvorik.

Rising from his chair, he gestured for Rosinsky to place it on the great wooden table that had been his father's from long ago. In due course the lid was pried open, and the most exquisite odor of fresh oranges entered the room. The crate contained two dozen perfect fruits, with the logo carefully stamped on the outer peel. There was a small envelope within; Julius opened the envelope and found a small card.

This is a new strain we have cultivated within the last few months, it read. *Rakov is a born genius. We call this one Yelena. The gospoda in Saint Helena will find them plenty sweet enough. — Lisimov.*

Julius withdrew his handkerchief from his pocket, and slowly peeled one of the Yelena oranges. It fell apart in his hand, eight perfect segments.

One taste was enough to evoke the pastoral landscape of the Saint Kyril Valley, and the sunshine of a summer day; and Julius Norton knew that, despite the grumblings of his directors, he had made the right choice.

It was, after all, a matter of business.

ENDS AND BEGINNINGS

1906

CHAPTER 1

When Mikhail Gyazin thought about it later, in his advanced old age, memories—little vignettes—floated to the surface, things and people and places that reminded him of the world he had known before everything changed.

* * *

Toward the end of 1905, the Japanese reopened their consulate in Alexander Square. The ink was scarcely dry on the treaty: the Baltic Fleet was at the bottom of the Tsushima Straits, and the Great Autocrat was dealing with unrest among the nobility and peasant revolts in the countryside. Mikhail was not expecting to exchange pleasantries with a nation that had just finished conducting a devastating war and inflicting a humiliating peace on his country. But there it was: an exquisitely polite letter requesting an audience with the Governor-General.

He had seen no merit in refusing the request. Count Sato Togawi, a punctilious but generally inoffensive bureaucrat, had been the Meiji Emperor's consul in Saint Helena for a dozen years before the war, and had returned as soon as was diplomatically feasible—he and Mikhail had been cordial, even friendly; Togawi had always been especially polite and respectful toward Mikhail's parents, making the effort to provide his mother with fresh flowers from the consulate's own garden once a week.

"Why don't you invite them to the Presidio?" Ekaterina had asked him when he showed her Togawi's letter. "Perhaps he will bring Akio with him."

"You'll have him in our home, Katja?"

"I don't see why not. Count Togawi did not sink the tsar's battleships, or attack his fortresses. He seems to want things to go back to the way they were."

"Things will never be the way they were, my heart."

"I don't see why not."

"It is a matter of politics, my dear—"

"Oh, don't use *that* argument on me, Mischa. Your father always trusted your mother's instincts—you should trust mine."

"And what do your instincts say?"

"That Gyazin is a name known for its courtesy and grace. Politics can be left at the door for an afternoon."

So it was decided; Sato and Akio Togawi were invited to the governor's residence, along with Grigori and Andrea, Mikhail's parents, to help emphasize the casual and personal nature of the visit. Politics were to be left at the door.

A few days before the planned dinner party, Count Togawi requested that one more person be added to the guest list: a visiting dignitary from Japan. Mikhail could not help but accept, and the party was increased from six to seven.

The Japanese visitors arrived in a brand-new motorcar, which huffed its way up the long hill and through the main gate, receiving the salutes of dress-uniformed Life Guards as it approached. Mikhail and Ekaterina waited on the veranda to receive their guests: old friends and the "visiting dignitary"—who, in sharp contrast to the diplomatic couple in their Western attire, was turned out in distinctly Japanese costume—though, Mikhail noted, he did not appear to be carrying the customary swords that accompanied his rank. He ignored any assistance in alighting from the car, and emerged to stand upright and stiff, as if checking the lay of the land and the strength of the wind. The Togawis showed great deference to this elderly man; Mikhail and Ekaterina exchanged a glance as the three of them approached, the distinguished visitor in the lead.

"Governor Lord Gyazin," Count Togawi said, as they reached the veranda. "It is my honor to introduce to you Count Takayuki Sasaki, privy councilor and senior *taifu* to His Serene Highness the Emperor Meiji."

Mikhail bowed and smiled. "My wife Ekaterina," he said, and Katja offered a curtsy. "I will be honored to introduce you to my parents, Prince and Princess Gyazin—"

"We have met," Sasaki said. His Russian was heavily accented but completely understandable. "Some years ago."

Mikhail looked from Sasaki to Togawi. "I see," he said, trying not to react to the interruption. "I am sure they will be glad to see you again."

"It remains to be seen," the dignitary answered, not smiling. "I came to your city with Baron Iwakura." He looked Mikhail up and down. "Things have changed a great deal since then."

In the awkward silence, Ekaterina stepped in. "Let us not stand out here when people are waiting. You are most welcome in our home, Count Sasaki. And it is so good to have our dear friends back to visit." She smiled and turned, leading the way, leaving the rest no alternative but to follow.

✳ ✳ ✳

Grigori Andreivich Gyazin would have liked to think that he was eternally young, but he knew better; while he still felt that he thought clearly, and he still found his wife Andrea to be the most beautiful woman on God's earth, there was no question that they had grown old: the children, and grandchildren, and now great-grandchildren were testament to that.

Still, when Sasaki entered the sunroom in the company of his daughter-in-law and son with the Japanese consul and his wife trailing behind, he felt as if thirty years had been peeled away.

In 1873, when he was governor, a delegation of Japanese diplomats led by Baron Iwakura had come to Saint Helena as a part of a worldwide tour—the opportunity for the Japanese Meiji Emperor to introduce his country to the world after it was opened by British naval power in the 1850s. It was a curious event: the large delegation, led by a few important principals, seemed wide-eyed with wonder at everything they saw, and uncomfortable in the Western dress they had chosen to adopt. They loved Saint Helena, and Gregori and Andrea loved showing it to them.

Sasaki was a minor functionary in that delegation. He was a very serious man who asked many questions and answered few. During the few conversations that Grigori had with him during the delegation's stay in Saint Helena he betrayed a haughty superiority, a strong belief in the strength of Japanese culture and the weakness of the West . . . or at least Russia.

And now here he was: likely in his mid-seventies, and here Grigori was, in his eighties, and the world had changed.

"Father, Mother," Mikhail was saying. "Count Sasaki tells me that you have met."

Count, Grigori thought. *That would be . . .* hakushaku. *Come up in the world.* "A pleasure to see you again," Grigori said, remembering not to extend his hand. "You remember my wife and dear heart Andrea."

"Of course," Sasaki said, bowing. "The delicate rose of Saint Helena. Your presence honors me."

"You are too kind."

"Shall we sit," Ekaterina said, gesturing to an arrangement of couches and chairs.

Sasaki remained the center of attention as he took his place. What might have been a light and casual social event was far more restrained with his presence; it lasted through the social period and the luncheon that followed.

After lunch, Ekaterina and Angela escorted the Japanese guests into the garden. Sasaki appeared as if he would have liked to remain, but allowed himself to be included in the stroll. Mikhail and Gregori remained behind.

"I feel as if there is something I do not know," Mikhail said.

"About Sasaki?"

"He is here for some purpose. I would like to know what it is, and if you know anything that would be helpful. . . ."

"This isn't diplomacy, Mischa. He's measuring the drapes."

"Measuring—"

"It is a term that sounds better in English, my son. Sasaki is here to be the eyes and ears of the Meiji Emperor, and if I were to guess—the Meiji Emperor expects to add Novaya Rossiya to his possessions in the very near future."

"The treaty has already been signed, Father."

"The treaty was only the beginning." Grigori looked old and tired. "The tsar is facing rebellion at home and has no ships in the Pacific. There is nothing to prevent the Meiji Emperor from changing all the maps and the street-signs to Japanese. The city . . . the world that I have known here in Novaya Rossiya is about to be swept away."

"The tsar would never give away Novaya Rossiya."

"Wouldn't he? I ask you, Mischa. What makes you think the Great Autocrat Nikolai cares a whit about Novaya Rossiya? He's never been here. None of them, none of the great *boyars* or courtiers, have ever been here. My uncle and cousin sent me to Saint Helena because they had no interest in traveling halfway around the world to a place so remote. Besides, the Japanese are rich now, and we are prostrate. They would pay, and we would surrender this land because those in power would no longer care about it."

Grigori's voice was strong, unchanged by years or circumstances, but there was pain in it, something that Mikhail recognized but could not identify.

"That makes no sense to me." Mikhail gestured toward the garden, the bay dappled in sunlight, the far shore shrouded in mist beyond. "This is the only place I've ever known, and it's a paradise. Who wouldn't want to be here?"

"You've never been to Moskva or Sankt-Petersburg, my son. You've never seen the rodina."

"*This* is the *rodina*, Father."

"No, it's not," Grigori said, with more intensity than Mikhail would have expected. "No, my dear boy. You have never known what the rodina is, what it means. There's no way you could know. Your mother and I . . ."

"You're saying that I am not a true Russian."

"That's not what I said."

He turned to face his father. "It's *exactly* what you said. That the tsar would never surrender the homeland, but he would give up Novaya Rossiya without a thought. Because it's not holy ground. It's not the rodina, which—not to put too fine a point on it, Father—I simply don't understand. I am not ready for that: I am not ready for this old samurai to, well, finish *measuring the drapes*."

By Walter H. Hunt

He wasn't sure what the reaction would be: his father rarely showed his temper—largely due to the heroic efforts of his mother. But she was in the garden with the Japanese visitors. He stiffened and waited for the response.

Instead, Grigori Gyazin, twenty-third (or twenty-fourth, or twenty-fifth) in line for the tsar's throne, turned to his son, smiling, and embraced him. After a moment he stepped back.

"Thank you, my son. That is what I hoped you would say."

* * *

The Japanese did not come calling over that winter, or into the spring. Things moved on much as they had done.

Mikhail went to the hills above Archangel on a bear hunt with Julius Norton, his man of business and the son of his father's man of business. Yulchik, a dozen years younger, had been his friend for most of his life—and unlike his father, he enjoyed hunting. It wasn't the same as it had been half a century ago, when thousands of emigres had rushed to Novaya Rossiya in search of quick wealth in the gold fields; that had significantly reduced the wild animal population in the unsettled areas of the East Bay, which overall was far more tame and orderly than it had been. But there were still bears in the high hills and deep forests, and by the time Mikhail and his little party reached the hunting lodge, they had material for four beautiful bear pelts.

The lodge had not gotten much use in recent years, but Mikhail had determined to come there more often now that the children were grown. He had first visited there when he was twelve, as a bearer for one of his father's many hunts; it had been the scene of the memorable exchange with Brigham Young, the patriarch of Deseret, when he came out under cover of night in 1861. The house servants had uncovered the furniture and laid a fire, then—at his explicit direction—retired to their quarters along with the rest of the hunting party, leaving Mikhail and Yulcha to fend for themselves.

Mikhail poured three glasses of excellent vodka, placed them carefully on a tray, and carried them to a low table near the fire. Juilius watched the entire process curiously but said nothing. A few moments later there was a knock at the door; Julius rose, but Mikhail waved his friend back to his seat and went to the door.

"Ah, excellent," he said, after opening it to reveal a distinguished middle-aged gentleman whom he knew well: Sir Courtenay Bennett, His Majesty's consul in Saint Helena. Bennett was dressed impeccably, but instead of his court or morning dress, he was attired as a proper British gentleman might be when going on the hunt—khaki trousers and jacket, dark-colored vest and cravat, and stout boots. Mikhail took Bennett's walking-stick and hat, and gestured for him to enter, shutting the door behind.

"You know Norton, of course," Mikhail said.

"Of course," Bennett answered, grasping Norton's hand as he rose to meet the visitor.

"Now we won't have to dice for that third glass," Julius said. The three men took up seats before the fire.

"Chilly day," Bennett said. "Nothing like a spot of warmth inside—and out. To the tsar," he said, raising his glass and drinking.

"And to the King," Mikhail replied. "Now. My man of business is itching to know what this is all about, but is far too proper to come out and ask. I suppose we'd best tell him."

"Indeed," Bennett said. "Mr. Norton, I know that the Governor-General reposes great trust in you, but I must clarify that any discussion we have here is highly privileged, and should never be discussed when it can be overheard." After Julius nodded, he continued. "I assume I have your word that you will keep these matters private."

"Of course, Sir Courtney. The governor would not have me present if I did not enjoy his trust."

"Then we'd best get to it," Bennett said. "I have received a communication from Count Togawi, on behalf of His Imperial Highness the Meiji Emperor. He has respectfully asked the intentions of His Majesty's Government regarding the colony of Novaya Rossiya and the Russian exclave in the Sandwich Islands; which is to say, if the Japanese government saw fit to claim these territories as concessions to prevent further conflict, would we go to war to prevent it?"

"That's outrageous," Julius said. "I assume you told him so."

Bennett smiled. "As a diplomat, sir, I assure you that I reserve outrage for the most egregious insults to king and country. After all, this is merely a back-channel inquiry, not a formal proposal to His Majesty's Government. Still, I agree with you: it's an outrageous notion, and I do not think that the prime minister would view it with favor."

"But he would also not lead the British Empire into war over it."

"I can't speak for the P. M.," Bennett said. "I don't know what he'd do."

"You do," Mikhail said, standing and taking his glass to the sideboard. "But you're too polite to say it."

Bennett didn't answer, but looked away into the fire. Mikhail poured another drink into his glass.

"If Novaya Rossiya was the bargaining chip that kept the world at peace, and kept Japan from making an alliance with the French, His Majesty's Government would stand by."

"I don't know that for certain," Bennett said. "But . . . yes, I suspect that would be the case."

"And that," Mikhail said, returning to his seat, "is a very shoddy way to treat a friend and ally."

"You didn't need to bring me out here in private to tell you that," Bennett said. "Unless you just wanted a witness."

"That's not why I asked you here, Courtnay. And you know that. I had a long talk with my father a few days ago, after Count Sasaki came out to the Presidio to . . . what did my father call it? To 'measure the drapes.' He showed me the correspondence. All of it."

"What correspondence?" Julius asked.

"Between himself and the tsar, and between the tsar and Queen Victoria."

"Regarding . . ."

"The transfer of Novaya Rossiya to British control."

Julius Norton maintained his composure well enough to place his glass on the tray instead of dropping it. Queen Victoria had been dead five years, and Mikhail had been Governor-General for five years before that; so in order for there to be correspondence involving Prince Gregori and the Queen of England, it would be at least ten years old.

"I can see him doing the math in his head," Mikhail said, leaning back in his chair. "Let me make it easier for you, Yulcha. The first letter was sent to Her Majesty in 1878. Such a transfer has been contemplated for nearly thirty years."

"I had no idea."

"Neither did I, not officially, until a few days ago. But there have been discussions on the subject. Russian influence is stretched thin this far from the rodina. I suspect that the tsar would hesitate to surrender Lahaina to the Japanese, but Saint Helena might be an entirely different matter."

"I find that hard to believe."

"So did I. But under the right circumstances . . . for example, if Russia had extremely favorable trading rights in Novaya Rossiya in general, and here in Saint Helena in particular, I would think that this land would prosper under British rule."

"It is prospering under Russian rule."

"It is prospering," Mikhail said, "under the administration of local government which rarely, if ever, receives any communication from the tsar, may he live long and remain far away. I fear, however, that the alternative is for it to become an outpost of the Empire of Japan."

The three men sat silently for some time, then Julius said, "It sounds as if you are resigned to this outcome, Mischa—give in to the Japanese or to the British."

"It's not my decision, Yulcha. It is up to the tsar and the King of England." He gestured to Courtnay Bennett with his glass; the consul nodded, smiling slightly. "Or, if there is no handshake between them, to the Meiji Emperor. No matter how much it means to all of us, the decision is out of our hands."

"Still," Bennett said, "those who make the decisions are wise enough to listen to us. For those of us who have affection for a place that our rulers have never seen, it is hopefully enough."

CHAPTER 2

A squadron of the Royal Navy came to port during the second week of April. It wasn't the first time British ships had visited Saint Helena, though there had been no such visit since the end of the war with Japan. Mikhail received the squadron commander and two of his captains, and they were unfailingly polite and completely apolitical.

They were still in port when the ground began to shake.

* * *

The first tremor was enough to awaken Mikhail and Ekaterina: they had been adolescents in 1866 and '68, when quakes had struck Saint Helena and Mikhail's father had sought to enforce stronger building codes. But as the city grew all around the bay, the desire for new land—recovered from the swamps and fens along the coastline—circumvented many of those codes.

Mikhail's first thought was that the shaking was relatively minor: nothing worse than any of a number of quakes in the last forty years. He and Ekaterina exchanged glances.

"That wasn't so bad," he said, "don't you—"

But then the first real shock hit, and continued. It might have been a few seconds or a few minutes: as they made their way away from their bedroom into the breakfast room in the predawn light, the ground continued to shake.

Antonin, the master butler, appeared in a doorway, clad only in a nightshirt, holding a lantern.

"Forgive me for the undress, my lord, but—"

"Bring that over here," Mikhail said, gesturing to the sideboard. The ground had stopped shaking. "Please check to see that no one is hurt." He squeezed his wife's shoulders. "I will be in my office."

"At once," Antonin said.

"Mischa—"

"Telephone," he said, and turned to walk down the corridor. She followed: usually she stayed out of official business, but she wanted to be near him, and he didn't object.

The device had only been installed a year or so earlier, connecting Saint Helena's City Hall with the Presidio. Mikhail didn't usually make connections—it was Antonin who took care of it—but he had watched the process. He took the receiver off the switchhook and waited for the operator to come on the line.

After several seconds of silence, he placed it down again. Whether that meant that there was no operator available, or that the line was down for some reason, it wasn't clear—but either explanation filled him with dread.

* * *

An hour and several small tremors later, Mikhail was dressed and standing in front of the house, waiting for his chauffeur to bring his car around. Katja had asked him not to go into the city, but he had reassured her with gentle words and prepared to depart. The telephone had not rung, and no messenger of any kind had arrived—even from his parents. He feared that something terrible had happened, but did not share that with Katja either.

As he waited, he heard the door open behind him and Katja appeared, dressed for travel. She had a defiant expression on her face that he knew very well.

"My heart, this may be dangerous. I—"

"Where are you going?"

"To the city."

"Yes, yes, of course to the city. But where are you going *first*?"

He wanted to say, *City Hall*, because it was the correct answer: it was where the governor should go first. But he knew that it was not true, and Katja knew it, too.

"Odessa Street. To make sure father and mother are safe."

"Then I am most certainly going with you. And then we will go to the Embarcadero, and to Fort Vladimir, and to Alexander Square, to make sure our own children are safe. I know they can take of themselves, but still."

"'We'."

"Yes. Absolutely, 'we'."

"Katja—"

"<u>Mischa</u>," she interrupted. "Mikhail Gregorivich Gyazin. I accede to your direction on almost all things. But not this." The car came around the corner and stopped in front of the house; the chauffeur, Alexander, jumped out of the driver's seat and opened the rear door, one eyebrow slightly raised at Katja.

Mikhail sighed, and handed his wife up into the seat and followed her into the car. A few moments later they were on their way, taking the winding road eastward toward the city.

✳ ✳ ✳

It was as if some giant had torn the land apart. Streets had large cracks and deep potholes, making the car's progress slow and in some cases impossible. But even worse, when they crept slowly up to the top of the Tula Heights east of the Presidio, they had their first look at what the quake had wrought.

Saint Helena was on fire. A pall of smoke was already hanging over the downtown area, and they were presented with a scene of devastation that left them speechless.

Alexander handed Mikhail a pair of binoculars. As he surveyed the scene more closely, his heart sank even further. Odessa Street was much too far away to see, as was Alexander Square: the long diagonal boulevard, the Prospekt, disappeared into the smoke and gloom.

"We have to get closer."

"I don't think we can drive down there, Governor," the chauffeur said. "And I'm not sure I'd try to go on foot." He glanced into the car, where Ekaterina sat upright, looking out the window, worry and fear on her face.

"Well then," Mikhail said. "We will establish a command post up here." Already he could see residents of the neighborhood approaching, perhaps expecting him to do something about the fire. Suddenly, the earth shifted and shook again for several seconds, and then after a pause it shook a second time.

"This is not a safe place," the chauffeur said, looking in again at Ekaterina.

"There may not be a safe place. All right then, Alexander. Return to the Presidio with my wife; get the staff working on supplies. We're going to need to set up a first aid station. I'll remain here and try to organize these people." He waved toward the little crowd gathering nearby.

"She's not going to like that."

"You are driving the car, _da_? Go and return. She will return with you, but this will keep her busy for the next hour. Come back as soon as you can."

Mikhail was able to put the locals to work. One of them was a streetcar gripman, well acquainted with the city's geography and in possession of a bicycle that he used to go to and from work; Mikhail gave him a calling-card bearing his own seal, with instructions to get as close to City Hall as possible, make contact with anyone official, and report back. The man was eager to serve and dashed off downhill toward the smoke-shrouded city. He hoped that his messenger would be careful and return safely.

The ground shook three more times before Alexander returned with two footmen and Katja; the car was full of all sorts of supplies. Katja had changed clothes, replacing her usual walking dress with a more practical riding outfit. She looked somewhat peeved at Mikhail, but he was not in the mood for argument.

"A messenger reached the Presidio about twenty minutes ago, Mischa," she said. "He brought this." She handed him a sealed letter; he immediately recognized his father's script on the outside. Katja had no doubt recognized it as well, but hadn't opened the note.

He pulled it open and read.

Mischa
Your mother and I are safe and are trying to gather up people
on our street. Much of the city is on fire and we will have to
abandon our little house; the Prospekt is completely in ruins.
We are going to the Basilica and will send word when we
arrive.

We are sure you are on duty and all will be well, but we shall
all have to offer extra prayers.

Your loving parents G and A

Through his binoculars he could just make out the domes of Saint Helena's, and he hoped that Telegraph Hill was high enough to be out of danger from the fire.

*   *   *

Messengers and runners came to Mikhail's Tula Heights command post. Slowly a picture began to form: in a matter of a few minutes, the quakes had wrought enormous destruction—worse, far worse, than any previous event—perhaps there had been no tremor as violent since the town's settlement in 1816, when the cathedral construction had begun and the town had been given its name.

Meanwhile, the fires were still burning, and the means to combat them had been severely hindered by disruption of water mains and destruction of firefighting equipment. By midday, it wasn't clear how much of Saint Helena was going to be consumed.

Antonin returned and brought him something to eat, but Mikhail left it largely untouched. He felt helpless and disheartened; messages to his sons had been sent and answered, but there was much that he did not know, and what he saw through his binoculars was the end of most everything he had known all his life.

In the early afternoon, a small group on horseback came riding up the hill. Mikhail saw at once that it was led by Count Togawi, the Japanese consul; he was accompanied by a junior diplomat and three soldiers, who were more heavily armed than Mikhail would have expected.

Togawi dismounted and walked to where the governor was standing, offered a polite bow.

"I am relieved to see you, Sato-*san*," Mikhail said. "We have heard nothing about the consulates."

"I wish I had better news, my friend. Much of the city is on fire."

"Yes, I can see that."

"I would be happy to offer my assistance."

"Really, I'm not sure—"

"Governor," Togawi interrupted, a surprising break with his usual polite restraint. "Please. If there is anyone in Saint Helena who understands earthquakes and fires, it is one who has survived them. Tokyo has suffered many such. This is . . . all too familiar." Togawi turned away to look at the distant fires, his expression empty of emotion.

"I don't know what to do."

"I apologize for being trite, Gyazin-san, but the only way to fight fire is with fire. You must starve the fire of fuel so that it can no longer burn."

"How would that be accomplished?"

"There." Togawi pointed into the distance. "Choose a line across the city, and remove every structure and close off every gas main. Wherever you choose to do so, the fire will come to an end."

"Destroy—you mean, tear buildings down?"

"You do not have time to 'tear down' anything, my friend. You must destroy those buildings, and rapidly. The longer you wait, the more will be destroyed."

"The outrage would be tremendous. I would be burned in effigy—or worse."

"You will be praised for having saved part of Saint Helena, Gyazin-san. Whatever anger you face will be set aside in time." Togawi looked back at Mikhail. "Or, my friend, you can watch it burn until the entire city is destroyed."

"This is a terrible choice, Togawi-san."

"Life is full of terrible choices."

It crossed Mikhail's mind that the Japanese consul might have some ulterior motive: obviously they had nothing to do with the actual quake event, but it would not be hard to imagine the Empire of Japan wanting to take advantage of Saint Helena's distress.

But he could not imagine what benefit might be derived from destroying part of the city—unless it was merely to rebuild it in some more amenable—some more *Japanese*—form.

"It will take some time to arrange this. Assuming I could locate enough materiel to do what you suggest."

"What about the British squadron? They would certainly be well-equipped to assist."

"This is like a bad Russian novel, Togawi-san. Asking a British military force to follow the advice of a Japanese diplomat to help destroy part of a Russian city."

"It spreads around the responsibility, I suppose."

* * *

From his headquarters on Tula Heights, Mikhail Gyazin watched as a line of buildings stretching from the old Spanish mission to the southern end of the Embarcadero were leveled by explosives provided by the British squadron. He imagined that his parents were watching it too from the cathedral of Saint Helena on Telegraph Hill: it did not make him happy, and he knew that it would not make them happy either. It was a scene that would be forever etched on his memory.

The fires continued to spread, but they only crossed the line of destruction in a few places. The firefighters of Saint Helena worked all day and all night and into the next day, dealing with the fickle winds coming off the bay—but eventually the terrible fire burned itself out, leaving destruction behind.

The fire never reached the Presidio, but over the next few days the lower part of the governor's estate became the temporary home of a few thousand Saint Helena citizens who had nowhere else to go.

CHAPTER 3

Five days after the day of the quake, the Metropolitan of Saint Helena held a service of Thanksgiving at the cathedral, from which the vista of destruction could be readily seen. Mikhail and Ekaterina, as well as Mikhail's parents, were prominently in attendance, along with the rest of the Gyazin family.

The religious celebration left Mikhail unmoved. Though he was a less regular churchgoer now that his children were grown, he had always found such solemnities reassuring—God was in His heaven, and Christ Pantocrator supervised Earth from behind the altar . . . but somehow the destruction of his city, in the context of everything else that had recently transpired, left him disturbed and uneasy.

Katja sensed his discomfort, and realized his need to be alone. His mother, however, had no such reticence. After the service, Andrea came up beside her son, and tucked her arm firmly into his.

"Walk with me, Mischa," she said, more an order than a request. There was a beautiful manicured garden on the north side of the cathedral, which gave a view of the smoldering ruin of Saint Helena. It was the very last place that Mikhail wanted to be—and he could not imagine why his mother would want to see it: after all, she had made Saint Helena her home for more than sixty years, and now it lay in this condition at her very feet.

"Mother, I—"

"Do you know the story of how this cathedral was built, Mischa?"

His protests left off, and he looked at her curiously. "No. Why do you ask?"

"Do you know that you share a name with the very first priest of this settlement? He came here almost a century ago, and according to the stories written about him, he thought he had been exiled to a far place, where he would be forgotten."

"Father has reminded me that this is not the rodina."

"Oh, your father," Andrea said, smiling, dismissing it with a wave. "He thinks about such things too much. This is our home, just as it has always been *your* home, Mischa. But you are distracting me from my story."

"I am sorry. Please continue."

She looked at him owlishly, as if to say, *are you mocking me, little Mischa?* It made him smile, despite the scene spread before him.

"Father Mikhail built a church. Not this one, mind you—a less impressive one, but still dedicated to the holy Saint Helena, the mother of Constantine the Great, who found Our Lord's sepulchre in the Holy Land. He built his church despite the wishes of the governor, and despite every obstacle that was placed before him: and on the day it was dedicated there was an earthquake. The church fell and he died trying to rescue the *ikon* of the holy Saint."

"An omen, surely."

"A *sacrifice*," his mother answered. "Brother Gennady—*Father* Gennady, the first Metropolitan of Novaya Rossiya, but that was all in the future—demanded that a new church be built. That would be *this* church, which bore the blessed Helena's name and gave the name to our beautiful city."

"It's not so beautiful now, Mother. And you know what I had to do to keep it all from being destroyed."

"I know what you had to do, and yes, I weep for the city that has been taken down by the wiggling of the Lord's smallest finger. We are all fragile creatures, Mischa, from the smallest infant to the old woman I am surprised to have become. We fool ourselves if we think anything else.

"But to say this is not beautiful, even in its prostrate condition, is to see with half-closed eyes. Look around you, my son. The beauty of the Lord's work still remains. This—" she waved her hand at the city below. "This is man's work, destroyed in a day just as it was built in a day. At least in the measure of the God in which we believe."

"That's very sweet, Mother. But it does not rebuild this city. It does not save us from—"

"From what? What do we need to be saved from?"

"I should think that would be obvious. It's obvious to Father. At one time, he discussed everything with you."

Andrea Gyazin walked to the railing and looked back across the ruined city.

"The vultures have been circling for some time, Mischa. I don't know if we can avoid becoming a meal for either the Japanese or the British. But we knew that when Grisha—your father—and I were your age. It is, it has for a long time, been more a matter of *when*, not *if*."

"So tell me what Father would do."

"Will you do what he would do?"

"I don't know yet. But I value his advice."

"He favors the United Kingdom, Mischa. He does not trust the Japanese, and I tend to agree."

"It isn't completely up to me, of course. It will be the decision of the tsar."

"His Highness will listen to you. It is best that you are ready with your recommendation."

"As the Governor of . . . this. What is left of it."

"You have heard nothing of what I have said," Andrea responded, turning to face him. "I have wasted my breath."

"No, Mother, you have not. I just don't see what you see. You see with optimistic eyes."

"After all I have seen, Mischa, it is all that remains for me to see. You should not have to wait long to weigh in with your opinion."

✳ ✳ ✳

It was not long in coming, as his mother had said. He was in his shirt-sleeves, his desk covered with reports and documents, the office filled with staff: his secretary entered looking flustered and came over to Mikhail and whispered in his ear.

"Everyone leave," he said. "At once. You too, Pyotr," he added to the secretary. "Then send in our visitor."

When his staff had departed, Pyotr turned at the door and nodded. A conservatively-dressed middle-aged man stepped past the secretary, who closed the door behind him.

The man approached Mikhail's desk, removing his hat. He reached inside his jacket and handed a document to Mikhail.

He unfolded and examined it. It bore an official seal with the inscription Охранное отделение—'the guard'.

Okhrana.

"Excellency," Mikhail said.

"I do not merit such a title, Governor. What is more, I am merely here to represent my superior."

"Gospodin Trepov, I presume." Dmitri Feodorovich Trepov was the head of the Okhrana, the organization that had replaced the feared Third Section, the tsar's secret police. This gentleman was one of Trepov's operatives here in Saint Helena, and while Mikhail thought he was reasonably familiar with such officials, this was one he had never seen.

"Yes, of course. I am directed to convey information from the director, which you may take as a message directly from the highest authority. Confirmation will follow shortly."

"The . . . *highest* authority."

"You know what I mean, gospodin. There are negotiations taking place. May we speak plainly?"

"I assumed we already were."

"Your secretary, Pyotr. Is he trustworthy?"

"I would not employ him otherwise."

"I commend your sense of trust. He is listening at the door."

Mikhail thought for a moment and then shrugged.

"It is likely that this province will be conveyed—for a price—to another polity, gospodin. It is possible that you, and some of your staff, will have an opportunity to assist with that transition."

"Are you able to reveal which one?"

"Which what?"

"Which nation will become our suzerain. I thought we were speaking plainly."

"It should be obvious."

"Humor me."

"The Supreme Autocrat favors his royal cousin King Edward. He would rather place Novaya Rossiya in the hands of . . ."

"Of Westerners."

"Just so. But, of course, it is not that simple. To do so presents a grave insult to the Japanese, with whom we have so recently been at war; and whose favor the English crave. It might not be too unreasonable to imagine that the King of England might convey the province to them for some consideration."

"So it doesn't matter who—"

"*Might*, gospodin. It is not clear what could happen. Naturally, gospodin Trepov seeks your advice before advising the supreme authority."

"He wants to know what I would do."

"It seems so."

"We are better off remaining Russian," Mikhail said. "But if that is not to be, I think it is far more reasonable to allow the British Empire to annex Novaya Rossiya—better for the people here, at least. And I assume that His Highness King Edward would offer better compensation to his imperial cousin than—"

"Than a non-Westerner."

"Just so," Mikhail said.

"It would encourage Japan to seek alliance with the French, don't you think?"

"All of this is beyond my scope," Mikhail said carefully. "But the Japanese do not have much love for the rodina or its people. If they chose to ally themselves with our ally's enemy, I don't think it would come as a surprise to anyone."

"A very astute answer, gospodin," the Okhrana man said. He picked up something from the crowded table—a glass paperweight in the form of an orange, a gift from Yulcha. "The notion that a worldwide war would be caused by the decision of a declining Empire . . . it is ironic, nyet?"

"I don't know if I would characterize Russia as a 'declining Empire'."

"You are a loyal servant of the tsar, Governor. He would appreciate your allegiance."

"I assume he knows nothing of it," Mikhail said, "just as he knows nothing of anything else here in Novaya Rossiya."

"You underestimate his level of interest."

"That may be. But his willingness to sell us off to the highest or best bidder suggests that he really doesn't know much about us at all."

"So the tiger has teeth after all," the Okhrana agent said, smiling. He put the paperweight down on the table. "But I should not be surprised that you care a great deal about your land. Still, you are right in one respect: the highest authority is intending to sell Novaya Rossiya, because it is impossible to keep it.

"You should welcome this, gospodin. Either of the great polities has more to offer to restore Saint Helena to its former beauty, while the—highest authority—is far away."

Beauty, Mikhail thought, and it echoed what his mother had said: that the land was still beautiful.

It would still be beautiful if it belonged to Britain or to Japan. The flag that flew over the land would make no difference.

"So," Mikhail said at last. "My English is reasonably good. Should I plan to take lessons in Japanese?"

"You will be kept informed." The Okhrana man put his hat on his head, nodded to Mikhail, and walked to the door, opened it, and let himself out.

CHAPTER 4

In the end, Mikhail did not need to learn Japanese.

Sixteen days after the destruction of Saint Helena, Mikhail Georgiovich Gyazin, Governor-General of Novaya Rossiya, stood in his morning suit staring up at the white-blue-red flag of the Russian Empire. Sir Courtenay Bennett, similarly attired, stood next to him.

"I have mixed emotions about this, Governor," he said.

"Things have changed." Mikhail looked away from the flag and at the British ambassador. "Your nation inherits a ruin instead of the Saint Helena I have known all my life."

"Ruins can be rebuilt. London was destroyed by a terrible fire three hundred and fifty years ago, and it was made over into an even greater city. This is all temporary."

"You sound like my mother."

"The Lady Andrea is as wise as she is beautiful," Bennett said. "She speaks the truth."

"She usually does. But I don't think she sees the long-term consequences."

"For Novaya Rossiya—for Pacifica, as the P. M. designates it—to join the Empire will not materially affect the lives of most people here in Saint Helena. The government has offered you the post of governor, for at least the near future; there is no one better suited to the task. *Especially* in the near future."

"Things will change. Perhaps not for a short while, but they will change. In a generation, this will no longer be the city it has always been. It is what your empire does; what is it that Tacitus said? 'They make a wasteland and call it peace'."

"That is rather a depressing view, my friend. We do not wish to make a wasteland."

"My mother and father are giving serious thought to returning to Russia, Sir Courtenay. Their house, along with every house on Odessa Street, is a pile of rubble; their city is gone. They have friends in Saint Petersburg."

"Surely they have friends here."

"They wish to live and die Russian. They cannot do that here, expatriates in the place they called home."

"What about you?"

"I have no friends in Saint Petersburg." Mikhail smiled. "Wasteland or not, this is the only home I know. I am honored by the confidence His Majesty's government places in me, and I have been assured of the tsar's endorsement of my . . . employment. Your king can be assured of my best intentions."

"I know you will remain a subject of the tsar. Eventually there will be a British governor, but it was thought that continuity was more important."

"For the near future."

"Yes. For the near future. It is as far as any of us can see."

Mikhail glanced at the row of diplomats, all finely attired, waiting in the morning sun. The French ambassador, General Brunet, was in polite conversation with Count Togawi; neither seemed to want to look in his direction, and neither looked happy.

"I would like to believe that we have outgrown war, my friend," Mikhail said. "But you and I know better, even though we are too old to charge into battle. I do not think this ends well."

"Perhaps not," Bennett said. "But at least it begins well."

An order to the honor guard brought them to attention; the group of diplomats became quiet and attentive as the band began to play *Bozhe, Tsarya khrani*—"God save the Tsar"—as the standard of the Russian Empire was slowly lowered, catching its last breeze in the city by the bay.

CHARACTER LIST

A * indicates that the character is based on a real historical figure.

Alcantár y Rodriguez, Don Domingo. (1796-1848) Captain of *Reina Isabella*; Spanish nobleman in the Viceroyalty of New Spain.

Alexiev, Gennady. (1791-1862) First Metropolitan of Saint Helena; after the earthquake in 1816, became priest of the Russian settlement, and was the prime mover in the building of the cathedral on Telegraph Hill.

*Astor, John Jacob.** (1763-1848) Merchant, real estate mogul and entrepreneur. Emigrated from the Palatinate around 1800, became wealthy in the fur trade in the Pacific Northwest. He took British citizenship, and by the 1830s was the wealthiest man in British North America due to real estate investments in New York.

*Astor, John Jacob, III.** (1822-1890) Merchant, factor of the Astor Company. In the 1850s he was executive for the Company in Saint Helena. His wife was named *Charlotte* (1826-1887).

*Astor, William Backhouse.** (1792-1875) Son of John Jacob Astor; first chief executive of the Astor Company in

Saint Helena. After 1849, chairman of Astor in New York. His wife was *Margaret** (d. 1872).

*Bartlett, Franklin Allen.** (1816-1865) In our time line, his name was "Washington Allen Bartlett". An army officer, in our timeline the first American mayor of San Francisco. In this time line, he is an ambitious British officer.

*Bennett, Sir Courtnay Walter**. (1855-1937) A member of the Diplomatic Service; assigned to Saint Helena in 1901, served through the assumption of British Rule in 1906.

*Brunet, Jules**. (1838-1911) French general and diplomat. Posted to Japan in the 1860s as an adjutant, he served at numerous important diplomatic posts, and was French consul in Saint Helena at the time of the transfer to British rule.

*Clemens, Samuel Langhorne**. *(Mark Twain)* (1835-1910) British American humorist and author. One of the best-known writers of his day. Visits Saint Helena in 1878 during his world tour.

Damon, Jacques. (possibly an alias.) (b. about 1825) A spy for the King of France, involved in the entrapment plot with Joshua Norton.

Donatiev, Gyorgy Mikhailovich. (1774-1855) Commander of the Russian settlement from 1816 to 1822; son of Baron Donatiev.

Drentln, Alexander. (1815?-1902) General. Head of the Okhrana during the 1870s and 1880s.

*Elssler, Fanny (Franziska).** (1810-1884) Austrian ballerina. A friend of Dorothea Lieven. Martin Van Buren, Jr. was infatuated with her.

Gonzalo, Brother. (1790?-1840?) Franciscan monk at the Misión San Francisco; friend of Brother, later Father, Gennady of Saint Helena.

Gros, Étienne-Louis* (1819-1892) French gentleman, son of *(Baron) Jean-Baptiste-Louis Gros* (1793-1870), French consul in Saint Helena.

Gyazin, Andrea. (1825-1911) Wife of *Gregori* (whom she calls 'Grisha'); the "Rose of Saint Helena" – a beautiful, talented, intelligent woman. She planted the gardens at the Presidio. She is artistic and graceful, and speaks excellent French.

Gyazin, Gregori Alexandrovich. (1822-1916) Russian nobleman, distantly related to the Tsar. He comes to Saint Helena with his wife in the early 1850s to manage property belonging to his uncle. Later he is appointed Governor-General and serves in that capacity for many years and is succeeded by his son *Mikhail.* He has five other children, including *Konstantin*, who is a customs officer, and *Helena*, who is married to *Gyorgy Sharovsky's* son.

Gyazin, Mikhail Gregorivich. (1844-1927) "Mischa". Russian nobleman, son of *Gregori*, whom he succeeds as Governor-General. His wife is *Ekaterina* (1844-1919).

Hackfeld, Heinrich (1814-1879). Proprietor of H. Hackfeld & Company in Honolulu.

Halleck, Fitz-Greene*. (1790-1867) Poet and author; from 1832, personal secretary and amanuensis to John Jacob Astor from 1832.

Ionescu, Alexander. (1858-1934) Butler to Mikhail Gyazin.

Kalakaua, David*. (1836-1891) King of Hawai'i (the "Sandwich Islands") from 1874 until his death in 1891. King Kalakaua did make a world tour in 1881; it has been moved to 1878 to allow him to be in Saint Helena to

273

meet Mark Twain. His wife was named *Kapi'olani* (1834-1899).

Kirov, Pyotr. (1862-1937) Businessman, employed by Norton & Company until about 1892; "managing a factory in Archangel".

Lafayette, Gilbert du Motier, Marquis (later Duc) de* (1757-1834). French nobleman, became a part of government after the French Reform in the 1770s. The *bête noire* of the Earl of Schuylkill, his ministry overhauled and modernized the French economy in the early part of the 19th century.

Lee, Robert Edward, 5th Baron Lee.* (1807-1886) Virginia general and aristocrat. Served in the War of Texian Annexation; Governor-General of British North America in the 1860s and 1870s.

Lieven, Dorothea* (1785-1857). Noblewoman and socialite. A daughter of General Van Benckendorff; married *Count Christoph von Lieven* (d. 1839). A patroness of the arts and of society; a Lady Patroness of Almack's, and later the Caspian Sea Rooms in Saint Helena. *Konstantin Van Benckendorff** (1783-1844), head of the Secret Chancellery, was her brother.

Lisimov, Ivan Kyrilovich. (1852-1909) Businessman, employed by Norton & Company; a "dour Ukranian", good with figures.

Mikhail, Father. (1752-1816). First priest of the Russian settlement, later St. Helena. Died in the earthquake.

Norton, Joshua.* (1818-1903) Merchant and 'man of business' in Saint Helena. He was of Jewish ancestry and grew up in Cape Colony, coming to Saint Helena in the 1840s. He was a Freemason. A friend of Gregori Gyazin. In the real world timeline, Norton's business is ruined and he becomes unhinged, eventually proclaiming himself Emperor; his life in this one is significantly different. In both timelines he has the notion of building a bridge over the East Bay; in this timeline it is built in the 1860s.

Norton, Julius. (1855-1932) "Yulchik". Son of Joshua Norton, and head of Norton and Company after his father's retirement. Close friends with Mikhail Gyazin.

Orlov, Alexey Fyodorovich*. (1787-1862) Head of the Third Section (the "Secret Chancellory"), the Tsarist secret police, from 1844 to 1856.

Pico, Don Pío de Jesús.* (1801-1894) Royal governor of Alta California

Pietrewski, Wladislaw. (1790-1836) Officer aboard *Strelka*; employed by the Russian-American Company.

Rakov, Istvan. (1855-1912) Citrus worker, leader among the laborers at *Raiskiy Dvorik*. His wife *Yelena* died of cholera in 1891.

Rosinsky, Ilya. (1867-1916) Businessman, employed by Norton & Company. An avid birdwatcher.

Sasaki, Takayuki*. (1830-1910) *Taifu* to the Meiji Emperor. A member of Iwakura's delegation that visited North America in the 1870s, where he first met Grigori and Andrea Gyazin.

Schönberg, Karl Heinrich. (1849-1911) Prussian-born businessman, employed by Norton & Company at *Raiskiy Dvorik* plantation as manager.

Seratova, Vasileva. (1807-1891) Lady companion to Dorothea Lieven.

Sharovsky, Gyorgy Stefanovich. (1805-1882). Able seaman, later ship's captain. Served with Volkov aboard *Strelka* and *Lady Helen*. Had some connections with the Tsar's government later in his career.

Sherwood, John ("Ivan Shevrud"). (1804-1877) British spy and adventurer; double agent in service to the Secret Chancellery.

Sutter, John. (1803-1880) Swiss pioneer, an employee of the Astor Company; with his subordinate James Marshall, discovered gold in 1841.

Thorne, Zachariah. (1803-1864) Merchant and businessman; Joshua Norton's business partner, and possibly a closet Catholic. Originally from Connecticut Colony; escaped to New Spain after absconding with much of the funds from Norton & Thorne.

Togawi, Sato (Count Togawi). (1852-1917) Japanese consul in Saint Helena, before and after the Russo-Japanese War. His wife is named *Akio* (1868-1934)

Trepov, Dmitri Feodorovich.* (1850-1906) Head of the Okhrana from 1895 to 1906. A strong advocate of repression of dissent against the Tsar.

Tromelin, Louis-François Marie Nicolas, Baron de.* (1786-1867). Admiral in the French Pacific fleet.

Twichell, Joseph Hopkins, Reverend.* (1838-1918) Congregational minister from Hartford, Connecticut; companion to Sam Clemens during his world tour in 1878. Immortalized as 'Harris' in *A Tramp Abroad*, though the source of the name in the text is fictional.

*Van Buren, Martin** (1782-1862). Barrister, Court of King's Bench (then Queen's Bench), Crown Colony of New York. Employed by John J. Astor to perfect land claims in Novaya Rossiya in 1843. Father of Martin Jr. His wife was Hannah Hoss, whom he married in 1807 and who died in 1819. His other sons, who appear briefly, were:

*Abraham Van Buren** (1807-1873) Captain in the New York colonial militia.

John Van Buren* (1810-1863) City councilman in New York.

Smith Thompson Van Buren* (1817-1876) Bureaucrat; aide to Governor Bouck.

There was also another son, *Laurence**, who died very young.

Van Buren, Martin, Jr.* (1812-1855). Clerk. Son of Martin Van Buren; accompanies his father to Saint Helena in 1843.

Volkov, Leonid. (1794-1843). Ship's captain, originally in the service of the Russian-American Company, later with Astor & Son. One of the original commanders in the Vigilance Squadron.

Voznesensky, Ilya Gavrilovich*. (1816-1871) Russian explorer and naturalist; an expert on biological and cultural artifacts, a member of the Russian Geological Society. Employed by Andrea Gyazin to help create "Andrea's Garden" at the Presidio in the late 1850s.

Water Carrier. (1800?-1870?) Ohlone shaman, who helped create "Andrea's Garden".

Young, Brigham*. (1801-1877) Head of the Church of Latter-Day Saints after Joseph Smith's death in 1844, Royal Governor of Deseret.

GEOGRAPHICAL NOTES

Novaya Rossiya is the Russian colony on the Pacific coast, extending from Alaska to 34° 30' North Latitude, and bounded by the Sierra Nevada Mountains. Its capital, Saint Helena, corresponds to San Francisco. Archangel, located on the east side of the Bay, corresponds to Oakland.

The Saint Stanislaus River, described in Water of Life, is the San Joaquin; in addition to agriculture, there was a limited amount of oil exploration during the nineteenth century; but Valley farmers in our world were more careful regarding the water supply. New Odessa is Antioch, near the river delta. The Bay Bridge was not constructed in our world until 1933, but was conceived three-quarters of a century earlier, and commanded to be built by Emperor Norton; in this world, it is built long before that. Based on the Eads Bridge, constructed in 1868, it might well have been feasible, and British (and British American) engineering could be put to use here.

In British North America, locations are largely as in our world (except that Washington, D. C. is of course not there). The Colonial Parliament represents colonies stretching from Nova Scotia to Cuba (conquered in 1762) on the Atlantic Coast, and a number of large, sparser ones inland; for example, Franklin Colony is roughly Illinois and Iowa, and the city of Franklin (the eastern terminus of the Crown Pacific transcontinental railway, built in the early 1850s) corresponds to Chicago; and Vandalia is Kentucky and Tennessee. Louisiana becomes a British colony in 1815 in part due to the heroism of General Andrew Jackson, leading his colonial troops against the French; Texas was added in a war with Spain in the 1830s (the "War of Texian Annexation"). Deseret is somewhat larger than Utah, and is a colony reserved (by act of Parliament) for the Latter-Day Saints from 1847. Zion City is Salt Lake City. There are two autonomous native enclaves: Iroquoia (the western third of the colony of New York) and Cherokeeia (eastern Vandalia and western North Carolina).

Both Britain and Russia maintain treaty ports in the Sandwich Islands (Hawai'i): Britain is in Honolulu, Russia in Lahaina. As of 1906, the French have no toehold in the Islands, and their Pacific fleet is stationed in New Caledonia.

A BRIEF TIMELINE

1736. Death of King George II at sea; accession of King
Frederick Louis on Christmas Day.

1737. Battle of Rotherham; defeat of the Jacobites and death
of the Old Pretender. Prince Charles Stuart exiled to
Louisiana. Separation of the crowns of Britain and
Hanover.

1740-46. First Anglo-French War. (the "War of Jenkins'
Ear").

1754-66. Second Anglo-French War (the "Twelve Years'
War").

1754. Prince Charles Stuart defeated at Edenton (North
Carolina).

1762. Great Britain captures Havana; Cuba becomes a crown
colony.

1768. Sir Benjamin Franklin ennobled as 1st Earl of
Schuylkill, appointed Governor-General of North
America.

1776-87. Third Anglo-French War ("King George's War").

1777. Burgoyne defeats Montcalm at the Battle of Saratoga.
Made Lord Burgoyne.

1784. Lord Burgoyne appointed Governor-General.

1786. Marquis de Lafayette becomes First Minister for King
Louis XVI. Negotiates the cessation of hostilities with
Britain.

1790. Death of Lord Schuylkill.

1792-1820. Regency of Prince George for King George III.

1807. Passage of British Slave Trade Act. Exception for slavery in the southern American colonies.

1809. Anglo-Russian Treaty assigns Novaya Rossiya to Russian Empire.

1811. Russian treaty port established in Lahaina (Sandwich Islands).

1812-1815. Fourth Anglo-French War ("War of 1812").

1815. Battle of New Orleans, won by General Andrew Jackson for Britain against France, which cedes Louisiana at the end of the war. Spain cedes Florida to Britain.

1816. Founding of Saint Helena.

1816-1818. Seminole War. Jackson knighted by British crown.

1820. Jackson ennobled as Lord Nashville by the new King George IV; becomes Governor-General.

1821-30. Slave holders begin settlement in the New Spanish colony of Texas.

1822. Astor & Son established in Saint Helena.

1829. Founding of the Church of Latter-Day Saints in the Crown Colony of New York.

1831. Formation of the Vigilance Squadron in Saint Helena.

1833. Manumission Act signed by Lord Nashville, ending slavery in America.

1834 Death of the Duc de Richelieu.

1835-37. Texian rebellion by British emigrées aided by anti-government insurgents led by Santa Anna.

1836. Battles of San Jacinto and San Antonio de Béxar, securing Texian independence.

1838. Caspian Sea Rooms opened in Saint Helena.

Death of William III; Victoria becomes Queen of the Empire.

1841. Completion of the railroad across the Isthmus of Darien (Panama).

1843. Discovery of gold on the American River in Novaya Rossiya.

1844. Latter Day Saints driven from Nauvoo in Illinois Colony; emigration begins to Missouri and ultimately to the western part of Louisiana.

1845. Texas joins the British Empire. General Houston made Lord Houston, as the first Governor.

1849. Foundation of Salt Lake City by the Latter-Day Saints.

1851. Completion of the first transcontinental rail line from Franklin (Illinois Colony) to Archangel (Novaya Rossiya).

1853. French plot against Novaya Rossiya thwarted with the assistance of Joshua Norton.

1878. Completion of the railroad bridge from Archangel to Saint Helena.

1901. Death of Queen Victoria; Edward VII becomes King.

1904-05. War between Russia and Japan.

1906. Great earthquake and fire destroys much of Saint Helena. Novaya Rossiya ceded to the British Empire.

Made in the USA
Middletown, DE
30 July 2021